MORE THAN
HUMAN

MORE THAN HUMAN

Theodore Sturgeon

A Del Rey Gold Seal Selection

BALLANTINE BOOKS • NEW YORK

A Del Rey Book
Published by Ballantine Books
Copyright © 1953 by Theodore Sturgeon

Cover illustration by Paul Giovanopoulous

Library of Congress Catalog Card Number: 53-11211

ISBN 0-345-29886-1

Manufactured in the United States of America

Originally published simultaneously with Farrar, Straus and Cudahy, Inc.

U.S. Printing History
First Edition: October 1953
Twelfth Printing: June 1981

Canadian Printing History
First Edition: October 1972

First Ballantine Books Trade Edition: October 1981

9 8 7 6 5 4 3 2 1

To His Gestaltitude
NICHOLAS SAMSTAG

Contents

PART ONE
The Fabulous Idiot

THE idiot lived in a black and gray world, punctuated by the white lightning of hunger and the flickering of fear. His clothes were old and many-windowed. Here peeped a shinbone, sharp as a cold chisel, and there in the torn coat were ribs like the fingers of a fist. He was tall and flat. His eyes were calm and his face was dead.

Men turned away from him, women would not look, children stopped and watched him. It did not seem to matter to the idiot. He expected nothing from any of them. When the white lightning struck, he was fed. He fed himself when he could, he went without when he could. When he could do neither of these things he was fed by the first person who came face to face with him. The idiot never knew why, and never wondered. He did not beg. He would simply stand and wait. When someone met his eyes there would be a coin in his hand, a piece of bread, a fruit. He would eat and his benefactor would hurry away, disturbed, not understanding. Sometimes, nervously, they would speak to him; they would speak about him to each other. The idiot heard the sounds but they had no meaning for him. He lived inside somewhere, apart, and the little link between word and significance hung broken. His eyes were excellent, and could readily distinguish between a smile and a snarl; but neither

: any impact on a creature so lacking in sympathy, who
.ad never laughed and never snarled and so could not com-
.1 the feelings of his gay or angry fellows.

had exactly enough fear to keep his bones together and oiled.
/as incapable of anticipating anything. The stick that raised, the
.1e that flew found him unaware. But at their touch he would
.spond. He would escape. He would start to escape at the first blow
and he would keep on trying to escape until the blows ceased. He
escaped storms this way, rockfalls, men, dogs, traffic and hunger.

He had no preferences. It happened that where he was there was
more wilderness than town; since he lived wherever he found himself, he lived more in the forest than anywhere else.

They had locked him up four times. It had not mattered to him
any of the times, nor had it changed him in any way. Once he had
been badly beaten by an inmate and once, even worse, by a guard.
In the other two places there had been the hunger. When there was
food and he was left to himself, he stayed. When it was time for
escape, he escaped. The means to escape were in his outer husk; the
inner thing that it carried either did not care or could not command.
But when the time came, a guard or a warden would find himself
face to face with the idiot and the idiot's eyes whose irises seemed on
the trembling point of spinning like wheels. The gates would open
and the idiot would go, and as always the benefactor would run to do
something else, anything else, deeply troubled.

He was purely animal—a degrading thing to be among men. But
most of the time he was an animal away from men. As an animal in
the woods he moved like an animal, beautifully. He killed like an
animal, without hate and without joy. He ate like an animal, everything edible he could find, and he ate (when he could) only enough
and never more. He slept like an animal, well and lightly, faced in
the opposite direction from that of a man; for a man going to sleep is
about to escape into it while animals are prepared to escape out of it.
He had an animal's maturity, in which the play of kittens and pup-
pies no longer has a function. He was without humor and without
joy. His spectrum lay between terror and contentment.

He was twenty-five years old.

Like a stone in a peach, a yolk in an egg, he carried another thing.
It was passive, it was receptive, it was awake and alive. If it was
connected in any way to the animal integument, it ignored the

connections. It drew its substance from the idiot and was otherwise unaware of him. He was often hungry, but he rarely starved. When he did starve, the inner thing shrank a little perhaps; but it hardly noticed its own shrinking. It must die when the idiot died but it contained no motivation to delay that event by one second.

It had no function specific to the idiot. A spleen, a kidney, an adrenal—these have definite functions and an optimum level for those functions. But this was a thing which only received and recorded. It did this without words, without a code system of any kind; without translation, without distortion, and without operable outgoing conduits. It took what it took and gave out nothing.

All around it, to its special senses, was a murmur, a sending. It soaked itself in the murmur, absorbed it as it came, all of it. Perhaps it matched and classified, or perhaps it simply fed, taking what it needed and discarding the rest in some intangible way. The idiot was unaware. The thing inside. . . .

Without words: *Warm when the wet comes for a little but not enough for long enough.* (Sadly): *Never dark again.* A feeling of pleasure. A sense of subtle crushing and *Take away the pink, the scratchy. Wait, wait, you can go back, yes, you can go back. Different, but almost as good.* (Sleep feelings): *Yes, that's it! That's the—oh!* (Alarm): *You've gone too far, come back, come back, come—* (A twisting, a sudden cessation; and one less "voice.") . . . *It all rushes up, faster, faster, carrying me.* (Answer): *No, no. Nothing rushes. It's still; something pulls you down on to it, that's all.* (Fury): *They don't hear us, stupid, stupid. . . . They do. . . . They don't, only crying, only noises.*

Without words, though. Impression, depression, dialogue. Radiation of fear, tense fields of awareness, discontent. Murmuring, sending, speaking, sharing, from hundreds, from thousands of voices. None, though, for the idiot. Nothing that related to him; nothing he could use. He was unaware of his inner ear because it was useless to him. He was a poor example of a man, but he was a man; and these were the voices of the children, the very young children, who had not yet learned to stop crying to be heard. *Only crying, only noises.*

Mr. Kew was a good father, the very best of fathers. He told his daughter Alicia so, on her nineteenth birthday. He had said as much to Alicia ever since she was four. She was four when little Evelyn

had been born and their mother had died cursing him, her indigna-
tion at last awake and greater than her agony and her fear.

Only a good father, the very finest of fathers, could have delivered
his second child with his own hands. No ordinary father could have
nursed and nurtured the two, the baby and the infant, so tenderly
and so well. No child was ever so protected from evil as Alicia; and
when she joined forces with her father, a mighty structure of purity
was created for Evelyn. "Purity triple-distilled," Mr. Kew said to
Alicia on her nineteenth birthday. "I know good through the study of
evil, and have taught you only the good. And that good teaching has
become your good living, and your way of life is Evelyn's star. I
know all the evil there is and you know all the evil which must be
avoided; but Evelyn knows no evil at all."

At nineteen, of course, Alicia was mature enough to understand
these abstracts, this "way of life" and "distillation" and the inclusive
"good" and "evil." When she was sixteen he had explained to her
how a man went mad if he was alone with a woman, and how the
poison sweat appeared on his body, and how he would put it on her,
and then it would cause the horror on her skin. He had pictures of
skin like that in his books. When she was thirteen she had a trouble
and told her father about it and he told her with tears in his eyes that
this was because she had been thinking about her body, as indeed
she had been. She confessed it and he punished her body until she
wished she had never owned one. And she tried, she tried not to
think like that again, but she did in spite of herself; and regularly,
regretfully, her father helped her in her efforts to discipline her
intrusive flesh. When she was eight he taught her how to bathe in
darkness, so she would be spared the blindness of those white eyes of
which he also had magnificent pictures. And when she was six he
had hung in her bedroom the picture of a woman, called Angel, and
the picture of a man, called Devil. The woman held her palms up
and smiled and the man had his arms out to her, his hands like
hooks, and protruding point-outward from his breastbone was a
crooked knife blade with a wetness on it.

They lived alone in a heavy house on a wooded knoll. There was
no driveway, but a path which turned and turned again, so that from
the windows no one could see where it went. It went to a wall and in
the wall was an iron gate which had not been opened in eighteen
years and beside the gate was a steel panel. Once a day Alicia's father

went down the path to the wall and with two keys opened the two locks in the panel. He would swing it up and take out food and letters, put money and mail in, and lock it again.

There was a narrow road outside which Alicia and Evelyn had never seen. The woods concealed the wall and the wall concealed the road. The wall ran by the road for two hundred yards, east and west; it mounted the hill then until it bracketed the house. Here it met iron pickets, fifteen feet high and so close together a man could hardly press a fist between them. The tops of the pickets curved out and down, and between them was cement, and in the cement was broken glass. The pickets ran east and west, connecting the house to the wall; and where they joined, more pickets ran back and back into the woods in a circle. The wall and the house, then, were a rectangle and that was forbidden territory. And behind the house were the two square miles of fenced woodland, and that belonged to Evelyn, with Alicia to watch. There was a brook there; wild flowers and a little pond; friendly oaks and little hidden glades. The sky above was fresh and near and the pickets could not be seen for the shouldering masses of holly which grew next to them, all the way around, blocking the view, breaking the breeze. This closed circle was all the world to Evelyn, all the world she knew, and all in the world she loved lay in it.

On Alicia's nineteenth birthday Evelyn was alone by her pond. She could not see the house, she could not see the holly hedge nor the pickets, but the sky was there, up and up, and the water was there, by and by. Alicia was in the library with her father; on birthdays he always had special things planned for Alicia in the library. Evelyn had never been in the library. The library was a place where her father lived, and where Alicia went at special times. Evelyn never thought of going there, any more than she thought of breathing water like a speckled trout. She had not been taught to read, but only to listen and obey. She had never learned to seek, but only to accept. Knowledge was given to her when she was ready for it and only her father and sister knew just when that might be.

She sat on the bank, smoothing her long skirts. She saw her ankle and gasped and covered it as Alicia would do if she were here. She set her back against a willow-trunk and watched the water.

It was spring, the part of spring where the bursting is done, the held-in pressures of desiccated sap-veins and gum-sealed buds are gone, and all the world's in a rush to be beautiful. The air was heavy and sweet; it lay upon lips until they parted, pressed them until they smiled, entered boldly to beat in the throat like a second heart. It was air with a puzzle to it, for it was still and full of the colors of dreams, all motionless; yet it had a hurry to it. The stillness and the hurry were alive and laced together and how could that be? That was the puzzle.

A dazzle of bird notes stitched through the green. Evelyn's eyes stung and the wonder misted the wood. Something tensed in her lap. She looked down in time to see her hands attack one another, and off came her long gloves. Her naked hands fled to the sides of her neck, not to hide something but to share something. She bent her head and the hands laughed at one another under the iron order of her hair. They found four hooks and scampered down them. Her high collar eased and the enchanted air rushed in with a soundless shout. Evelyn breathed as if she had been running. She put out her hand hesitantly, futilely, patted the grass beside her as if somehow the act might release the inexpressible confusion of delight within her. It would not, and she turned and flung herself face down in a bed of early mint and wept because the spring was too beautiful to be borne.

He was in the wood, numbly prying the bark from a dead oak, when it happened. His hands were still and his head came up hunting, harking. He was as aware of the pressures of spring as an animal, and slightly more than an animal could be. But abruptly the spring was more than heavy, hopeful air and the shifting of earth with life. A hard hand on his shoulder could have been no more tangible than this call.

He rose carefully, as if something around him might break if he were clumsy. His strange eyes glowed. He began to move—he who had never called nor been called, nor responded before. He moved toward the thing he sensed and it was a matter of will, not of external compulsion. Without analysis he was aware of the bursting within him of an encysted need. It had been a part of him all his life but there was no hope in him that he might express it. And bursting so, it flung a thread across his internal gulf, linking his alive and independent core to the half-dead animal around it. It was a sending straight to what was human in him, received by an instrument which, up to now, had accepted only the incomprehensible radiations of the new-born, and so had been ignored. But now it spoke, as it were, in his own tongue.

He was careful and swift, careful and silent. He turned his wide shoulders to one side and the other as he moved, slipping through the alders, passing the pines closely as if it were intolerable to leave the direct line between himself and his call. The sun was high; the woods were homogeneously the woods, front, right, left; yet he followed his course without swerving, not from knowledge, not by any compass, but purely in conscious response.

He arrived suddenly, for the clearing was, in the forest, a sudden thing. For fifty feet outward the earth around the closet pickets had been leached and all trees felled years ago, so that none might overhang the fence. The idiot slipped out of the wood and trotted across the bare ground to the serried iron. He put out his arms as he ran, slid his hands between the pickets and when they caught on his starved bony forearms, his legs kept moving, his feet sliding, as if his need empowered him to walk through the fence and the impenetrable holly beyond it.

The fact that the barrier would not yield came to him slowly. It was as if his feet understood it first and stopped trying and then his hands, which withdrew. His eyes, however, would not give up at all. From his dead face they yearned through the iron, through the holly, ready to burst with answering. His mouth opened and a scratching sound emerged. He had never tried to speak before and could not now; the gesture was an end, not a means, like the starting of tears at a crescendo of music.

He began to move along the fence walking sidewise, finding it unbearable to turn away from the call.

It rained for a day and a night and for half the next day, and when the sun came out it rained again, upward; it rained light from the heavy jewels which lay on the rich new green. Some jewels shrank and some fell and then the earth in a voice of softness, and leaves in a voice of texture, and flowers speaking in color, were grateful.

Evelyn crouched on the window seat, elbows on the sill, her hands cupped to the curve of her cheeks, their pressure making it easy to smile. Softly, she sang. It was strange to hear for she did not know music; she did not read and had never been told of music. But there were birds, there was the bassoon of wind in the eaves sometimes; there were the calls and cooings of small creatures in that part of the wood which was hers and, distantly, from the part which was not. Her singing was made of these things, with strange and effortless fluctuations in pitch from an instrument unbound by the diatonic scale, freely phrased.

> *But I never touch the gladness*
> *May not touch the gladness*
> *Beauty, oh beauty of touchness*
> *Spread like a leaf, nothing between me and the sky but*
> *light,*
> *Rain touches me*
> *Wind touches me*
> *Leaves, other leaves, touch and touch me. . . .*

She made music without words for a long moment and was silent, making music without sound, watching the raindrops fall in the glowing noon.

Harshly, "What are you doing?"

Evelyn started and turned. Alicia stood behind her, her face strangely tight. "What are you doing?" she repeated.

Evelyn made a vague gesture toward the window, tried to speak. "Well?"

Evelyn made the gesture again. "Out there," she said. "I—I—" She slipped off the window seat and stood. She stood as tall as she could. Her face was hot.

"Button up your collar," said Alicia. "What is it, Evelyn? Tell me!"

"I'm trying to," said Evelyn, soft and urgent. She buttoned her collar and her hands fell to her waist. She pressed herself, hard. Alicia stepped near and pushed the hands away. "Don't do that. What was that . . . what you were doing? Were you talking?"

"Talking, yes. Not you, though. Not Father."

"There isn't anyone else."

"There is," said Evelyn. Suddenly breathless, she said, "Touch me, Alicia."

"*Touch* you?"

"Yes, I . . . want you to. Just . . ." She held out her arms. Alicia backed away.

"We don't touch one another," she said, as gently as she could through her shock. "What is it, Evelyn? Aren't you well?"

"Yes," said Evelyn. "No. I don't know." She turned to the window. "It isn't raining. It's dark here. There's so much sun, so much—I want the sun on me, like a bath, warm all over."

"Silly. Then it would be all light in your bath. . . . We don't talk about bathing, dear."

Evelyn picked up a cushion from the window seat. She put her arms around it and with all her strength hugged it to her breast.

"Evelyn! Stop that!"

Evelyn whirled and looked at her sister in a way she had never used before. Her mouth twisted. She squeezed her eyes tight closed and when she opened them, tears fell. "I want to," she cried, "I want to!"

"Evelyn!" Alicia whispered. Wide-eyed, she backed away to the door. "I shall have to tell Father."

Evelyn nodded, and drew her arms even tighter around the cushion.

When he came to the brook, the idiot squatted down beside it and stared. A leaf danced past, stopped and curtsied, then made its way through the pickets and disappeared in the low gap the holly had made for it.

He had never thought deductively before and perhaps his effort to follow the leaf was not thought-born. Yet he did, only to find that the pickets were set in a concrete channel here. They combed the water from one side to the other; nothing larger than a twig or a leaf could slip through. He wallowed in the water, pressing against the iron, beating at the submerged cement. He swallowed water and choked and kept trying, blindly, insistently. He put both his hands on one of the pickets and shook it. It tore his palm. He tried another and another and suddenly one rattled against the lower cross-member.

It was a different result from that of any other attack. It is doubtful whether he realized that this difference meant that the iron here had rusted and was therefore weaker; it simply gave hope because it was different.

He sat down on the bottom of the brook and in water up to his armpits, he placed a foot on each side of the picket which had rattled. He got his hands on it again, took a deep breath and pulled with all his strength. A stain of red rose in the water and whirled downstream. He leaned forward, then back with a tremendous jerk. The rusted underwater segment snapped. He hurtled backward, striking his head stingingly on the edge of the channel. He went limp for a moment and his body half rolled, half floated back to the pickets. He inhaled water, coughed painfully, and raised his head. When the spinning world righted itself, he fumbled under the water. He found an opening a foot high but only about seven inches wide. He put his arm in it, right up to the shoulder, his head submerged. He sat up again and put a leg into it.

Again he was dimly aware of the inexorable fact that will alone was not enough; that pressure alone upon the barrier would not make it yield. He moved to the next picket and tried to break it as he had the one before. It would not move, nor would the one on the other side.

At last he rested. He looked up hopelessly at the fifteen-foot top of the fence with its close-set, outcurving fangs and its hungry rows of broken glass. Something hurt him; he moved and fumbled and found himself with the eleven-inch piece of iron he had broken away. He sat with it in his hands, staring stupidly at the fence.

Touch me, touch me. It was that, and a great swelling of emotion behind it; it was a hunger, a demand, a flood of sweetness and of need. The call had never ceased, but this was something different. It was as if the call were a carrier and this a signal suddenly impressed upon it.

When it happened that thread within him, bridging his two selves, trembled and swelled. Falteringly, it began to conduct. Fragments and flickerings of inner power shot across, were laden with awareness and information, shot back. The strange eyes fell to the piece of iron, the hands turned it. His reason itself ached with disuse as it stirred; then for the first time came into play on such a problem.

He sat in the water, close by the fence, and with the piece of iron he began to rub against the picket just under the cross-member.

It began to rain. It rained all day and all night and half the next day.

"She *was* here," said Alicia. Her face was flushed.

Mr. Kew circled the room, his deepset eyes alight. He ran his whip through his fingers. There were four lashes. Alicia said, remembering, "And she wanted me to touch her. She asked me to."

"She'll be touched," he said. "Evil, evil," he muttered. "Evil can't be filtered out," he chanted. "I thought it could, I thought it could. You're evil, Alicia, as you know, because a woman touched you, for years she handled you. But not Evelyn . . . it's in the blood and the blood must be let. Where is she, do you think?"

"Perhaps outdoors . . . the pool, that will be it. She likes the pool. I'll go with you."

He looked at her, her hot face, bright eyes. "This is for me to do. Stay here!"

"Please . . ."

He whirled the heavy-handled whip. "You too, Alicia?"

She half turned from him, biting into a huge excitement. "Later," he growled. He ran out.

Alicia stood a moment trembling, then plunged to the window. She saw her father outside, striding purposefully away. Her hands spread and curled against the sash. Her lips writhed apart and she uttered a strange wordless bleat.

When Evelyn reached the pool, she was out of breath. Something—an invisible smoke, a magic—lay over the water. She took it in hungrily, and was filled with a sense of nearness. Whether it was a thing which was near or an event, she did not know; but it was near and she welcomed it. Her nostrils arched and trembled. She ran to the water's edge and reached out toward it.

There was a boiling in the upstream end and up from under the holly stems he came. He thrashed to the bank and lay there gasping, looking up at her. He was wide and flat, covered with scratches. His hands were puffy and water-wrinkled; he was gaunt and worn. Shreds of clothing clung to him here and there, covering him not at all.

She leaned over him, spellbound, and from her came the call—floods of it, loneliness and expectancy and hunger, gladness and sympathy. There was a great amazement in her but no shock and no surprise. She had been aware of him for days and he of her, and now their silent radiations reached out to each other, mixed and mingled and meshed. Silently they lived in each other and then she bent and touched him, touched his face and shaggy hair.

He trembled violently, and kicked his way up out of the water.

She sank down beside him. They sat close together, and at last she met those eyes. The eyes seemed to swell up and fill the air; she wept for joy and sank forward into them, wanting to live there, perhaps to die there, but at very least to be a part of them.

She had never spoken to a man and he had never spoken to anyone. She did not know what a kiss was and any he might have seen had no significance to him. But they had a better thing. They stayed close, one of her hands on his bare shoulder, and the currents of their inner selves surged between them. They did not hear her father's resolute footsteps, nor his gasp, nor his terrible bellow of outrage. They were aware of nothing but each other until he leapt on them, caught her up, lifted her high, threw her behind him. He did not look to see where or how she struck the ground. He stood over the idiot, his lips white, his eyes staring. His lips parted and again he made the terrible sound. And then he lifted the whip.

So dazed was the idiot that the first multiple blow, and the second, seemed not to affect him at all, though his flesh, already soaked and cut and beaten, split and spouted. He lay staring dully at that midair point which had contained Evelyn's eyes and did not move.

Then the lashes whistled and clacked and buried their braided tips in his back again and the old reflex returned to him. He pressed himself backward trying to slide feet-first into the water. The man dropped his whip and caught the idiot's bony wrist in both his hands. He literally ran a dozen steps up the bank, the idiot's long tattered body flailing along behind him. He kicked the creature's head, ran back for his whip. When he returned with it the idiot had managed to rear up on his elbows. The man kicked him again, rolled him over on his back. He put one foot on the idiot's shoulder and pinned him down and slashed at the naked belly with the whip.

There was a devil's shriek behind him and it was as if a bullock with tiger's claws had attacked him. He fell heavily and twisted, to look up into the crazed face of his younger daughter. She had bitten her lips and she drooled and bled. She clawed at his face; one of her fingers slipped into his left eye. He screamed in agony, sat up, twined his fingers in the complexity of lace at her throat, and clubbed her twice with the loaded whip-handle.

Blubbering, whining, he turned to the idiot again. But now the implacable demands of escape had risen, flushing away everything else. And perhaps another thing was broken as the whip-handle crushed the consciousness from the girl. In any case there was nothing left but escape, and there could be nothing else until it was achieved. The long body flexed like a snap-beetle, flung itself up and over in a half-somersault. The idiot struck the bank on all fours and sprang as he struck. The lash caught him in midair; his flying body curled around it, for a brief instant capturing the lashes between the lower ribs and the hipbone. The handle slipped from the man's grasp. He screamed and dove after the idiot, who plunged into the arch at the holly roots. The man's face buried itself in the leaves and tore; he sank and surged forward again in the water. With one hand he caught a naked foot. It kicked him on the ear as he pulled it toward him. And then the man's head struck the iron pickets.

The idiot was under and through already and lay half out of the brook, twitching feebly in an exhausted effort to bring his broken body to its feet. He turned to look back and saw the man clinging to the bars, raging, not understanding about the underwater gap in the fence.

The idiot clung to the earth, pink bloody water swirling away from him and down on his pursuer. Slowly the escape reflex left him. There was a period of blankness and then a strange new feeling came to him. It was as new an experience as the call which had brought him here and very nearly as strong. It was a feeling like fear but where fear was a fog to him, clammy and blinding, this was something with a thirsty edge to it, hard and purposeful.

He relaxed his grasp on the poisoned weeds which grew sickly in the leached ground by the brook. He let the water help him and drifted down again to the bars, where the insane father mouthed and yammered at him. He brought his dead face close to the fence and widened his eyes. The screaming stopped.

For the first time he used the eyes consciously, purposely, for something other than a crust of bread.

When the man was gone he dragged himself out of the brook and, faltering, crawled toward the woods.

When Alicia saw her father returning, she put the heel of her hand in her mouth and bit down until her teeth met. It was not his clothes, wet and torn, nor even his ruined eye. It was something else, something which—"*Father!*"

He did not answer, but strode up to her. At the last possible instant before being walked down like a wheat stalk, she numbly stepped aside. He stamped past her and through the library doors, leaving them open. "Father!"

No answer. She ran to the library. He was across the room, at the cabinets which she had never seen open. One was open now. From it he took a long-barreled target revolver and a small box of cartridges. This he opened, spilling the cartridges across his desk. Methodically he began to load.

Alicia ran to him. "What is it? What is it? You're hurt, let me help you, what are you . . ."

His one good eye was fixed and glassy. He breathed slowly, too deeply, the air rushing in for too long, being held for too long, whistling out and out. He snapped the cylinder into place, clicked off the safety, looked at her and raised the gun.

She was never to forget that look. Terrible things happened then and later, but time softened the focus, elided the details. But that look was to be with her forever.

He fixed the one eye on her, caught and held her with it; she squirmed on it like an impaled insect. She knew with a horrifying certainty that he did not see her at all, but looked at some unknowable horror of his own. Still looking through her, he put the muzzle of the gun in his mouth and pulled the trigger.

There was not much noise. His hair fluffed upward on top. The eye still stared, she was still pierced by it. She screamed his name. He was no less reachable dead than he had been a moment before. He bent forward as if to show her the ruin which had replaced his hair and the thing that held her broke, and she ran.

Two hours, two whole hours passed before she found Evelyn. One of the hours was simply lost; it was a blackness and a pain. The other was too quiet, a time of wandering about the house followed by a soft little whimpering that she made herself: "What?" she whimpered, "what's that you say?" trying to understand, asking and asking the quiet house for the second hour.

She found Evelyn by the pool, lying on her back with her eyes wide open. On the side of Evelyn's head was a puffiness, and in the center of the puffiness was a hollow into which she could have laid three fingers.

"Don't," said Evelyn softly when Alicia tried to lift her head.

Alicia set it back gently and knelt and took her hands and squeezed them together. "Evelyn, oh, what happened?"

"Father hit me," Evelyn said calmly. "I'm going to go to sleep." Alicia whimpered.

Evelyn said, "What is it called when a person needs a . . . person . . . when you want to be touched and the . . . two are like one thing and there isn't anything else at all anywhere?"

Alicia, who had read books, thought about it. "Love," she said at length. She swallowed. "It's a madness. It's bad."

Evelyn's quiet face was suffused with a kind of wisdom. "It isn't bad," she said. "I had it."

"You have to get back to the house."

"I'll sleep here," said Evelyn. She looked up at her sister and smiled. "It's all right . . . Alicia?"

"Yes."

"I won't ever wake up," she said with that strange wisdom. "I wanted to do something and now I can't. Will you do it for me?"

"I'll do it," Alicia whispered.

"For me," Evelyn insisted. "You won't want to."

"I'll do it."

"When the sun is bright," Evelyn said, "take a bath in it. There's more, wait." She closed her eyes. A little furrow came and went on her brow. "Be in the sun like that. Move, run. Run and . . . jump high. Make a wind with running and moving. I so wanted that. I didn't know until now that I wanted it and now I . . . oh, *Alicia!*"

"What is it, what is it?"

"There it is, there it is, can't you see? The love, with the sun on its body!"

The soft wise eyes were wide, looking at the darkling sky. Alicia looked up and saw nothing. When she looked down again, she knew that Evelyn was also seeing nothing. Not any more.

Far off, in the woods beyond the fence, there was a rush of weeping.

Alicia stayed there listening to it and at last put out her hand and closed Evelyn's eyes. She rose and went toward the house and the weeping followed her and followed her, almost until she reached the door. And even then it seemed to go on inside her.

*   *   *

When Mrs. Prodd heard the hoof thuds in the yard, she muttered under her breath and peered out between the dimity kitchen curtains. By a combination of starlight and deep familiarity with the yard itself, she discerned the horse and stoneboat, with her husband plodding beside it, coming through the gate. He'll get what for, she mumbled, off to the woods so long and letting her burn dinner.

He didn't get what for, though. One look at his broad face precluded it. "What is it, Prodd?" she asked, alarmed.

"Gimme a blanket."

"Why on earth—"

"Hurry now. Feller bad hurt. Picked him up in the woods. Looks like a bear chewed him. Got the clo'es ripped off him."

She brought the blanket, running, and he snatched it and went out. In a moment he was back, carrying a man. "Here," said Mrs. Prodd. She flung open the door to Jack's room. When Prodd hesitated, the long limp body dangling in his arms, she said, "Go on, go on, never mind the spread. It'll wash."

"Get a rag, hot water," he grunted. She went out and he gently lifted off the blanket. "Oh my God."

He stopped her at the door. "He won't last the night. Maybe we shouldn't plague him with that." He indicated the steaming basin she carried.

"We got to try." She went in. She stopped and he deftly took the basin from her as she stood, white-faced, her eyes closed. "Ma—"

"Come," she said softly. She went to the bed and began to clean the tattered body.

He lasted the night. He lasted the week too and it was only then that the Prodds began to have hope for him. He lay motionless in the room called Jack's room, interested in nothing, aware of nothing except perhaps the light as it came and went at the window. He would stare out as he lay, perhaps seeing, perhaps watching, perhaps not. There was little to be seen out there. A distant mountain, a few of Prodd's sparse acres; occasionally Prodd himself, a doll in the distance, scratching the stubborn soil with a broken harrow, stooping for weed-shoots. His inner self was encysted and silent in sorrow. His outer self seemed shrunken, unreachable also. When Mrs. Prodd brought food—eggs and warm sweet milk, homecured ham and johnny-cake—he would eat if she urged him, ignore both her and the food if she did not.

In the evenings, "He say anything yet?" Prodd would ask, and his wife would shake her head. After ten days he had a thought; after two weeks he voiced it. "You don't suppose he's tetched, do you, Ma?"

She was unaccountably angry. "How do you mean tetched?"

He gestured. "You know. Like feeble-minded. I mean, maybe he don't talk because he can't."

"No!" she said postively. She looked up to see the question in Prodd's face. She said, "You ever look in his eyes? He's no idiot."

He had noticed the eyes. They disturbed him; that was all he could say of them. "Well, I wish he'd say something."

She touched a thick coffee cup. "You know Grace."

"Well, you told me. Your cousin that lost her little ones."

"Yes. Well, after the fire, Grace was almost like that, lying quiet all day. Talk to her, it was like she didn't hear. Show her something, she might've been blind. Had to spoon-feed her, wash her face."

"Maybe it's that then," he allowed. "That feller, he sure walked into something worth forgetting, up there . . . Grace, she got better, didn't she?"

"Well, she was never the same," said his wife. "But she got over it. I guess sometimes the world's too much to live with and a body sort of has to turn away from it to rest."

The weeks went by and broken tissues knit and the wide flat body soaked up nourishment like a cactus absorbing moisture. Never in his life had he had rest and food and . . .

She sat with him, talked to him. She sang songs, "Flow Gently, Sweet Afton" and "Home on the Range." She was a little brown woman with colorless hair and bleached eyes, and there was about her a hunger very like one he had felt. She told the moveless, silent face all about the folks back East and second grade and the time Prodd had come courting in his boss's Model T and him not even knowing how to drive it yet. She told him all the little things that would never be altogether in the past for her; the dress she wore to her confirmation, with a bow here and little gores here and here, and the time Grace's husband came home drunk with his Sunday pants all tore and a live pig under his arm, squealing to wake the dead. She read to him from the prayer book and told him Bible stories. She chattered out everything that was in her mind, except about Jack.

He never smiled nor answered and the only difference it made in him was that he kept his eyes on her face when she was in the room and patiently on the door when she was not. What a profound difference this was, she could not know; but the flat starved body tissues were not all that were slowly filling out.

A day came at last when the Prodds were at lunch—"dinner," they called it—and there was a fumbling at the inside of the door of Jack's room. Prodd exchanged a glance with his wife, then rose and opened it.

"Here, now, you can't come out like that." He called, "Ma, throw in my other overalls."

He was weak and very uncertain, but he was on his feet. They helped him to the table and he slumped there, his eyes cloaked and stupid, ignoring the food until Mrs. Prodd tantalized his nostrils with a spoonful. Then he took the spoon in his broad fist and got his mouth on it and looked past his hand at her. She patted his shoulder and told him it was just wonderful, how well he did.

"Well, Ma, you don't have to treat him like a two-year-old," said Prodd. Perhaps it was the eyes, but he was troubled again.

She pressed his hand warningly; he understood and said no more about it just then. But later in the night when he thought she was asleep, she said suddenly, "I do so have to treat him like a two-year-old, Prodd. Maybe even younger."

"How's that?"

"With Grace," she said, "it was like that. Not so bad, though. She was like six, when she started to get better. Dolls. When she didn't get apple pie with the rest of us one time, she cried her heart out. It was like growing up all over again. Faster, I mean, but like traveling the same road again."

"You think he's going to be like that?"

"Isn't he like a two-year-old?"

"First I ever saw six foot tall."

She snorted in half-pretended annoyance. "We'll raise him up just like a child."

He was quiet for a time. Then, "What'll we call him?"

"Not Jack," she said before she could stop herself.

He grunted an agreement. He didn't know quite what to say then.

She said, "We'll bide our time about that. He's got his own name.

It wouldn't be right to put another to him. You just wait. He'll get back to where he remembers it."

He thought about it for a long time. He said, "Ma, I hope we're doing the right thing." But by then she was asleep.

There were miracles.

The Prodds thought of them as achievements, as successes, but they were miracles. There was the time when Prodd found two strong hands at the other end of a piece of 12x12 he was snaking out of the barn. There was the time Mrs. Prodd found her patient holding a ball of yarn, holding it and looking at it only because it was red. There was the time he found a full bucket by the pump and brought it inside. It was a long while, however, before he learned to work the handle.

When he had been there a year, Mrs. Prodd remembered and baked him a cake. Impulsively she put four candles on it. The Prodds beamed at him as he stared at the little flames, fascinated. His strange eyes caught and held hers, then Prodd's. "Blow it out, son."

Perhaps he visualized the act. Perhaps it was the result of the warmth outflowing from the couple, the wishing for him, the warmth of caring. He bent his head and blew. They laughed together and rose and came to him, and Prodd thumped his shoulder and Mrs. Prodd kissed his cheek.

Something twisted inside him. His eyes rolled up until, for a moment, only the whites showed. The frozen grief he carried slumped and flooded him. This wasn't the call, the contact, the exchange he had experienced with Evelyn. It was not even like it, except in degree. But because he could now feel to such a degree, he was aware of his loss, and he did just what he had done when first he lost it. He cried.

It was the same shrill tortured weeping that had led Prodd to him in the darkening wood a year ago. This room was too small to contain it. Mrs. Prodd had never heard him make a sound before. Prodd had, that first night. It would be hard to say whether it was worse to listen to such a sound or to listen to it again.

Mrs. Prodd put her arms around his head and cooed small syllables to him. Prodd balanced himself awkwardly nearby, put out a hand, changed his mind, and finally retreated into a futile reiteration: "Aw. Aw. . . . Aw, now."

In its own time, the weeping stopped. Sniffling, he looked at them each in turn. Something new was in his face; it was as if the bronze mask over which his facial skin was stretched had disappeared. "I'm sorry," Prodd said. "Reckon we did something wrong."

"It wasn't wrong," said his wife. "You'll see."

He got a name.

The night he cried, he discovered consciously that if he wished, he could absorb a message, a meaning, from those about him. It had happened before, but it happened as the wind happened to blow on him, as reflexively as a sneeze or a shiver. He began to hold and turn this ability, as once he had held and turned the ball of yarn. The sounds called speech still meant little to him, but he began to detect the difference between speech directed to him and that which did not concern him. He never really learned to hear speech; instead, ideas were transmitted to him directly. Ideas in themselves are formless and it is hardly surprising that he learned very slowly to give ideas the form of speech.

"What's your name?" Prodd asked him suddenly one day. They were filling the horse trough from the cistern and there was that about water running and running in the sun which tugged deeply at the idiot. Utterly absorbed, he was jolted by the question. He looked up and found his gaze locked with Prodd's.

Name. He made a reaching, a flash of demand, and it returned to him carrying what might be called a definition. It came, though, as pure concept. *"Name" is the single thing which is me and what I have done and been and learned.*

It was all there, waiting for that single symbol, a name. All the wandering, the hunger, the loss, the thing which is worse than loss, called back. There was a dim and subtle awareness that even here, with the Prodds, he was not a something, but a substitute for something.

All alone.

He tried to say it. Directly from Prodd he took the concept and its verbal coding and the way it ought to sound. But understanding and expressing were one thing; the physical act of enunciation was something else again. His tongue might have been a shoe sole and his larynx a rusty whistle. His lips writhed. He said, "Ul . . . ul . . ."

"What is it, son?"

All alone. It was transmitted clear and clean, complete, but as a

thought only and he sensed instantly that a thought sent this way had
no impact whatever on Prodd, though the farmer strained to receive
what he was trying to convey. "Ul-ul . . . lone," he gasped.

"Lone?" said Prodd.

It could be seen that the syllable meant something to Prodd,
something like the codification he offered, though far less.

But it would do.

He tried to repeat the sound, but his unaccustomed tongue became spastic. Saliva spurted annoyingly and ran from his lips. He
sent a desperate demand for help, for some other way to express it,
found it, used it. He nodded.

"Lone," repeated Prodd.

And again he nodded; and this was his first word and his first
conversation; another miracle.

It took him five years to learn to talk and always he preferred not
to. He never did learn to read. He was simply not equipped.

There were two boys for whom the smell of disinfectant on tile was
the smell of hate.

For Gerry Thompson it was the smell of hunger, too, and of
loneliness. All food was spiced with it, all sleep permeated with
disinfectant, hunger, cold, fear . . . all components of hatred.
Hatred was the only warmth in the world, the only certainty. A man
clings to certainties, especially when he has only one; most especially
when he is six years old. And at six Gerry was very largely a man—at
least, he had a grown man's appreciation of that gray pleasure which
comes merely with the absence of pain; he had an implacable patience, found usually only in men of purpose who must appear
broken until their time of decision arrives. One does not realize that
for a six-year-old the path of memory stretches back for just as long a
lifetime as it does for anyone, and is as full of detail and incident.
Gerry had had trouble enough, loss enough, illness enough, to make
a man of anyone. At six he looked it, too; it was then that he began to
accept, to be obedient, and to wait. His small, seamed face became
just another face, and his voice no longer protested. He lived like this
for two years, until his day of decision.

Then he ran away from the state orphanage, to live by himself, to
be the color of gutters and garbage so he would not be picked up; to
kill if cornered; to hate.

*   *   *

For Hip there was no hunger, no cold, and no precocious maturity. There was the smell of hate, though. It surrounded his father the doctor, the deft and merciless hands, the somber clothes. Even Hip's memory of Doctor Barrows' voice was the memory of chlorine and carbolic.

Little Hip Barrows was a brilliant and beautiful child, to whom the world refused to be a straight, hard path of disinfected tile. Everything came easily to him, except control of his curiosity—and "everything" included the cold injections of rectitude administered by his father the doctor, who was a successful man, a moral man, a man who had made a career of being sure and of being right.

Hip rose through childhood like a rocket, burnished, swift, afire. His gifts brought him anything a young man might want, and his conditioning constantly chanted to him that he was a kind of thief, not entitled to that which he had not earned; for such was the philosophy of his father the doctor, who had worked hard for everything. So Hip's talents brought him friends and honors, and friendships and honors brought him uneasiness and a sick humility of which he was quite unaware.

He was eight when he built his first radio, a crystal set for which he even wound the coils. He suspended it from the bedsprings so it could not be seen except by lifting the bed itself and buried an earphone inside the mattress so he could lie awake at night and hear it. His father the doctor discovered it and forbade his ever touching so much as a piece of wire in the house again. He was nine when his father the doctor located his cache of radio and electronics texts and magazines and piled them all up in front of the fireplace and made him burn them, one by one; they were up all night. He was twelve when he won a Science Search engineering scholarship for his secretly designed tubeless oscilloscope, and his father the doctor dictated his letter of refusal. He was a brilliant fifteen when he was expelled from premedical school for playfully cross-wiring the relays in the staff elevators and adding some sequence switches, so that every touch of a control button was an unappreciated adventure. At sixteen, happily disowned, he was making his own living in a research laboratory and attending engineering school.

He was big and bright and very popular. He needed to be very popular and this, like all his other needs, he accomplished with ease.

He played the piano with a surprisingly delicate touch and played swift and subtle chess. He learned to lose skilfully and never too often at chess and at tennis and once at the harassing game of being "first in the Class, first in the School." He always had time—time to talk and to read, time to wonder quietly, time to listen to those who valued his listening, time to rephrase pedantries for those who found them arduous in the original. He even had time for ROTC and it was through this that he got his commission.

He found the Air Force a rather different institution from any school he had ever attended and it took him a while to learn that the Colonel could not be softened by humility or won by a witticism like the Dean of Men. It took him even longer to learn that in Service it is the majority, not the minority, who tend to regard physical perfection, conversational brilliance and easy achievement as defects rather than assets. He found himself alone more than he liked and avoided more than he could bear.

It was on the anti-aircraft range that he found an answer, a dream, and a disaster. . . .

Alicia Kew stood in the deepest shade by the edge of the meadow. "Father, Father, forgive me!" she cried. She sank down on the grass, blind with grief and terror, torn, shaken with conflict.

"Forgive me," she whispered with passion. "Forgive me," she whispered with scorn.

She thought, Devil, why won't you be dead? Five years ago you killed yourself, you killed my sister, and still it's "Father, forgive me." Sadist, pervert, murderer, devil . . . *man*, dirty poisonous *man!*

I've come a long way, she thought, I've come no way at all. How I ran from Jacobs, gentle Lawyer Jacobs, when he came to help with the bodies; oh, how I ran, to keep from being alone with him, so that he might not go mad and poison me. And when he brought his wife, how I fled from her too, thinking women were evil and must not touch me. They had a time with me, indeed they did; it was so long before I could understand that I was mad, not they . . . it was so long before I knew how very good, how very patient, Mother Jacobs was with me; how much she had to do with me, for me. "But child, no one's worn clothes like those for forty years!" And in the cab, when I screamed and couldn't stop, for the people, the hurry, the *bodies*, so many bodies, all touching and so achingly visible; bodies on the streets, the stairs, great pictures of bodies in the magazines, men holding women who laughed and were brazenly unfrightened . . . Dr. Rothstein who explained and explained and went back and explained again; there is no poison sweat, and there must be men and women else there would be no people at all. . . . I had to learn this, Father, dear devil Father, because of you; because of you I had never seen an automobile or a breast or a newspaper or a railroad train or a sanitary napkin or a kiss or a restaurant or an elevator or a bathing suit or the hair on—oh forgive me, Father.

I'm not afraid of a whip, I'm afraid of hands and eyes, thank you Father. One day, one day, you'll see, Father, I shall live with people all around me, I shall ride on their trains and drive my own motorcar; I shall go among thousands on a beach at the edge of a sea which goes out and out without walls, I shall step in and out among them with a tiny strip of cloth here and there and let them see my navel, I shall meet a man with white teeth, Father, and round strong arms, Father, and I shall oh what will become of me, what have I become now, Father forgive me.

I live in a house you never saw, one with windows overlooking a road, where the bright gentle cars whisper past and children play outside the hedge. The hedge is not a wall and, twice for the drive and once for the walk, it is open to anyone. I look through the curtains whenever I choose, and see strangers. There is no way to make the bathroom black dark and in the bathroom is a mirror as tall as I am; and one day, Father, I shall leave the towel off.

But all that will come later, the moving about among strangers, the touchings without fear. Now I must live alone, and think; I must read and read of the world and its works, yes, and of madmen like you, Father, and what twists them so terribly; Dr. Rothstein insists that you were not the only one, that you were so rare, really, only because you were so rich.

Evelyn . . .

Evelyn never knew her father was mad. Evelyn never saw the pictures of the poisoned flesh. I lived in a world different from this one, but her world was just as different, the world Father and I made for her, to keep her pure. . . .

I wonder, I wonder how it happened that you had the decency to blow your rotten brains out. . . .

The picture of her father, dead, calmed her strangely. She rose and looked back into the woods, looked carefully around the meadow, shadow by shadow, tree by tree. "All right, Evelyn, I will, I will. . . ."

She took a deep breath and held it. She shut her eyes so tight there was red in the blackness of it. Her hands flickered over the buttons on her dress. It fell away. She slid out of underwear and stockings with a single movement. The air stirred and its touch on her body was indescribable; it seemed to blow through her. She stepped forward into the sun and with tears of terror pressing through her closed lids, she danced naked, for Evelyn, and begged and begged her dead father's pardon.

When Janie was four, she hurled a paperweight at a Lieutenant because of an unanalyzed but accurate feeling that he had no business around the house while her father was overseas. The Lieutenant's skull was fractured and, as is often the case in concussion, he was forever unable to recall the fact that Janie stood ten feet away from the object when she threw it. Janie's mother whaled the tar out of her for it, an episode which Janie accepted with her usual composure. She added it, however, to the proofs given her by similar occasions that power without control has its demerits.

"She gives me the creeps," her mother told her other Lieutenant later. "I can't stand her. You think there's something wrong with me for talking like that, don't you?"

"No I don't," said the other Lieutenant, who did. So she invited him in for the following afternoon, quite sure that once he had seen the child, he would understand.

He saw her and he did understand. Not the child, nobody understood her; it was the mother's feelings he understood. Janie stood straight up, with her shoulders back and her face lifted, legs apart as if they wore jackboots, and she swung a doll by one of its feet as if it were a swagger-stick. There was a rightness about the child which, in a child, was wrong. She was, if anything, a little smaller than average. She was sharp featured and narrow eyed; her eyebrows were heavy. Her proportions were not quite those of most four-year-olds, who can bend forward from the waist and touch their foreheads to the floor. Janie's torso was a little too short or her legs a little too long for that. She spoke with a sweet clarity and a devastating lack of tact.

When the other Lieutenant squatted clumsily and said, "*Hel*-lo, Janie. Are we going to be friends?" she said, "No. You smell like Major Grenfell." Major Grenfell had immediately preceded the injured Lieutenant.

"Janie!" her mother shouted, too late. More quietly, she said, "You know perfectly well the Major was only in for cocktails." Janie accepted this without comment, which left an appalling gap in the dialogue. The other Lieutenant seemed to realize all in a rush that it was foolish to squat there on the parquet and sprang to his feet so abruptly he knocked over the coffee table. Janie achieved a wolfish smile and watched his scarlet ears while he picked up the pieces. He left early and never came back.

Nor, for Janie's mother, was there safety in numbers. Against the strictest orders, Janie strode into the midst of the fourth round of Gibsons one evening and stood at one end of the living room, flicking an insultingly sober gray-green gaze across the flushed faces. A round yellow-haired man who had his hand on her mother's neck extended his glass and bellowed, "You're Wima's little girl!"

Every head in the room swung at once like a bank of servo-switches, turning off the noise, and into the silence Janie said, "You're the one with the—"

"*Janie!*" her mother shouted. Someone laughed. Janie waited for it to finish. "—big, fat—" she enunciated. The man took his hand off Wima's neck. Someone whooped, "Big fat what, Janie?"

Topically, for it was wartime, Janie said, "—meat market."

Wima bared her teeth. "Run along back to your room, darling. I'll come and tuck you in in a minute." Someone looked straight at the blond man and laughed. Someone said in an echoing whisper, "There goes the Sunday sirloin." A drawstring could not have pulled the fat man's mouth so round and tight and from it his lower lip bloomed like strawberry jam from a squeezed sandwich.

Janie walked quietly toward the door and stopped as soon as she was out of her mother's line of sight. A sallow young man with brilliant black eyes leaned forward suddenly. Janie met his gaze. An expression of bewilderment crossed the young man's face. His hand faltered out and upward and came to rest on his forehead. It slid down and covered the black eyes.

Janie said, just loud enough for him to hear, "Don't you ever do that again." She left the room.

"Wima," said the young man hoarsely, "that child is telepathic."

"Nonsense," said Wima absently, concentrating on the fat man's pout. "She gets her vitamins every single day."

The young man started to rise, looking after the child, then sank back again. "God," he said, and began to brood.

When Janie was five she began playing with some other little girls. It was quite a while before they were aware of it. They were toddlers, perhaps two and a half years old, and they looked like twins. They conversed, if conversation it was, in high-pitched squeaks, and tumbled about on the concrete courtyard as if it were a haymow. At first Janie hung over her windowsill, four and a half stories above, and contemplatively squirted saliva in and out between her tongue and her hard palate until she had a satisfactory charge. Then she would crane her neck and, cheeks bulging, let it go. The twins ignored the bombardment when it merely smacked the concrete, but yielded up a most satisfying foofaraw of chitterings and squeals when she scored a hit. They never looked up but would race around in wild excitement, squealing.

Then there was another game. On warm days the twins could skin out of their rompers faster than the eye could follow. One moment they were as decent as a deacon and in the next one or both would be fifteen feet away from the little scrap of cloth. They would squeak and scramble and claw back into them, casting deliciously frightened glances at the basement door. Janie discovered that with a little concentration she could move the rompers—that is, when they were unoccupied. She practiced diligently, lying across the windowsill, her chest and chin on a cushion, her eyes puckered with effort. At first the garment would simply lie there and flutter weakly, as if a small dust-devil had crossed it. But soon she had the rompers scuttling across the concrete like little flat crabs. It was a marvel to watch those two little girls move when that happened, and the noise was a pleasure. They became a little more cautious about taking them off and sometimes Janie would lie in wait for forty minutes before she had a chance. And sometimes, even then, she held off and the twins, one clothed, one bare, would circle around the romper, and stalk it like two kittens after a beetle. Then she would strike, the romper would fly, the twins would pounce; and sometimes they caught it immediately, and sometimes they had to chase it until their little lungs were going like a toy steam engine.

Janie learned the reason for their preoccupation with the basement door when one afternoon she had mastered the knack of lifting the rompers instead of just pushing them around. She held off until the twins were lulled into carelessness and were shucking out of their clothes, wandering away, ambling back again, as if to challenge her. And still she waited, until at last both rompers were lying together in a little pink-and-white mound. Then she struck. The rompers rose from the ground in a steep climbing turn and fluttered to the sill of a first-floor window. Since the courtyard was slightly below street level, this put the garments six feet high and well out of reach. There she left them.

One of the twins ran to the center of the courtyard and jumped up and down in agitation, stretching and craning to see the rompers. The other ran to the building under the first-floor window and reached her little hands up as high as she could get them, patting at the bricks fully twenty-eight inches under her goal. Then they ran to each other and twittered anxiously. After a time they tried reaching up the wall again, side by side. More and more they threw those terrified glances at the basement door; less and less was there any pleasure mixed with the terror.

At last they hunkered down as far as possible away from the door, put their arms about one another and stared numbly. They slowly quieted down, from chatters to twitters to cooings, and at last were silent, two tiny tuffets of terror.

It seemed hours—weeks—of fascinated anticipation before Janie heard a thump and saw the door move. Out came the janitor, as usual a little bottle-weary. She could see the red crescents under his sagging yellow-whited eyes. "Bonnie!" he bellowed, "Beanie! Wha y'all?" He lurched out into the open and peered around. "Come out yeah! Look at *yew*! I gwine snatch yew bald-headed! Wheah's yo' clo'es?" He swooped down on them and caught them, each huge hand on a tiny biceps. He held them high, so that each had one toe barely touching the concrete and their little captured elbows pointed skyward. He turned around, once, twice, seeking, and at last his eye caught the glimmer of the rompers on the sill. "How you do dat?" he demanded. "You trine th'ow away yo' 'spensive clo'es? Oh, I gwine whop you."

He dropped to one knee and hung the two little bodies across the other thigh. It is probable that he had the nack of cupping his hand so that he produced more sound than fury, but however he did it, the noise was impressive. Janie giggled.

The janitor administered four equal swats to each twin and set them on their feet. They stood silently side by side with their hands pressed to their bottoms and watched him stride to the windowsill and snatch the rompers off. He threw them down at their feet and waggled his right forefinger at them. "Cotch you do dat once mo', I'll get Mr. Milton the conductah come punch yo' ears fulla holes. *Heah?*" he roared. They shrank together, their eyes round. He lurched back to the door and slammed it shut behind him.

The twins slowly climbed into their rompers. Then they went back to the shadows by the wall and hunkered down, supporting themselves with their back and their feet. They whispered to one another. There was no more fun for Janie that day.

Across the street from Janie's apartment house was a park. It had a bandstand, a brook, a moulting peacock in a wire enclosure and a thick little copse of dwarf oak. In the copse was a hidden patch of bare earth, known only to Janie and several thousand people who were wont to use it in pairs at night. Since Janie was never there at night she felt herself its discoverer and its proprietor.

Some four days after the spanking episode, she thought of the place. She was bored with the twins; they never did anything interesting any more. Her mother had gone to lunch somewhere after locking her in her room. (One of her admirers, when she did this, had once asked, "What about the kid? Suppose there's a fire or something?" "Fat chance!" Wima had said with regret.)

The door of her room was fastened with a hook-and-eye on the outside. She walked to the door and looked up at the corresponding spot inside. She heard the hook rise and fall. She opened the door and walked down the hall and out to the elevators. When the self-service car arrived, she got in and pressed the third-, second- and first-floor buttons. One floor at a time the elevator descended, stopped, opened its gate, closed its gate, descended, stopped, opened its gate . . . it amused her, it was so stupid. At the bottom she pushed all of the buttons and slid out. Up the stupid elevator started. Janie clucked pityingly and went outdoors.

She crossed the street carefully, looking both ways. But when she got to the copse she was a little less ladylike. She climbed into the lower branches of the oak and across the multiple crotches to a branch she knew which overhung the hidden sanctuary. She thought she saw a movement in the bushes, but she was not sure. She hung from the branch, went hand over hand until it started to bend, waited until she had stopped swinging, and then let go.

It was an eight-inch drop to the earthen floor—usually. This time . . .

The very instant her fingers left the branch, her feet were caught and snatched violently backward. She struck the ground flat on her stomach. Her hands happened to be together, at her midriff; the impact turned them inward and drove her own fist into her solar plexus. For an unbearably long time she was nothing but one tangled knot of pain. She fought and fought and at long last sucked a tearing breath into her lungs. It would come out through her nostrils but she could get no more in. She fought again in a series of sucking sobs and blowing hisses, until the pain started to leave her.

She managed to get up on her elbows. She spat out dirt, part dusty, part muddy. She got her eyes open just enough to see one of the twins squatting before her, inches away. "Ho-ho," said the twin, grabbed her wrists, and pulled hard. Down she went on her face again. Reflexively she drew up her knees. She received a stinging blow on the rump. She looked down past her shoulder as she flung herself sideways and saw the other twin just in the midst of the follow-through with the stave from a nail keg which she held in her little hands. "He-hee," said the twin.

Janie did what she had done to the sallow, black-eyed man at the cocktail party. "Eeep," said the twin and disappeared, flickered out the way a squeezed appleseed disappears from between the fingers. The little cask stave clattered to the packed earth. Janie caught it up, whirled, and brought it down on the head of the twin who had pulled her arms. But the stave whooshed down to strike the ground; there was no one there.

Janie whimpered and got slowly to her feet. She was alone in the shadowed sanctuary. She turned and turned back. Nothing. No one.

Something plurped just on the center part of her hair. She clapped her hand to it. Wet. She looked up and the other twin spit too. It hit her on the forehead. "Ho-ho," said one. "He-hee," said the other.

Janie's upper lip curled away from her teeth, exactly the way her mother's did. She still held the cask stave. She slung it upward with all her might. One twin did not even attempt to move. The other disappeared.

"Ho-ho." There she was, on another branch. Both were grinning widely.

She hurled a bolt of hatred at them the like of which she had never even imagined before.

"Ooop," said one. The other said "Eeep." Then they were both gone.

Clenching her teeth, she leapt for the branch and swarmed up into the tree.

"*Ho-ho.*"

It was very distant. She looked up and around and down and back; and something made her look across the street.

Two little figures sat like gargoyles on top of the courtyard wall. They waved to her and were gone.

For a long time Janie clung to the tree and stared at the wall. Then she let herself slide down into the crotch where she could put her back against the trunk and straddle a limb. She unbuttoned her pocket and got her handkerchief. She licked a fold of it good and wet and began wiping the dirt off her face with little feline dabs.

They're only three years old, she told herself from the astonished altitude of her seniority. Then, *They knew who it was all along, that moved those rompers.*

She said aloud, in admiration, "Ho-ho . . ." There was no anger left in her. Four days ago the twins couldn't even reach a six-foot sill. They couldn't even get away from a spanking. And now look.

She got down on the street side of the tree and stepped daintily across the street. In the vestibule, she stretched up and pressed the shiny brass button marked JANITOR. While waiting she stepped off the pattern of tiles in the floor, heel and toe.

"Who push dat? You push dat?" His voice filled the whole world.

She went and stood in front of him and pushed up her lips the way her mother did when she made her voice all croony, like sometimes on the telephone. "Mister Widdecombe, my mother says I can play with your little girls."

"She say dat? *Well!*" The janitor took off his round hat and whacked it against his palm and put it on again. "Well. Dat's mighty nice . . . little gal," he said sternly, "is yo' mother to home?"

"Oh *yes*," said Janie, fairly radiating candor.

"You wait raht cheer," he said, and pounded away down the cellar steps.

She had to wait more than ten minutes this time. When he came back with the twins he was fairly out of breath. They looked very solemn.

"Now don't you let 'em get in any mischief. And see ef you cain't keep them clo'es on 'em. They ain't got no more use for clo'es than a jungle monkey. Gwan, now, hole hands, chillun, an' mine you don't leave go tel you git there."

The twins approached guardedly. She took their hands. They watched her face. She began to move toward the elevators, and they followed. The janitor beamed after them.

Janie's whole life shaped itself from that afternoon. It was a time of belonging, of thinking alike, of transcendent sharing. For her age, Janie had what was probably a unique vocabulary, yet she spoke hardly a word. The twins had not yet learned to talk. Their private vocabulary of squeaks and whimpers was incidental to another kind of communion. Janie got a sign of it, a touch of it, a sudden opening, growing rush of it. Her mother hated her and feared her; her father was a remote and angry entity, always away or shouting at mother or closed sulkily about himself. She was talked to, never spoken to.

But here was converse, detailed, fluent, fascinating, with no sound but laughter. They would be silent; they would all squat suddenly and paw through Janie's beautiful books; then suddenly it was the dolls. Janie showed them how she could get chocolates from the box in the other room without going in there and how she could throw a pillow clear up to the ceiling without touching it. They liked that, though the paintbox and easel impressed them more.

It was a thing together, binding, immortal; it would always be new for them and it would never be repeated.

The afternoon slid by, as smooth and soft and lovely as a passing gull, and as swift. When the hall door banged open and Wima's voice clanged out, the twins were still there.

"All righty, all righty, come in for a drink then, who wants to stand out there all night." She pawed her hat off and her hair swung raggedly over her face. The man caught her roughly and pulled her close and bit her face. She howled. "You're crazy, you old crazy you." Then she saw them, all three of them peering out. "Dear old Jesus be to God," she said, "she's got the place filled with niggers."

"They're going home," said Janie resolutely. "I'll take 'em home right now."

"Honest to God, Pete," she said to the man, "this is the God's honest first time this ever happened. You got to believe that, Pete. What kind of a place you must think I run here, I hate to think how it looks to you. Well get them the hell out!" she screamed at Janie. "Honest to God, Pete, so help me, never before—"

Janie walked down the hall to the elevators. She looked at Bonnie and at Beanie. Their eyes were round. Janie's mouth was as dry as a carpet and she was so embarrassed her legs cramped. She put the twins into an elevator and pressed the bottom button. She did not say goodbye, though she felt nothing else.

She walked slowly back to the apartment and went in and closed the door. Her mother got up from the man's lap and clattered across the room. Her teeth shone and her chin was wet. She raised claws—not a hand, not a fist, but red, pointed claws.

Something happened inside Janie like the grinding of teeth, but deeper inside her than that. She was walking and she did not stop. She put her hands behind her and tilted her chin up so she could meet her mother's eyes.

Wima's voice ceased, snatched away. She loomed over the five-year-old, her claws out and forward, hanging, curving over, a blood-tipped wave about to break.

Janie walked past her and into her room, and quietly closed the door.

Wima's arms drew back, strangely, as if they must follow the exact trajectory of their going. She repossessed them and the dissolving balance of her body and finally her voice. Behind her the man's teeth clattered swiftly against a glass.

Wima turned and crossed the room to him, using the furniture like a series of canes and crutches. "Oh God," she murmured, "but she gives me the creeps. . . ."

He said, "You got lots going on around here."

Janie lay in bed as stiff and smooth and contained as a round toothpick. Nothing would get in, nothing could get out; somewhere she had found this surface that went all the way through, and as long as she had it, nothing was going to happen.

But if anything happens, came a whisper, *you'll break.*

But if I don't break, nothing will happen, she answered.

But if anything . . .

The dark hours came and grew black and the black hours labored by.

Her door crashed open and the light blazed. "He's gone and baby, I've got business with you. Get out here!" Wima's bathrobe swirled against the doorpost as she turned and went away.

Janie pushed back the covers and thumped her feet down. Without understanding quite why, she began to get dressed. She got her good plaid dress and the shoes with two buckles, and the knit pants and the slip with the lace rabbits. There were little rabbits on her socks too, and on the sweater, the buttons were rabbits' fuzzy nubbin tails.

Wima was on the couch, pounding and pounding with her fist. "You wrecked my cel," she said, and drank from a square-stemmed glass, "ebration, so you ought to know what I'm celebrating. You don't know it but I've had a big trouble and I didn't know how to hannel it, and now it's all done for me. And I'll tell you all about it right now, little baby Miss Big Ears. Big Mouth. Smarty. Because your father, I can hannel him any time, but what I was going to do with your big mouth going day and night? That was my trouble, what was I going to do about your big mouth when he got back. Well it's all fixed, he won't be back, the Heinies fixed it up for me." She waved a yellow sheet. "Smart girls know that's a telegram, and the telegram says, says here, 'Regret to inform you that your husband.' They shot your father, that's what they regret to say, and now this is the way it's going to be from now on between you and me. Whatever I want to do I do, an' whatever you want to nose into, nose away. Now isn't that fair?"

She turned to be answered but there was no answer. Janie was gone.

Wima knew before she started that there wasn't any use looking, but something made her run to the hall closet and look in the top shelf. There wasn't anything up there but Christmas tree ornaments and they hadn't been touched in three years.

She stood in the middle of the living room, not knowing which way to go. She whispered, "Janie?"

She put her hands on the sides of her face and lifted her hair away from it. She turned around and around, and asked, "What's the matter with me?"

Prodd used to say, "There's this about a farm: when the market's good there's money, and when it's bad there's food." Actually the principle hardly operated here, for his contract with markets was slight. It was a long haul to town and what if there's a tooth off the hayrake? "We've still got a workin' majority." Two off, eight, twelve? "Then make another pass. No road will go by here, not ever. Place will never get too big, get out of hand." Even the war passed them by, Prodd being over age and Lone—well, the sheriff was by once and had a look at the halfwit working on Prodd's, and one look was enough.

When Prodd was young the little farmhouse was there, and when he married they built on to it—a little, not a lot, just a room. If the room had ever been used the land wouldn't have been enough. Lone slept in the room of course but that wasn't quite the same thing. That's not what the room was for.

Lone sensed the change before anyone else, even before Mrs. Prodd. It was a difference in the nature of one of her silences. It was a treasure-proud silence, and Lone felt it change as a man's kind of pride might change when he turned from a jewel he treasured to a green shoot he treasured. He said nothing and concluded nothing; he just knew.

He went on with his work as before. He worked well; Prodd used to say that whatever anyone might think, that boy was a farmer before his accident. He said it not knowing that his own style of farming was as available to Lone as water from his pump. So was anything else Lone wanted to take.

So the day Prodd came down to the south meadow, where Lone was stepping and turning tirelessly, a very part of his whispering scythe, Lone knew what it was that he wanted to say. He caught Prodd's gaze for half a breath in those disturbing eyes and knew as well that saying it would pain Prodd more than a little.

Understanding was hardly one of his troubles any more, but niceties of expression were. He stopped mowing and went to the forest margin nearby and let the scythe-point drop into a rotten stump. It gave him time to rehearse his tongue, still thick and unwieldy after eight years here.

Prodd followed slowly. He was rehearsing too.

Suddenly, Lone found it. "Been thinking," he said.

Prodd waited, glad to wait. Lone said, "I should go." That wasn't quite it. "Move along," he said, watching. That was better.

"Ah, Lone. Why?"

Lone looked at him. *Because you want me to go.*

"Don't you like it here?" said Prodd, not wanting to say that at all.

"Sure." From Prodd's mind, he caught, *Does he know?* and his own answered, *Of course I know!* But Prodd couldn't hear that. Lone said slowly, "Just time to be moving along."

"Well." Prodd kicked a stone. He turned to look at the house and that turned him away from Lone, and that made it easier. "When we came here, we built Jack's, *your* room, the room you're using. We call it Jack's room. You know why, you know who Jack is?"

Yes, Lone thought. He said nothing.

"Long as you're . . . long as you want to leave anyway, it won't make no difference to you. Jack's our son." He squeezed his hands together. "I guess it sounds funny. Jack was the little guy we were so sure about, we built that room with seed money. Jack, he—"

He looked up at the house, at its stub of a built-on wing, and around at the rock-toothed forest rim. "—never got born," he finished.

"Ah," said Lone. He's picked that up from Prodd. It was useful.

"He's coming now, though," said Prodd in a rush. His face was alight. "We're a bit old for it, but there's a daddy or two quite a bit older, and mothers too." Again he looked up at the barn, the house. "Makes sense in a sort of way, you know, Lone. Now, if he'd been along when we planned it, the place would've been too small when he was growed enough to work it with me, and me with no place else to go. But now, why, I reckon when he's growed we just naturally won't be here any more, and he'll take him a nice little wife and start out just about like we did. So you see it does make a kind of sense?" He seemed to be pleading. Lone made no attempt to understand this.

"Lone, listen to me, I don't want you to feel we're turning you out."

"Said I was going." Searching, he found something and amended, " 'Fore you told me." *That,* he thought, *was very right.*

"Look, I got to say something," said Prodd. "I heard tell of folks who want kids and can't have 'em, sometimes they just give up trying and take in somebody else's. And sometimes, with a kid in the house, they turn right round and have one of their own after all."

"Ah," said Lone.

"So what I mean is, we taken you in, didn't we, and now look."

Lone did not know what to say. "Ah" seemed wrong.

"We got a lot to thank you for, is what I mean, so we don't want you to feel we're turning you out."

"I already said."

"Good then." Prodd smiled. He had a lot of wrinkles on his face, mostly from smiling.

"Good," said Lone. "About Jack." He nodded vehemently. "Good." He picked up the scythe. When he reached his window, he looked after Prodd. *Walks slower than he used to,* he thought.

Lone's next conscious thought was, Well, that's finished.

What's finished? he asked himself.

He looked around. "Mowing," he said. Only then he realized that he had been working for more than three hours since Prodd spoke to him, and it was as if some other person had done it. He himself had been—*gone* in some way.

Absently he took his whetstone and began to dress the scythe. It made a sound like a pot boiling over when he moved it slowly, and like a shrew dying when he moved it fast.

Where had he known this feeling of time passing, as it were, behind his back?

He moved the stone slowly. Cooking and warmth and work. A birthday cake. A clean bed. A sense of . . . "Membership" was not a word he possessed but that was his thought.

No, obliterated time didn't exist in those memories. He moved the stone faster.

Death-cries in the wood. Lonely hunter and its solitary prey. The sap falls and the bear sleeps and the birds fly south, all doing it together, not because they are all members of the same thing, but only because they are all solitary things hurt by the same thing.

That was where time had passed without his awareness of it. Almost always, before he came here. That was how he had lived.

Why should it come back to him now, then?

He swept his gaze around the land, as Prodd had done, taking in the house and its imbalancing bulge, and the land, and the woods which held the farm like water in a basin. When I was alone, he thought, time passed me like that. Time passes like that now, so it must be that I am alone again.

And then he knew that he had been alone the whole time. Mrs. Prodd hadn't raised him up, not really. She had been raising up her Jack the whole time.

Once in the wood, in water and agony, he had been a part of something, and in wetness and pain it had been torn from him. And if, for eight years now, he had thought he had found something else to belong to, then for eight years he had been wrong.

Anger was foreign to him; he had only felt it once before. But now it came, a wash of it that made him swell, that drained and left him weak. And he himself was the object of it. For hadn't he known? Hadn't he taken a name for himself, knowing that the name was a crystallization of all he had ever been and done? All he had ever been and done was *alone*. Why should he have let himself feel any other way?

Wrong. Wrong as a squirrel with feathers, or a wolf with wooden teeth; not injustice, not unfairness—just a wrongness that, under the sky, could not exist . . . the idea that such as he could belong to anything.

Hear that, *son?* Hear, that, *man?*

Hear that, Lone?

He picked up three long fresh stalks of timothy and braided them together. He upended the scythe and thrust the handle deep enough into the soft earth so it would stand upright. He tied the braided grass to one of the grips and slipped the whetstone into the loops so it would stay. Then he walked off into the woods.

It was too late even for the copse's nocturnal habitants. It was cold at the hidden foot of the dwarf oak and as dark as the chambers of a dead man's heart.

She sat on the bare earth. As time went on, she had slid down a little and her plaid skirt had moved up. Her legs were icy, especially when the night air moved on them. But she didn't pull the skirt down because it didn't matter. Her hand lay on one of the fuzzy buttons of her sweater because, two hours ago, she had been fingering it and wondering what it was like to be a bunny. Now she didn't care whether or not the button was a bunny's tail or where her hand happened to be.

She had learned all she could from being there. She had learned that if you leave your eyes open until you have to blink and you don't blink, they start to hurt. Then if you leave them open even longer, they hurt worse and worse. And if you still leave them open, they suddenly stop hurting.

It was too dark there to know whether they could still see after that.

And she had learned that if you sit absolutely still for long enough it hurts too, and then stops. But then you mustn't move, not the tiniest little bit, because if you do it will hurt worse than anything.

When a top spins it stands up straight and walks around. When it slows a little it stands in one place and wobbles. When it slows a lot it waggles around like Major Grenfell after a cocktail party. Then it almost stops and lies down and bumps and thumps and thrashes around. After that it won't move any more.

When she had the happy time with the twins she had been spinning like that. When Mother came home the top inside didn't walk any more, it stood still and waggled. When Mother called her out of her bed she was waving and weaving. When she hid here her spinner inside bumped and kicked. Well, it wasn't doing it any more and it wouldn't.

She started to see how long she could hold her breath. Not with a big deep lungful first, but just breathing quieter and quieter and missing an *in* and quieter and quieter still, and missing an *out*. She got to where the misses took longer than the breathings.

The wind stirred her skirt. All she could feel was the movement and that too was remote, as if she had a thin pillow between it and her legs.

Her spinner, with the lift gone out of it, went round and round with its rim on the floor and went slower and slower and at last

stopped

. . . and began to roll back the other way, but not very far, not fast and

stopped

and a little way back, it was too dark for anything to roll, and even if it did you wouldn't be able to see it, you couldn't even hear it, it was so dark.

But anyway, she rolled. She rolled over on her stomach and on

her back and pain squeezed her nostrils together and filled up her
stomach like too much soda water. She gasped with the pain and
gasping was breathing and when she breathed she remembered who
she was. She rolled over again without wanting to, and something
like little animals ran on her face. She fought them weakly. They
weren't pretend-things, she discovered; they were real as real. They
whispered and cooed. She tried to sit up and the little animals ran
behind her and helped. She dangled her head down and felt the
warmth of her breath falling into the front of her dress. One of the
little animals stroked her cheek and she put up a hand and caught it.

"Ho-ho," it said.

On the other side, something soft and small and strong wriggled
and snuggled tight up against her. She felt it, smooth and alive. It
said "He-hee."

She put one arm around Bonnie and one arm around Beanie and
began to cry.

Lone came back to borrow an ax. You can do just so much with
your bare hands.

When he broke out of the woods he saw the difference in the
farm. It was as if every day it existed had been a gray day, and now
the sun was on it. All the colors were brighter by an immeasurable
amount; the barn-smells, growth-smells, stove-smoke smells were
clearer and purer. The corn stretched skyward with such intensity in
its lines that it seemed to be threatening its roots.

Prodd's venerable stake-bed pick-up truck was grunting and howl-
ing somewhere down the slope. Following the margins, Lone went
downhill until he could see the truck. It was in the fallow field
which, apparently, Prodd had decided to turn. The truck was
hitched to a gang plow with all the shares but one removed. The
right rear wheel had run too close to the furrow, dropped in, and
buried, so that the truck rested on its rear axle and the wheel spun
almost free. Prodd was pounding stones under it with the end of a
pick-handle. When he saw Lone he dropped it and ran toward him,
his face beaming like firelight. He took Lone's upper arms in his
hands and read his face like the page of a book, slowly, a line at a
time, moving his lips. "Man, I thought I wouldn't see you again,
going off like you did."

"You want help," said Lone, meaning the truck.

Prodd misunderstood. "Now wouldn't you know," he said happily. "Come all the way back to see if you could lend a hand. Oh, I been doing fine by myself, Lone, believe me. Not that I don't appreciate it. But I feel like it these days. Working, I mean."

Lone went and picked up the pick-handle. He prodded at the stones under the wheel. "Drive," he said.

"Wait'll Ma sees you," said Prodd "Like old times." He got in and started the truck. Lone put the small of his back against the rear edge of the truck-bed, clamped his hands on it, and as the clutch engaged, he heaved. The body came up as high as the rear springs would let it, and still higher. He leaned back. The wheel found purchase and the truck jolted up and forward onto firm ground.

Prodd climbed out and came back to look into the hole, the irresistible and useless act of a man who picks up broken china and puts its edges together. "I used to say, I bet you were a farmer once," he grinned. "But now I know. You were a hydraulic jack."

Lone did not smile. He never smiled. Prodd went to the plow and Lone helped him wrestle the hitch back to the truck. "Horse dropped dead," Prodd explained. "Truck's all right but sometimes I wish there was some way to keep this from happening. Spend half my time diggin' it out. I'd get another horse, but you know—hold everything till after Jack gets here. You'd think that would bother me, losing the horse." He looked up at the house and smiled. "Nothing bothers me now. Had breakfast?"

"Yes."

"Well come have some more. You know Ma. Wouldn't forgive either of us if she wasn't to feed you."

They went back to the house, and when Ma saw Lone she hugged him hard. Something stirred uncomfortably in Lone. He wanted an ax. He thought all these other things were settled. "You sit right down there and I'll get you some breakfast."

"Told you," said Prodd, watching her, smiling. Lone watched her too. She was heavier and happy as a kitten in a cowshed. "What you doing now, Lone?"

Lone looked into his eyes to find some sort of an answer. "Working," he said. He moved his hand. "Up there."

"In the woods?"

"Yes."

"What you doing?" When Lone waited, Prodd asked, "You hired out? No? Then what—trapping?"

"Trapping," said Lone, knowing that this would be sufficient.

He ate. From where he sat he could see Jack's room. The bed was gone. There was a new one in there, not much longer than his forearm, all draped with pale-blue cotton and cheese-cloth with dozens of little tucks sewn into it.

When he was finished they all sat around the table and for a time nobody said anything. Lone looked into Prodd's eyes and found *He's a good boy but not the kind to set around and visit.* He couldn't understand the *visit* image, a vague and happy blur of conversation-sounds and laughter. He recognized this as one of the many lacks he was aware of in himself—lacks, rather than inadequacies; things he could not do and would never be able to do. So he just asked Prodd for the ax and went out.

"You don't s'pose e's mad at us?" asked Mrs. Prodd, looking anxiously after Lone.

"Him?" said Prodd. "He wouldn't have come back here if he was. I was afraid of that myself until today." He went to the door. "Don't you lift nothing heavy, hear?"

Janie read as slowly and carefully as she could. She didn't have to read aloud, but only carefully enough so the twins could understand. She had reached the part where the woman tied the man to the pillar and then let the other man, the "my rival, her laughing lover" one, out of the closet where he had been hidden and gave him the whip. Janie looked up at that point and found Bonnie gone and Beanie in the cold fireplace, pretending there was a mouse hiding in the ashes. "Oh, you're not listening," she said.

Want the one with the pictures, the silent message came.

"I'm getting so tired of that one," said Janie petulantly. But she closed *Venus in Furs* by von Sacher-Masoch and put it on the table. "This's anyway got a story to it," she complained, going to the shelves. She found the wanted volume between *My Gun Is Quick* and *The Illustrated Ivan Bloch,* and hefted it back to the armchair. Bonnie disappeared from the fireplace and reappeared by the chair. Beanie stood on the other side; wherever she had been, she had been aware of what was happening. If anything, she liked this book even better than Bonnie.

Janie opened the book at random. The twins leaned forward breathless, their eyes bugging.

Read it.

"Oh, all right," said Janie. " 'D34556. Tieback. Double shirred. 90 inches long. Maize, burgundy, hunter green and white. $24.68. D34557. Cottage style. Stuart or Argyll plaid, see illus. $4.92 pair. D34—' "

And they were happy again.

They had been happy ever since they got here and much of the hectic time before that. They had learned how to open the back of a trailer-truck and how to lie without moving under hay, and Janie could pull clothespins off a line and the twins could appear inside a room, like a store at night, and unlock the door from the inside when it was fastened with some kind of lock that Janie couldn't move, the way she could a hook-and-eye or a tower bolt which was shot but not turned. The best thing they had learned, though, was the way the twins could attract attention when somebody was chasing Janie. They'd found out for sure that to have two little girls throwing rocks from second-floor windows and appearing under their feet to trip them and suddenly sitting on their shoulders and wetting into their collars, made it impossible to catch Janie, who was just ordinarily running. Ho-ho.

And this house was just the happiest thing of all. It was miles and miles away from anything or anybody and no one ever came here. It was a big house on a hill, in forest so thick you hardly knew it was there. It had a big high wall around it on the road side, and a big high fence on the woods side and a brook ran through. Bonnie had found it one day when they had gotten tired and gone to sleep by the road. Bonnie woke up and went exploring by herself and found the fence and went along it until she saw the house. They'd had a terrible time finding some way to get Janie in, though, until Beanie fell into the brook where it went through the fence, and came up on the inside.

There were zillions of books in the biggest room and plenty of old sheets they could wrap around themselves when it was cold. Down in the cold dark cellar rooms they had found a half-dozen cases of canned vegetables and some bottles of wine, which later they smashed all over because, although it tasted bad, it smelled just wonderful. There was a pool out back to swim in that was more fun than the bathrooms, which had no windows. There were plenty of places for hide-and-seek. There was even a little room with chains on the walls, and bars.

It went much faster with the ax.

He never would have found the place at all if he had not hurt himself. In all the years he had wandered the forests, often blindly and uncaring, he had never fallen into such a trap. One moment he was stepping over the crest of an out-cropping, and next he was twenty feet down, in a bramble-choked, humus-floored pitfall. He hurt one of his eyes and his left arm hurt unbearably at the elbow.

Once he had thrashed his way out, he surveyed the place. Perhaps it had once been a pool in the slope with the lower side thin and erosible. It was gone, however, and what was left was a depression in the hillside, thickly grown inside, ever more thickly screened on both sides and at the front. The rock over which he had stepped rose out of the hill and overhung the depression.

At one time it had not mattered in the least to Lone whether he was near men or not. Now, he wanted only to be able to be what he knew he was—alone. But eight years at the farm had changed his way of life. He needed shelter. And the more he looked at this hidden place, with its overhanging rock wall-ceiling and the two earthen wings which flanked it, the more shelterlike it seemed.

At first his work on it was primitive. He cleared out enough brush so that he might lie down comfortably and pulled up a bush or two so that the brambles would not flay him as he went in and out. Then it rained and he had to channel the inside so that water would not stand inside, and he made a rough thatch at the crest.

But as time went on he became increasingly absorbed in the place. He pulled up more bush and pounded the earth until he had a level floor. He removed all the rock he could find loose on the rear wall, and discovered that some of the wall had ready-made shelves and nooks for the few things he might want to store. He began raiding the farms that skirted the foot of the mountain, operating at night, taking only a very little at each place, never coming back to any one place if he could help it. He got carrots and potatoes and tenpenny spikes and haywire, a broken hammer and a cast-iron pot. Once he found a side of bacon that had fallen from an abattoir truck. He stored it and when he came back he found that a lynx had been at it. That determined him to make walls, which was why he went back for the ax.

He felled trees, the biggest he could handle after trimming, and snaked them up to the hillside. He buried the first three so that they bounded the floor, and the side ones butted against the rock. He found a red clay which, when mixed with peat moss, made a mortar that was vermin-proof and would not wash away. He built up his walls and a door. He did not bother with a window, but simply left out a yard of mortar between six of the wall logs, on each side, and trimmed long side-tapered sticks to wedge in them when he wanted them closed.

His first fireplace was Indian-style, out near the center of the enclosure, with a hole at the top to let the smoke out. High up were hooks embedded in rock fissures, for hanging meat where the smoke could get to it, if he were ever fortunate enough to get some.

He was out hunting for flagstones for the fireplace when an invisible something began to tug at him. He recoiled as if he had been burned and shrank back against a tree and cast about him like a cornered elk.

It had been a long time since he had been aware of his inner sensitivity to the useless (to him) communication of infants. He was losing it; he had begun to be insensitive to it when he began to gain speech.

But someone had called to him this way—someone who "sent" like a child, but who was not a child. And though what he felt now was faint, it was in substance unbearably similar. It was sweet and needful, yes; but it was also the restimulation of a stinging lash and a terror of crushing kicks and obscene shouting, and the greatest loss he had ever known.

There was nothing to be seen. Slowly he left the tree and went back to the slab of stone he had been pawing at to free it from the earth. For perhaps half an hour he worked doggedly, trying to ignore the call. And he failed.

He rose, shaken, and began to walk to the call in a world turned dreamlike. The longer he walked, the more irresistible the call became and the deeper his enchantment. He walked for an hour, never going around anything if he could possibly go over it or through it, and by the time he reached the leached clearing he was nearly somnambulant. To permit himself any more consciousness would have been to kindle such an inferno of conflict that he could not have gone on. Stumbling blindly, he walked right up to and into the rusting fence which struck him cruelly over his hurt eye. He clung to it until his vision cleared, looked around to see where he was, and began to tremble.

He had one moment of clear, conscious determination: to get out of this terrible place and stay out of it. And even as he felt this touch of reason, he heard the brook and was turning toward it.

Where brook and fence met, he lowered himself in the water and made his way to the foot of the pickets. Yes, the opening was still here.

He peered in through the fence, but the ancient holly was thicker than ever. There was nothing to be heard, either—aurally. But the call . . .

Like the one he had heard before, it was a hunger, an aloneness, a wanting. The difference was in what it wanted. It said without words that it was a little afraid, and burdened, and was solicitous of the burden. It said in effect *who will take care of me now?*

Perhaps the cold water helped. Lone's mind suddenly became as clear as it ever could. He took a deep breath and submerged. Immediately on the other side he stopped and raised his head. He listened carefully, then lay on his stomach with only his nostrils above the water. With exquisite care, he inched forward on his elbows, until his head was inside the arch and he could see through.

There was a little girl on the bank, dressed in a torn plaid dress. She was about six. Her sharp-planed, unchildlike face was down-drawn and worried. And if he thought his caution was effective, he was quite wrong. She was looking directly at him.

"Bonnie!" she called sharply.

Nothing happened.

He stayed where he was. She continued to watch him, but she continued to worry. He realized two things: that it was this worriment of hers which was the essence of the call; and that although she was on her guard, she did not consider him important enough to divert her from her thoughts.

For the first time in his life he felt that edged and spicy mixture of anger and amusement called pique. This was followed by a great surge of relief, much like what one would feel on setting down a forty-pound pack after forty years. He had not known . . . he had not *known* the size of his burden!

And away went the restimulation. Back into the past went the whip and the bellowing, the magic and the loss—remembered still, but back where they belonged, with their raw-nerve tendrils severed so that never again could they reach into his present. The call was no maelstrom of blood and emotion, but the aimless chunterings of a hungry brat.

He sank and shot backward like a great lean crawfish, under the fence. He slogged up out of the brook, turned his back on the call and went back to his work.

When he got back to his shelter, streaming with perspiration, an eighteen-inch flagstone on his shoulder, he was weary enough to forget his usual caution. He crashed in through the underbrush to the tiny clearing before his door, and stopped dead.

There was a small naked infant about four years old squatting in front of his door.

She looked up at him and her eyes—her whole dark face—seemed to twinkle. "He-hee!" she said happily.

He tipped the stone off his shoulder and let it fall. He loomed over her, shadowed her; sky-high and full of the threats of thunder.

She seemed completely unafraid. She turned her eyes away from him and busily began nibbling at a carrot, turning it squirrel-wise, around and around as she ate.

A high movement caught his eye. Another carrot was emerging from the ventilation chinks in the long wall. It fell to the ground and was followed by still another.

"Ho-ho." He looked down, and there were *two* little girls.

The only advantage which Lone possessed under these circumstances was a valuable one: he had no impulse whatever to question his sanity and start a confusing debate with himself on the matter. He bent down and scooped one of the children up. But when he straightened she wasn't there any more.

The other was. She grinned enchantingly and started on one of the new carrots.

Lone said, "What you doing?" His voice was harsh and ill-toned, like that of a deaf-mute. It startled the child. She stopped eating and looked up at him open-mouthed. The open mouth was filled with carrot chips and gave her rather the appearance of a pot-bellied stove with the door open.

He sank down on his knees. Her eyes were fixed on his and his were eyes which had once commanded a man to kill himself and which, many times, violated the instincts of others who had not wanted to feed him. Without knowing why he was careful. There was no anger in him or fear; he simply wanted her to stay still.

When he was done, he reached for her. She exhaled noisily, blowing tiny wet chips of raw carrot into his eyes and nostrils, and vanished.

He was filled with astonishment—a strange thing in itself, for he had seldom been interested enough in anything to be astonished. Stranger still, it was a respectful astonishment.

He rose and put his back against the log wall, and looked for them. They stood side by side, hand in hand, looking up at him out of little wooden wondering faces, waiting for him to do something else.

Once, years ago, he had run to catch a deer. Once he had reached up from the ground to catch a bird in a treetop. Once he had plunged into a stream after a trout.

Once.

Lone was simply not constituted to chase something he knew empirically that he could not catch. He bent and picked up his flagstone, reached up and slid aside the outside bar which fastened his door and shouldered into the house.

He bedded his flagstone by the fire and swept the guttering embers over part of it. He threw on more wood and blew it up brightly, set up his green-stick crane and swung the iron pot on it. All the while there were two little white-eyed knobs silhouetted in the doorway, watching him. He ignored them.

The skinned rabbit swung on the high hook by the smoke hole. He got it down, tore off the quarters, broke the back and dropped it all into the pot. From a niche he took potatoes and a few grains of rock salt. The salt went into the pot and so did the potatoes after he had split them in two on his ax-blade. He reached for his carrots. Somebody had been at his carrots.

He wheeled and frowned at the doorway. The two heads whipped back out of sight. From outdoors came small soprano giggles.

Lone let the pot boil for an hour while he honed the ax and tied up a witch's broom like Mrs. Prodd's. And slowly, a fraction of an inch at a time, his visitors edged into the room. Their eyes were fixed on the seething pot. They fairly drooled.

He went about his business without looking at them. When he came close they retreated and when he crossed the room they entered again—that little fraction more each time. Soon their retreats were smaller and their advances larger until at last Lone had a chance to slam the door shut—which he did.

In the sudden darkness, the simmer of the pot and the small hiss of the flames sounded very loud. There was no other sound. Lone stood with his back against the door and closed his eyes very tight to adjust them more quickly to the darkness. When he opened them, the bars of waning daylight at the vents and the fireglow were quite sufficient for him to see everything in the room.

The little girls were gone.

He put on the inner bar and slowly circled the room. Nothing.

He opened the door cautiously, then flung it wide. They were not outside either.

He shrugged. He pulled on his lower lip and wished he had more carrots. Then he set the pot aside to cool enough so that he could eat and finished honing the ax.

At length he ate. He had reached the point of licking his fingers by way of having dessert, when a sharp knock on the door caused him to leap eighteen inches higher than upright, so utterly unexpected was it.

In the doorway stood the little girl in the plaid dress. Her hair was combed, her face scrubbed. She carried with a superb air an object which seemed to be a handbag but which at second glance revealed itself as a teakwood cigarette box with a piece of binder-twine fastened to it with four-inch nails. "Good evening," she said concisely. "I was passing by and thought I would come to call. You *are* at home?"

This parroting of a penurious beldame who once was in the habit of cadging meals by this means was completely incomprehensible to Lone. He resumed licking his fingers but he kept his eyes on the child's face. Behind the girl, suddenly, appeared the heads of his two previous visitors peeping around the doorpost.

The child's nostrils, then her eyes, found the stew pot. She wooed it with her gaze, yearned. She yawned, too, suddenly. "I beg your pardon," she said demurely. She pried open the lid of the cigarette box, drew out a white object and folded it quickly but not quickly enough to conceal the fact that it was a large man's sock, and patted her lips with it.

Lone rose and got a piece of wood and placed it carefully on the fire and sat down again. The girl took another step. The other two scuttled in and stood, one on each side of the doorway like toy soldiers. Their faces were little knots of apprehension. And they were clothed this time. One wore a pair of lady's linen bloomers, the like of which has not been seen since cars had tillers. It came up to her armpits, and was supported by two short lengths of the same hairy binder-twine, poked through holes torn in the waistband and acting as shoulder straps. The other one wore a heavy cotton slip, or at least the top third of it. It fell to her ankles where it showed a fringe of torn and unhemmed material.

With the exact air of a lady crossing a drawing room toward the bonbons, the white child approached the stewpot, flashed Lone a small smile, lowered her eyelids and reached down with a thumb and forefinger, murmuring, "May I?"

Lone stretched out one long leg and hooked the pot away from her and into his grasp. He set it on the floor on the side away from her and looked at her woodenly.

"You're a real cheap stingy son of a bitch," the child quoted.

This also missed Lone completely. Before he had learned to be aware of what men said, such remarks had been meaningless. Since, he had not been exposed to them. He stared at her blankly and pulled the pot protectively closer.

The child's eyes narrowed and her color rose. Suddenly she began to cry. "Please," she said. "I'm hungry. *We're* hungry. The stuff in the cans, it's all gone." Her voice failed her but she could still whisper. "Please," she whispered, "please."

Lone regarded her stonily. At length she took a timid step toward him. He lifted the pot into his lap and hugged it defiantly. She said, "Well, I didn't want any of your old . . ." but then her voice broke. She turned away and went to the door. The others watched her face as she came. They radiated silent disappointment; their eloquent expressions took the white girl to task far more than they did him. She had the status of provider and she had failed them, and they were merciless in their expression of it.

He sat with the warm pot in his lap and looked out the open door into the thickening night. Unbidden, an image appeared to him—Mrs. Prodd, a steaming platter of baked ham flanked by the orange gaze of perfect eggs, saying, "Now you set right down and have some breakfast." An emotion he was unequipped to define reached up from his solar plexus and tugged at his throat.

He snorted, reached into the pot, scooped out half a potato and opened his mouth to receive it. His hand would not deliver. He bent his head slowly and looked at the potato as if he could not quite recognize it or its function.

He snorted again, flung the potato back into the pot, thumped the pot back on the floor and leapt to his feet. He put one hand on each side of the door and sent his flat harsh voice hurtling out: "*Wait!*"

The corn should have been husked long since. Most of it still stood but here and there the stalks lay broken and yellowing, and soldier-ants were prospecting them and scurrying off with rumors. Out in the fallow field the truck lay forlornly, bogged, with the seeder behind it, tipped forward over its hitch and the winter wheat spilling out. No smoke came from the chimney up at the house and the half-door into the barn, askew and perverted amid the misery, hollowly applauded.

Lone approached the house, mounted the stoop. Prodd sat on the porch glider which now would not glide, for one set of end-chains was broken. His eyes were not closed but they were more closed than open.

"Hi," said Lone.

Prodd stirred, looked full into Lone's face. There was no sign of recognition. He dropped his gaze, pushed back to sit upright, felt aimlessly around his chest, found a suspender strap, pulled it forward and let it snap back. A troubled expression passed through his features and left it. He looked up again at Lone, who could sense self-awareness returning to the farmer like coffee soaking upward into a lump of sugar.

"Well, Lone, boy!" said Prodd. The old words were there but the tone behind them behaved like his broken hay rake. He rose, beaming, came to Lone, raised his fist to thump Lone's arm but then apparently forgot it. The fist hovered there for a moment and then gravitated downward.

"Corn's for husking," said Lone.

"Yeah, yeah, I know," Prodd half said, half sighed. "I'll get to it. I can handle it all right. One way or 'tother, always get done by the first frost. Ain't missed milkin' once," he added with wan pride.

Lone glanced through the door pane and saw, for the very first time, crusted dishes, heavy flies in the kitchen. "The baby come," he said, remembering.

"Oh, yes. Fine little feller, just like we . . ." Again he seemed to forget. The words slowed and were left suspended as his fist had been. "Ma!" he shrieked suddenly, "fix a bite for the boy, here!" He turned to Lone, embarrassedly. "She's yonder," he said pointing. "Yell loud enough, I reckon she'd hear. Maybe."

Lone looked where Prodd pointed, but saw nothing. He caught Prodd's gaze and for a split second started to probe. He recoiled violently at the very nature of what was there before he got close enough to identify it. He turned away quickly. "Brought your ax."

"Oh, that's all right. You could've kept it."

"Got my own. Want to get that corn in?"

Prodd gazed mistily at the corn patch. "Never missed a milking," he said.

Lone left him and went to the barn for a corn hook. He found one. He also discovered that the cow was dead. He went up to the corn patch and got to work. After a time he saw Prodd down the line, working too, working hard.

Well past midday and just before they had the corn all cut, Prodd disappeared into the house. Twenty minutes later he emerged with a pitcher and a platter of sandwiches. The bread was dry and the sandwiches were corned beef from, as Lone recalled, Mrs. Prodd's practically untouched "rainy day" shelf. The pitcher contained warm lemonade and dead flies. Lone asked no questions. They perched on the edge of the horse trough and ate.

Afterward Lone went down to the fallow field and got the truck dug out. Prodd followed him down in time to drive it out. The rest of the day was devoted to the seeding with Lone loading the seeder and helping four different times to free the truck from the traps it insisted upon digging for itself. When that was finished, Lone waved Prodd up to the barn where he got a rope around the dead cow's neck and hauled it as near as the truck would go to the edge of the wood. When at last they ran the truck into the barn for the night, Prodd said, "Sure miss that horse."

"You said you didn't miss it a-tall," Lone recalled tactlessly.

"Did I now." Prodd turned inward and smiled, remembering. "Yeah, nothing bothered me none, because of, you know." Still smiling, he turned to Lone and said, "Come back to the house." He smiled all the way back.

They went through the kitchen. It was even worse than it had looked from outside and the clock was stopped, too. Prodd, smiling, threw open the door of Jack's room. Smiling, he said, "Have a look, boy. Go right on in, have a look."

Lone went in and looked into the bassinet. The cheesecloth was torn and the blue cotton was moist and reeking. The baby had eyes like upholstery tacks and skin the color of mustard. Short blue-black horsehair covered its skull, and it breathed noisily.

Lone did not change expression. He turned away and stood in the kitchen looking at one of the dimity curtains, the one which lay on the floor.

Smiling, Prodd came out of Jack's room and closed the door. "See, he's not Jack, that's the one blessing," he smiled. "Ma, she had to go off looking for Jack, I reckon, yes; that would be it. She wouldn't be happy with anything less; well, you know that your own self." He smiled twice. "What that in there is, that's what the doctor calls a mongoloid. Just leave it be; it'll grow up to maybe size three and stay so for thirty year. Get him to a big city specialist for treatments and he'll grow up to maybe size ten." He smiled as he talked. "That's what the doctor said anyway. Can't shovel him into the ground now, can you? That was all right for Ma, way she loved flowers and all."

Too many words, some hard to hear through the wide, tight smiling. Lone brought his eyes to bear on Prodd's.

He found out exactly what Prodd wanted—things that Prodd himself did not know. He did the things.

When he was finished he and Prodd cleaned up the kitchen and took the bassinet and burned it, along with the carefully sewn diapers made out of old sheets and piled in the linen closet and the new oval enamel bath pan and the celluloid rattle and the blue felt booties with the white puffballs in their clear cellophane box.

Prodd waved cheerfully to him from the porch. "Just you wait'll Ma gets back; she'll stuff you full of johnny-cake till we got to scrape you off the wall."

* * *

"Mind you fix that barn door," Lone rasped. "I'll come back."

With his burden he plodded up the hill and into the forest. He struggled numbly with thoughts that would not be words or pictures. About those kids, now; about the Prodds. The Prodds were one thing and when they took him in they became something else; he knew it now. And then when he was by himself he was one thing; but taking those kids in he was something else. He had no business going back to Prodd's today. But now, the way he was, he *had* to do it. He'd go back again too.

Alone. Lone Lone alone. Prodd was alone now and Janie was alone and the twins, well they had each other but they were like one split person who was alone. He himself, Lone, was still alone, it didn't make any difference about the kids being there.

Maybe Prodd and his wife had not been alone. He wouldn't have any way of knowing about that. But there was nothing like Lone anywhere in the world except right here inside him. The whole world threw Lone away, you know that? Even the Prodds did, when they got around to it. Janie got thrown out, the twins too, so Janie said.

Well, in a funny way it helps to know you're alone, thought Lone.

The night was sun-stained by the time he got home. He kneed the door open and came in. Janie was making pictures on an old china plate with spit and mud. The twins as usual were sitting on one of the high rock niches, whispering to one another.

Janie jumped up. "What's that? What'd you bring?"

Lone put it down carefully on the floor. The twins appeared, one on each side of it. "It's a baby," said Janie. She looked up at Lone. "Is it a baby?"

Lone nodded. Janie looked again. "Nastiest one I ever saw."

Lone said, "Well never mind that. Give him something to eat.

"What?"

"I don't know," said Lone. "You're a baby, almost. You should know."

"Where'd you get him?"

"A farm yonder."

"You're a kidnapper," said Janie. "Know that?"

"What's a kidnapper?"

"Man that steals babies, that's what. When they find out about it the policeman will come and shoot you dead and put you in the electric chair."

"Well," said Lone, relieved, "ain't nobody going to find out. Only man knows about it, I fixed it so he's forgotten. That's the daddy. The ma, she's dead, but he don't know that either. He thinks she's back East. He'll hang on waiting for her. Anyway, feed him."

He pulled off his jacket. The kids kept it too hot in here. The baby lay still with its dull button eyes open, breathing too loudly. Janie stood before the fire, staring thoughtfully at the stewpot. Finally she dipped into it with a ladle and dribbled the juice into a tin can. "Milk," she said while she worked. "You got to start swiping milk for him, Lone. Babies, they eat more milk'n a cat."

"All right," said Lone.

The twins watched, wall-eyed, as Janie slopped the broth on the baby's disinterested mouth.

"He's getting some," said Janie optimistically.

Without humor and only from visible evidence, Lone said, "Maybe through his ears."

Janie pulled at the baby's shirt and half sat him up. This favored the neck rather than the ears but still left the mouth intake in doubt.

"Oh, maybe I can!" said Janie suddenly, as if answering a comment. The twins giggled and jumped up and down. Janie drew the tin can a few inches away from the baby's face and narrowed her eyes. The baby immediately started to choke and spewed up what was unequivocally broth.

"That's not right yet but I'll get it," said Janie. She spent half an hour trying. At last the baby went to sleep.

One afternoon Lone watched for a while and then prodded Janie with his toe. "What's going on there?"

She looked. "He's talking to them."

Lone pondered. "I used to could do that. Hear babies."

"Bonnie says all babies can do it, and you were a baby, weren't you? I forget if I ever did," she added. "Except the twins."

"What I mean," said Lone laboriously, "when I was growed I could hear babies."

"You must've been an idiot, then," said Janie positively. "Idiots can't understand people but can understand babies. Mr. Widdecombe, he's the man the twins lived with, he had a girl friend once who was an idiot and Bonnie told me."

"Baby's s'posed to be some kind of a idiot," Lone said.

"Yes, Beanie, she says he's sort of different. He's like a adding machine."

"What's a adding machine?"

Janie exaggerated the supreme patience that her nursery school teacher had affected. "It's a thing you push buttons and it gives you the right answer."

Lone shook his head.

Janie essayed, "Well, if you have three cents and four cents and five cents and seven cents and eight cents—how many you got altogether?"

Lone shrugged hopelessly.

"Well if you have a adding machine, you push a button for *two* and a button for *three* and a button for all the other ones and then you pull a handle, the machine tells you how many you got altogether. And it's always right."

Lone sorted all this out slowly and finally nodded. Then he waved toward the orange crate that was now Baby's bassinet, and the twins hanging spellbound over him. "He got no buttons you push."

"That was just a finger of speech," Janie said loftily. "Look, you tell Baby something, and then you tell him something else. He will put the somethings together and tell you what they come out to, just like the adding machine does with one and two and—"

"All right but what kind of somethings?"

"Anything." She eyed him. "You're sort of stoopid, you know that, Lone. I got to tell you every little thing four times. Now listen, if you want to know something you tell me and I'll tell Baby and he'll get the answer and tell the twins and they'll tell me and I'll tell you, now what do you want to know?"

Lone stared at the fire. "I don't know anything I want to know."

"Well, you sure think up a lot of silly things to ask me."

Lone, not offended, sat and thought. Janie went to work on a scab on her knee, picking it gently round and round with fingernails the color and shape of parentheses.

"Suppose I got a truck," Lone said a half hour later, "it gets stuck in a field all the time, the ground's too tore up. Suppose I want to fix it so it won't stick no more. Baby tell me a thing like that?"

"Anything, I told you," said Janie sharply. She turned and looked at Baby. Baby lay as always, staring dully upward. In a moment she looked at the twins.

"He don't know what is a truck. If you're going to ask him anything you have to explain all the pieces before he can put 'em together."

"Well you know what a truck is," said Lone, "and soft ground and what stickin' is. You tell him."

"Oh all right," said Janie.

She went through the routine again, sending to Baby, receiving from the twins. Then she laughed. "He says stop driving on the field and you won't get stuck. You could of thought of that yourself, you dumbhead."

Lone said, "Well suppose you got to use it there, then what?"

"You 'spect me to go on askin' him silly questions all *night*?"

"All right, he can't answer like you said."

"He can too!" Her facts impugned, Janie went to the task with a will. The next answer was, "Put great big wide wheels on it."

"Suppose you ain't got money nor time nor tools for that?"

This time it was, "Make it real heavy where the ground is hard and real light where the ground is soft and anything in between."

Janie very nearly went on strike when Lone demanded to know how this could be accomplished and reached something of a peak of impatience when Lone rejected the suggestion of loading and unloading rocks. She complained that not only was this silly, but that Baby was matching every fact she fed him with every other fact he had been fed previously and was giving correct but unsolicited answers to situational sums of tires plus weight plus soup plus bird's nests, and babies plus soft dirt plus wheel diameters plus straw. Lone doggedly clung to his basic question and the day's impasse was reached when it was determined that there was such a way but it could not be expressed except by facts not in Lone's or Janie's possession. Janie said it sounded to her like radio tubes and with only that to go on, Lone proceeded by entering the next night a radio service shop and stealing a heavy armload of literature. He bulled along unswerving, unstoppable, until at last Janie relinquished her opposition because she had not energy for it and for the research as well. For days she scanned elementary electricity and radio texts which meant nothing to her but which apparently Baby could absorb faster than she scanned.

And at last the specifications were met: something which Lone could make himself, which would involve only a small knob you pushed to make the truck heavier and pulled to make it lighter, as well as an equally simple attachment to add power to the front wheels—according to Baby a *sine qua non*.

In the half-cave, half-cabin, with the fire smoking in the center of the room and the meat turning slowly in the updraft, with the help of two tongue-tied infants, a mongoloid baby and a sharp-tongued child who seemed to despise him but never failed him, Lone built the device. He did it, not because he was particularly interested in the thing for itself, nor because he wished to understand its principles (which were and would always be beyond him), but only because an old man who had taught him something he could not name was mad with bereavement and needed to work and could not afford a horse.

He walked most of the night with it and installed it in the dim early hours of the morning. The idea of "pleasant surprise" was far too whimsical a thing for Lone but it amounted to the same thing. He wanted it ready for the day's work, without any time lost by the old man prancing around asking questions that he couldn't answer.

The truck stood bogged in the field. Lone unwound the device from around his neck and shoulders and began to attach it according to the exact instructions he had winnowed out of Baby. There wasn't much to do. A slender wire wrapped twice around the clutch housing outside and led to clamps on the front spring shackles, the little brushes touching the insides of the front wheels; and that was the front-wheel drive. Then the little box with its four silvery cables, box clamped to sheering post, each cable leading to a corner of the frame.

He got in and pulled the knob toward him. The frame creaked as the truck seemed to raise itself on tiptoe. He pushed the knob forward. The truck settled its front axle and differential housing on solid ground with a bump that made his head rock. He looked at the little box and its lever admiringly, then returned the lever to a neutral position. He scanned the other controls there, the ones which came with the truck: pedals and knobs and sticks and buttons. He sighed.

He wished he had wit enough to drive a truck.

He got out and climbed the hill to the house to wake Prodd. Prodd wasn't there. The kitchen door swung in the breeze, the glass gone out of it and lying on the stoop. Mud wasps were building under the sink. There was a smell of dirty dry floorboards, mildew, and ancient sweat. Otherwise it was fairly neat, about the way it was when he and Prodd had cleaned up last time he was here. The only new thing there aside from the mud wasps' nest was a paper nailed to the wall by all four corners. It had writing all over it. Lone detached it as carefully as he could, and smoothed it out on the kitchen table, and turned it over twice. Then he folded it, put it in his pocket. Again he sighed.

He wished he had sense enough to learn to read.

He left the house without looking back and plunged into the forest. He never returned. The truck stood out in the sun, slowly deteriorating slowly weakening its already low resistance to rust, slowly falling to pieces around the bright, strong, strange silver cables. Powered inexhaustibly by the slow release of atomic binding energy, the device was the practical solution of flight without wings, the simple key to a new era in transportation, in materials handling, and in interplanetary travel. Made by an idiot, harnessed idiotically to replace a spavined horse, stupidly left, numbly forgotten . . . Earth's first anti-gravity generator.

The *idiot!*

Dear loan I'll nale this up wher you cant hep see it I am cleering ot of here I dont no why I stade as long as I did. Ma is back east Wmsport pennsilvana and she been gone a long time and I am tied of wating. And I was goin to sell the truck to hep me on the way but it is stuck so bad now I cant get it to town to sell it. So now I am jest goin to go whatever and I'll make it some way long as I no Ma is at the othr end. Dont take no trouble about the place I guess I had enuf of it Anyway. And borrow any thing you want if you should want any Thing. You are a good boy you been a good frend well goodbeye until I see you if I ever do god Bless you your old frend E. Prodd.

Lone made Janie read him the letter four times in a three-week period, and each reading seemed to add a fresh element to the yeasty seething inside him. Much of this happened silently; for some of it he asked help.

He had believed that Prodd was his only contact with anything outside himself and that the children were merely fellow occupants of a slag dump at the edge of mankind. The loss of Prodd—and he knew with unshakeable certainty that he would never see the old man again—was the loss of life itself. At the very least, it was the loss of everything conscious, directed, cooperative; everything above and beyond what a vegetable could do by way of living.

"Ask Baby what is a friend."

"He says it's somebody who goes on loving you whether he likes you or not."

But then, Prodd and his wife had shucked him off when he was in the way, after all those years, and that meant they were ready to do it the first year and the second and the fifth—all the time, any time. You can't say you're a part of anything, anybody, that feels free to do that to you. But friends . . . maybe they just don't like him for a while, maybe they loved him all the way through.

"Ask Baby can you be truly part of someone you love."

"He says only if you love yourself."

His bench-mark, his goal-point, had for years been that thing which happened to him on the bank of the pool. He had to understand that. If he could understand that, he was sure he could understand everything. Because for a second there was this *other*, and himself, and a flow between them without guards or screens or barriers—no language to stumble over, no ideas to misunderstand, nothing at all but a merging.

What had he been then? What was it Janie had said?

Idiot. An idiot.

An idiot, she had said, was a grown person who could hear only babies' silent speech. Then—what was the creature with whom he had merged on that terrible day?

"Ask Baby what is a grown person who can *talk* like the babies."

"He says, an innocent."

He had been an idiot who could hear the soundless murmur. She had been an innocent who, as an adult, could speak it.

"Ask Baby what if an idiot and an innocent are close together."

"He says when they so much as touched, the innocent would stop being an innocent and the idiot would stop being an idiot."

He thought. An innocent is the most beautiful thing there can be. Immediately he demanded of himself, What's so beautiful about an innocent? And the answer, for once almost as swift as Baby's: It's the waiting that's beautiful.

Waiting for the end of innocence. And an idiot is waiting for the end of idiocy too, but he's ugly doing it. So each ends himself in the meeting, in exchange for a merging.

Lone was suddenly deep-down glad. For if this was true, he had made something, rather than destroyed something . . . and when he had lost it, the pain of the loss was justified. When he had lost the Prodds the pain wasn't worth it.

What am I doing? What am I doing? he thought wildly. Trying and trying like this to find out what I am and what I belong to. . . . Is this another aspect of being outcast, monstrous, *different?*

"Ask Baby what kind of people are all the time trying to find out what they are and what they belong to."

"He says, *every* kind."

"What kind," Lone whispered, "am I, then?"

A full minute later he yelled, *"What kind?"*

"Shut up a while. He doesn't have a way to say it . . . uh . . . Here. He says he is a figure-outer brain and I am a body and the twins are arms and legs and you are the head. He says the 'I' is all of us."

"I belong. I belong. Part of you, part of you and you too."

"The head, silly."

Lone thought his heart was going to burst. He looked at them all, every one: arms to flex and reach, a body to care and repair, a brainless but faultless computer and—the head to direct it.

"And we'll grow, Baby. We just got born!"

"He says not on your life. He says not with a head like that. We can do practically *anything* but we most likely won't. He says we're a thing, all right, but the thing is an idiot."

So it was that Lone came to know himself; and like the handful of people who have done so before him he found, at this pinnacle, the rugged foot of a mountain.

PART TWO
Baby Is Three

I FINALLY got in to see this Stern. He wasn't an old man at all. He looked up from his desk, flicked his eyes over me once, and picked up a pencil. "Sit over there, Sonny."

I stood where I was until he looked up again. Then I said, "Look, if a midget walks in here, what do you say—sit over there, Shorty?"

He put the pencil down again and stood up. He smiled. His smile was as quick and sharp as his eyes. "I was wrong," he said, "but how am I supposed to know you don't want to be called Sonny?"

That was better, but I was still mad. "I'm fifteen and I don't have to like it. Don't rub my nose in it."

He smiled again and said okay, and I went and sat down.

"What's your name?"

"Gerard."

"First or last?"

"Both," I said.

"Is that the truth?"

I said, "No. And don't ask me where I live either."

He put down his pencil. "We're not going to get very far this way."

"That's up to you. What are you worried about? I got feelings of hostility? Well, sure I have. I got lots more things than that wrong with me or I wouldn't be here. Are you going to let that stop you?"

"Well, no, but—"

"So what else is bothering you? How you're going to get paid?" I took out a thousand-dollar bill and laid it on the desk. "That's so you won't have to bill me. *You* keep track of it. Tell me when it's used up and I'll give you more. So you don't need my address. Wait," I said, when he reached toward the money. "Let it lay here. I want to be sure you and I are going to get along."

He folded his hands. "I don't do business this way, Son—I mean, Gerard."

"Gerry," I told him. "You do, if you do business with me."

"You make things difficult, don't you? Where did you get a thousand dollars?"

"I won a contest. Twenty-five words or less about how much fun it is to do my daintier thing with Sudso." I leaned forward. "This time it's the truth."

"All right," he said.

I was surprised. I think he knew it, but he didn't say anything more. Just waited for me to go ahead.

"Before we start—*if* we start," I said, "I got to know something. The things I say to you—what comes out while you're working on me—is that just between us, like a priest or a lawyer?"

"Absolutely," he said.

"No matter what?"

"No matter what."

I watched him when he said it. I believed him.

"Pick up your money," I said. "You're on."

He didn't do it. He said, "As you remarked a minute ago, that is up to me. You can't buy these treatments like a candy bar. We have to work together. If either one of us can't do that, it's useless. You can't walk in on the first psychotherapist you find in the phone book and make any demand that occurs to you just because you can pay for it."

I said tiredly, "I didn't get you out of the phone book and I'm not just guessing that you can help me. I winnowed through a dozen or more head-shrinkers before I decided on you."

"Thanks," he said, and it looked as if he was going to laugh at me, which I never like. "Winnowed, did you say? Just how?"

"Things you hear, things you read. You know. I'm not saying, so just file that with my street address."

He looked at me for a long time. It was the first time he'd used his eyes on me for anything but a flash glance. Then he picked up the bill.

"What do I do first?" I demanded.

"What do you mean?"

"How do we start?"

"We started when you walked in here."

So then I had to laugh. "All right, you got me. All I had was an opening. I didn't know where you would go from there, so I couldn't be there ahead of you."

"That's very interesting," Stern said. "Do you usually figure everything out in advance?"

"Always."

"How often are you right?"

"All the time. Except—but I don't have to tell you about no exceptions."

He really grinned this time. "I see. One of my patients has been talking."

"One of your ex-patients. Your patients don't talk."

"I ask them not to. That applies to you, too. What did you hear?"

"That you know from what people say and do what they're about to say and do, and that sometimes you let'm do it and sometimes you don't. How did you learn to do that?"

He thought a minute. "I guess I was born with an eye for details, and then let myself make enough mistakes with enough people until I learned not to make too many more. How did you learn to do it?"

I said, "You answer that and I won't have to come back here."

"You really don't know?"

"I wish I did. Look, this isn't getting us anywhere, is it?"

He shrugged. "Depends on where you want to go." He paused, and I got the eyes full strength again. "Which thumbnail description of psychiatry do you believe at the moment?"

"I don't get you."

Stern slid open a desk drawer and took out a blackened pipe. He smelled it, turned it over while looking at me. "Psychiatry attacks the onion of the self, removing layer after layer until it gets down to the little sliver of unsullied ego. Or: psychiatry drills like an oil well, down and sidewise and down again, through all the muck and rock until it strikes a layer that yields. Or: psychiatry grabs a handful of sexual motivations and throws them on the pinball machine of your life, so they bounce on down against episodes. Want more?"

I had to laugh. "That last one was pretty good."

"That last one was pretty bad. They are all bad. They all try to simplify something which is complex by its very nature. The only thumbnail you'll get from me is this: no one knows what's really wrong with you but you; no one can find a cure for it but you; no one but you can identify it as a cure; and once you find it, no one but you can do anything about it."

"What are *you* here for?"

"To listen."

"I don't have to pay somebody no day's wages every hour just to listen."

"True. But you're convinced that I listen selectively."

"Am I?" I wondered about it. "I guess I am. Well, don't you?"

"No, but you'll never believe that."

I laughed. He asked me what that was for. I said, "You're not calling me Sonny."

"Not you." He shook his head slowly. He was watching me while he did it, so his eyes slid in their sockets as his head moved. "What is it you want to know about yourself, that made you worried I might tell people?"

"I want to find out why I killed somebody," I said right away.

It didn't faze him a bit. "Lie down over there."

I got up. "On that couch?"

He nodded.

As I stretched out self-consciously, I said, "I feel like I'm in some damn cartoon."

"What cartoon?"

"Guy's built like a bunch of grapes," I said, looking at the ceiling. It was pale gray.

"What's the caption?"

" 'I got trunks full of 'em.' "

"Very good," he said quietly. I looked at him carefully. I knew then he was the kind of guy who laughs way down deep when he laughs at all.

He said, "I'll use that in a book of case histories some time. But it won't include yours. What made you throw that in?" When I didn't answer, he got up and moved to a chair behind me where I couldn't see him. "You can quit testing, Sonny. I'm good enough for your purposes."

I clenched my jaw so hard, my back teeth hurt. Then I relaxed. I relaxed all over. It was wonderful. "All right," I said, "I'm sorry." He didn't say anything, but I had that feeling again that he was laughing. Not at me, though.

"How old are you?" he asked me suddenly.

"Uh—fifteen."

"Uh—fifteen," he repeated. "What does the 'uh' mean?"

"Nothing. I'm fifteen."

"When I asked your age, you hesitated because some other number popped up. You discarded that and substituted 'fifteen.' "

"The hell I did! I am fifteen!"

"I didn't say you weren't." His voice came patiently. "Now what was the other number?"

I got mad again. "There wasn't any other number! What do you want to go pryin' my grunts apart for, trying to plant this and that and make it mean what you think it ought to mean?"

He was silent.

"I'm fifteen," I said defiantly, and then, "I don't like being only fifteen. You know that. I'm not trying to insist I'm fifteen."

He just waited, still not saying anything.

I felt defeated. "The number was eight."

"So you're eight. And your name?"

"Gerry." I got up on one elbow, twisting my neck around so I could see him. He had his pipe apart and was sighting through the stem at the desk lamp. "Gerry, without no 'uh!' "

"All right," he said mildly, making me feel real foolish.

I leaned back and closed my eyes.

Eight, I thought. Eight.

"It's cold in here," I complained.

Eight. Eight, plate, state, hate. I ate from the plate of the state and I hate. I didn't like any of that and I snapped my eyes open. The ceiling was still gray. It was all right. Stern was somewhere behind me with his pipe, and he was all right. I took two deep breaths, three, and then let my eyes close. Eight. Eight years old. Eight, hate. Years, fears. Old, cold. *Damn* it! I twisted and twitched on the couch, trying to find a way to keep the cold out. I ate from the plate of the—

I grunted and with my mind I took all the eights and all the rhymes and everything they stood for, and made it all black. But it wouldn't stay black. I had to put something there, so I made a great big luminous figure eight and just let it hang there. But it turned on its side and inside the loops it began to shimmer. It was like one of those movie shots through binoculars. I was going to have to look through whether I liked it or not.

Suddenly I quit fighting it and let it wash over me. The binoculars came close, closer, and then I was there.

Eight. Eight years old, cold. Cold as a bitch in the ditch. The ditch was by a railroad. Last year's weeds were scratchy straw. The ground was red, and when it wasn't slippery, clingy mud, it was frozen hard like a flowerpot. It was hard like that now, dusted with hoar-frost, cold as the winter light that pushed up over the hills. At night the lights were warm, and they were all in other people's houses. In the daytime the sun was in somebody else's house too, for all the good it did me.

I was dying in that ditch. Last night it was as good a place as any to sleep and this morning it was as good a place as any to die. Just as well. Eight years old, the sick-sweet taste of pork fat and wet bread from somebody's garbage, the thrill of terror when you're stealing a gunnysack and you hear a footstep.

And I heard a footstep.

I'd been curled up on my side. I whipped over on my stomach because sometimes they kick your belly. I covered my head with my arms and that was as far as I could get.

After a while I rolled my eyes up and looked without moving. There was a big shoe there. There was an ankle in the shoe, and another shoe close by. I lay there waiting to get tromped. Not that I cared much any more, but it was such a damn shame. All these months on my own, and they'd never caught up with me, never even come close, and now this. It was such a shame I started to cry.

The shoe took me under the armpit, but it was not a kick. It rolled me over. I was so stiff from the cold, I went over like a plank. I just kept my arms over my face and head and lay there with my eyes closed. For some reason I stopped crying. I think people only cry when there's a chance of getting help from somewhere.

When nothing happened, I opened my eyes and shifted my fore-arms a little so I could see up. There was a man standing over me and he was a mile high. He had on faded dungarees and an old Eisenhower jacket with deep sweat-stains under the arms. His face was shaggy, like the guys who can't grow what you could call a beard, but still don't shave.

He said, "Get up."

I looked down at his shoe, but he wasn't going to kick me. I pushed up a little and almost fell down again, except he put his big hand where my back would hit it. I lay against it for a second because I had to, and then got up to where I had one knee on the ground.

"Come on," he said. "Let's go."

I swear I felt my bones creak, but I made it. I brought a round white stone up with me as I stood. I hefted the stone. I had to look at it to see if I was really holding it, my fingers were that cold. I told him, "Stay away from me or I'll bust you in the teeth with this rock."

His hand came out and down so fast I never saw the way he got one finger between my palm and the rock and flicked it out of my grasp. I started to cuss at him, but he just turned his back and walked up the embankment towards the tracks. He put his chin on his shoulder and said, "Come on, will you?"

He didn't chase me, so I didn't run. He didn't talk to me so I didn't argue. He didn't hit me, so I didn't get mad. I went along after him. He waited for me. He put out his hand to me and I spit at it. So he went on, up to the tracks, out of my sight. I clawed my way up. The blood was beginning to move in my hands and feet and they felt like four point-down porcupines. When I got up to the roadbed, the man was standing there waiting for me.

The track was level just there, but as I turned my head to look along it, it seemed to be a hill that was steeper and steeper and turned over above me. And next thing you know, I was lying flat on my back looking up at the cold sky.

The man came over and sat down on the rail near me. He didn't try to touch me. I gasped for breath a couple of times and suddenly felt I'd be all right if I could sleep for a minute—just a little minute. I closed my eyes. The man stuck his finger in my ribs, hard. It hurt.

"Don't sleep," he said.

I looked at him.

He said, "You're frozen stiff and weak with hunger. I want to take you home and get you warmed up and fed. But it's a long haul up that way, and you won't make it by yourself. If I carry you, will that be the same to you as if you walked it?"

"What are you going to do when you get me home?"

"I told you."

"All right," I said.

He picked me up and carried me down the track. If he'd said anything else in the world, I'd of laid right down where I was until I froze to death. Anyway, what did he want to ask me for, one way or the other? I couldn't of done anything.

I stopped thinking about it and dozed off.

I woke up once when he turned off the right of way. He dove into the woods. There was no path, but he seemed to know where he was going. The next time I woke from a crickling noise. He was carrying me over a frozen pond and the ice was giving under his feet. He didn't hurry. I looked down and saw the white cracks raying out under his feet, and it didn't seem to matter a bit. I bleared off again.

He put me down at last. We were there. "There" was inside a room. It was very warm. He put me on my feet and I snapped out of it in a hurry. The first thing I looked for was the door. I saw it and jumped over there and put my back against the wall beside it, in case I wanted to leave. Then I looked around.

It was a big room. One wall was rough rock and the rest was logs with stuff shoved between them. There was a big fire going in the rock wall, not in a fireplace, exactly; it was a sort of hollow place. There was an old auto battery on a shelf opposite, with two yellowing electric light bulbs dangling by wires from it. There was a table, some boxes and a couple of three-legged stools. The air had a haze of smoke and such a wonderful, heartbreaking, candy-and-crackling smell of food that a little hose squirted inside my mouth.

The man said, "What have I got here, Baby?"

And the room was full of kids. Well, three of them, but somehow they seemed to be more than three kids. There was a girl about my age—eight, I mean—with blue paint on the side of her face. She had an easel and a palette with lots of paint and a fistful of brushes, but she wasn't using the brushes. She was smearing the paint on with her hands. Then there was a little Negro girl about five with great big eyes who stood gaping at me. And in a wooden crate, set up on two sawhorses to make a kind of bassinet, was a baby. I guess about three or four months old. It did what babies do, drooling some, making small bubbles, waving its hands around very aimless, and kicking.

When the man spoke, the girl at the easel looked at me and then at the baby. The baby just kicked and drooled.

The girl said, "His name's Gerry. He's mad."

"What's he mad at?" the man asked. He was looking at the baby.

"Everything," said the girl. "Everything and everybody."

"Where'd he come from?"

I said, "Hey, what is this?" but nobody paid any attention. The man kept asking questions at the baby and the girl kept answering. Craziest thing I ever saw.

"He ran away from a state school," the girl said. "They fed him enough, but no one bleshed with him."

That's what she said—"bleshed."

I opened the door then and cold air hooted in. "You louse," I said to the man, "you're from the school."

"Close the door, Janie," said the man. The girl at the easel didn't move, but the door banged shut behind me. I tried to open it and it wouldn't move. I let out a howl, yanking at it.

"I think you ought to stand in the corner," said the man. "Stand him in the corner, Janie."

Janie looked at me. One of the three-legged stools sailed across to me. It hung in midair and turned on its side. It nudged me with its flat seat. I jumped back and it came after me. I dodged to the side, and that was the corner. The stool came on. I tried to bat it down and just hurt my hand. I ducked and it went lower than I did. I put one hand on it and tried to vault over it, but it just fell and so did I. I got up again and stood in the corner, trembling. The stool turned right side up and sank to the floor in front of me.

The man said, "Thank you, Janie." He turned to me. "Stand there and be quiet, you. I'll get to you later. You shouldn'ta kicked up all that fuss." And then, to the baby, he said, "He got anything we need?"

And again it was the little girl who answered. She said, "Sure. He's the one."

"Well," said the man. "What do you know!" He came over. "Gerry, you can live here. I don't come from no school. I'll never turn you in."

"Yeah, huh?"

"He hates you," said Janie.

"What am I supposed to do about that?" he wanted to know.

Janie turned her head to look into the bassinet. "Feed him." The man nodded and began fiddling around the fire.

Meanwhile, the little Negro girl had been standing in the one spot with her big eyes right out on her cheekbones, looking at me. Janie went back to her painting and the baby just lay there same as always, so I stared right back at the little Negro girl. I snapped, "What the hell are you gawking at?"

She grinned at me. "Gerry ho-ho," she said, and disappeared. I mean she really disappeared, went out like a light, leaving her clothes where she had been. Her little dress billowed in the air and fell in a heap where she had been, and that was that. She was gone.

"Gerry hee-hee," I heard. I looked up, and there she was, stark naked, wedged in a space where a little outcropping on the rock wall stuck out just below the ceiling. The second I saw her she disappeared again.

"Gerry ho-ho," she said. Now she was on top of the row of boxes they used as storage shelves, over on the other side of the room.

"Gerry hee-hee!" Now she was under the table. "Gerry ho-ho!" This time she was right in the corner with me, crowding me.

I yelped and tried to get out of the way and bumped the stool. I was afraid of it, so I shrank back again and the little girl was gone.

The man glanced over his shoulder from where he was working at the fire. "Cut it out, you kids," he said.

There was a silence, and then the girl came slowly out from the bottom row of shelves. She walked across to her dress and put it on.

"How did you do that?" I wanted to know.

"Ho-ho," she said.

Janie said, "It's easy. She's really twins."

"Oh," I said. Then another girl, exactly the same, came from somewhere in the shadows and stood beside the first. They were identical. They stood side by side and stared at me. This time I let them stare.

"That's Bonnie and Beanie," said the painter. "This is Baby and that—" she indicated the man—"that's Lone. And I'm Janie."

I couldn't think of what to say, so I said, "Yeah."

Lone said, "Water, Janie." He held up a pot. I heard water trickling, but didn't see anything. "That's enough," he said, and hung the pot on a crane. He picked up a cracked china plate and brought it over to me. It was full of stew with great big lumps of meat in it and thick gravy and dumplings and carrots. "Here, Gerry. Sit down."

I looked at the stool. "On that?"

"Sure."

"Not me," I said. I took the plate and hunkered down against the wall.

"Hey," he said after a time. "Take it easy. We've all had chow. No one's going to snatch it away from you. Slow down!"

I ate even faster than before. I was almost finished when I threw it all up. Then for some reason my head hit the edge of the stool. I dropped the plate and spoon and slumped there. I felt real bad.

Lone came over and looked at me. "Sorry, kid," he said. "Clean up, will you, Janie?"

Right in front of my eyes, the mess on the floor disappeared. I didn't care about that or anything else just then. I felt the man's hand on the side of my neck. Then he tousled my hair.

"Beanie, get him a blanket. Let's all go to sleep. He ought to rest a while."

I felt the blanket go around me, and I think I was asleep before he put me down.

I don't know how much later it was when I woke up. I didn't know where I was and that scared me. I raised my head and saw the dull glow of the embers in the fireplace. Lone was stretched out on it in his clothes. Janie's easel stood in the reddish blackness like some great preying insect. I saw the baby's head pop up out of the bassinet, but I couldn't tell whether he was looking straight at me or away. Janie was lying on the floor near the door and the twins were on the old table. Nothing moved except the baby's head, bobbing a little.

I got to my feet and look around the room. Just a room, only the one door. I tiptoed toward it. When I passed Janie, she opened her eyes.

"What's the matter?" she whispered.

"None of your business," I told her. I went to the door as if I didn't care, but I watched her. She didn't do anything. The door was as solid tight closed as when I'd tried it before.

I went back to Janie. She just looked up at me. She wasn't scared. I told her, "I got to go to the john."

"Oh," she said. "Why'n't you say so?"

Suddenly I grunted and grabbed my guts. The feeling I had I can't begin to talk about. I acted as if it was a pain, but it wasn't. It was like nothing else that ever happened to me before. Something went *splop* on the snow outside.

"Okay," Janie said. "Go on back to bed."

"But I got to—"

"You got to what?"

"Nothing." It was true. I didn't have to go no place.

"Next time tell me right away. I don't mind."

I didn't say anything. I went back to my blanket.

"That's all?" said Stern. I lay on the couch and looked up at the gray ceiling. He asked, "How old are you?"

"Fifteen," I said dreamily. He waited until, for me, the gray ceiling acquired walls and a floor, a rug and lamps and a desk and a chair with Stern in it. I sat up and held my head a second, and then I looked at him. He was fooling with his pipe and looking at me. "What did you do to me?"

"I told you. I don't do anything here. You do it."

"You hypnotized me."

"I did not." His voice was quiet, but he really meant it.

"What was all that, then? It was . . . it was like it was happening for real all over again."

"Feel anything?"

"Everything." I shuddered. "*Every* damn thing. What was it?"

"Anyone doing it feels better afterward. You can go over it all again now any time you want to, and every time you do, the hurt in it will be less. You'll see."

It was the first thing to amaze me in years. I chewed on it and then asked, "If I did it by myself, how come it never happened before?"

"It needs someone to listen."

"Listen? Was I talking?"

"A blue streak."

"Everything that happened?"

"How can I know? I wasn't there. You were."

"You don't believe it happened, do you? Those disappearing kids and the footstool and all?"

He shrugged. "I'm not in the business of believing or not believing. Was it real to you?"

"Oh, hell, yes!"

"Well, then, that's all that matters. Is that where you live, with those people?"

I bit off a fingernail that had been bothering me. "Not for a long time. Not since Baby was three." I looked at him. "You remind me of Lone."

"Why?"

"I don't know. No, you don't." I added suddenly. "I don't know what made me say that." I lay down abruptly.

The ceiling was gray and the lamps were dim. I heard the pipe-stem click against his teeth. I lay there for a long time.

"Nothing happens," I told him.

"What did you expect to happen?"

"Like before."

"There's something there that wants out. Just let it come."

It was as if there was a revolving drum in my head, and on it were photographed the places and things and people I was after. And it was as if the drum was spinning very fast, so fast I couldn't tell one picture from another. I made it stop, and it stopped at a blank segment. I spun it again, and stopped it again.

"Nothing happens," I said.

"Baby is three," he repeated.

"Oh," I said. "That." I closed my eyes.

That might be it. Might, sight, night, light. I might have the sight of a light in the night. Maybe the baby. Maybe the sight of the baby at night because of the light . . .

There was night after night when I lay on that blanket, and a lot of nights I didn't. Something was going on all the time in Lone's house. Sometimes I slept in the daytime. I guess the only time everybody slept at once was when someone was sick, like me the first time I arrived there. It was always sort of dark in the room, the same night and day, the fire going, the two old bulbs hanging yellow by their wires from the battery. When they got too dim, Janie fixed the battery and they got bright again.

Janie did everything that needed doing, whatever no one else felt like doing. Everybody else did things, too. Lone was out a lot. Sometimes he used the twins to help him, but you never missed them, because they'd be here and gone and back again *bing!* like that. And Baby, he just stayed in his bassinet.

I did things myself. I cut wood for the fire and I put up more shelves, and then I'd go swimming with Janie and the twins sometimes. And I talked to Lone. I didn't do a thing that the others couldn't do, but they all did things I couldn't do. I was mad, mad all the time about that. But I wouldn't of known what to do with myself if I wasn't mad all the time about something or other. It didn't keep us from bleshing. Bleshing, that was Janie's word. She said Baby told it to her. She said it meant everyone all together being something, even if they all did different things. Two arms, two legs, one body, one head, all working together, although a head can't walk and arms can't think. Lone said maybe it was a mixture of "blending" and "meshing," but I don't think he believed that himself. It was a lot more than that.

Baby talked all the time. He was like a broadcasting station that runs twenty-four hours a day, and you can get what it's sending any time you tune in, but it'll keep sending whether you tune in or not. When I say he talked, I don't mean exactly that. He semaphored mostly. You'd think those wandering vague movements of his hands and arms and legs and head were meaningless, but they weren't. It was semaphore, only instead of a symbol for a sound, or such like, the movements were whole thoughts.

I mean spread the left hand and shake the right high up, and thump with the left heel, and it means, "Anyone who thinks a starling is a pest just don't know anything about how a starling thinks" or something like that. Janie said she made Baby invent the semaphore business. She said she used to be able to hear the twins thinking—that's what she said; hear them thinking—and they could hear Baby. So she would ask the twins whatever she wanted to know, and they'd ask Baby, and then tell her what he said. But then as they grew up they began to lose the knack of it. Every young kid does. So Baby learned to understand when someone talked, and he'd answer with this semaphore stuff.

Lone couldn't read the stuff and neither could I. The twins didn't give a damn. Janie used to watch him all the time. He always knew what you meant if you wanted to ask him something, and he'd tell Janie and she'd say what it was. Part of it, anyway. Nobody could get it all, not even Janie.

All I know is Janie would sit there and paint her pictures and watch Baby, and sometimes she'd bust out laughing.

Baby never grew any. Janie did, and the twins, and so did I, but not Baby. He just lay there. Janie kept his stomach full and cleaned him up every two or three days. He didn't cry and he didn't make any trouble. No one ever went near him.

Janie showed every picture she painted to Baby, before she cleaned the boards and painted new ones. She had to clean them because she only had three of them. It was a good thing, too, because I'd hate to think what that place would of been like if she'd kept them all; she did four or five a day. Lone and the twins were kept hopping getting turpentine for her. She could shift the paints back into the little pots on her easel without any trouble, just by looking at the picture one color at a time, but turps was something else again. She told me that Baby remembered all her pictures and that's why she didn't have to keep them. They were all pictures of machines and gear-trains and mechanical linkages and what looked like electric circuits and things like that. I never thought too much about them.

I went out with Lone to get some turpentine and a couple picnic hams one time. We went through the woods to the railroad track and down a couple of miles to where we could see the glow of a town. Then the woods again, and some alleys, and a back street.

Lone was like always, walking along, thinking, thinking.

We came to a hardware store and he went up and looked at the lock and came back to where I was waiting, shaking his head. Then we found a general store. Lone grunted and we went and stood in the shadows by the door. I looked in.

All of a sudden Beanie was in there, naked like she always was when she traveled like that. She came and opened the door from the inside. We went in and Lone closed it and locked it.

"Get along home, Beanie," he said, "before you catch your death."

She grinned at me and said, "Ho-ho," and disappeared.

We found a pair of fine hams and a two-gallon can of turpentine. I took a bright yellow ballpoint pen and Lone cuffed me and made me put it back.

"We only take what we need," he told me.

After we left, Beanie came back and locked the door and went home again. I only went with Lone a few times, when he had more to get than he could carry easily.

I was there about three years. That's all I can remember about it. Lone was there or he was out, and you could hardly tell the difference. The twins were with each other most of the time. I got to like Janie a lot, but we never talked much. Baby talked all the time, only I don't know what about.

We were all busy and we bleshed.

I sat up on the couch suddenly.

Stern said, "What's the matter?"

"Nothing's the matter. This isn't getting me any place."

"You said that when you'd barely started. Do you think you've accomplished anything since then?"

"Oh, yeah, but—"

"Then how can you be sure you're right this time?" When I didn't say anything, he asked me, "Didn't you like this last stretch?"

I said angrily, "I didn't like or not like. It didn't mean nothing. It was just—just talk."

"So what was the difference between this last session and what happened before?"

"My gosh, plenty! The first one, I felt everything. It was all really happening to me. But this time—nothing."

"Why do you suppose that was?"

"I don't know. You tell me."

"Suppose," he said thoughtfully, "that there was some episode so unpleasant to you that you wouldn't dare relive it."

"Unpleasant? You think freezing to death isn't unpleasant?"

"There are all kinds of unpleasantness. Sometimes the very thing you're looking for—the thing that'll clear up your trouble—is so revolting to you that you won't go near it. Or you try to hide it. Wait," he said suddenly, "maybe 'revolting' and 'unpleasant' are inaccurate words to use. It might be something very desirable to you. It's just that you don't want to get straightened out."

"I *want* to get straightened out."

He waited as if he had to clear something up in his mind, and then said, "There's something in that 'Baby is three' phrase that bounces you away. Why is that?"

"Damn if I know."

"Who said it!"

"I dunno . . . uh . . ."

He grinned. "Uh?"

I grinned back at him. "I said it."

"Okay. When?"

I quit grinning. He leaned forward, then got up.

"What's the matter?" I asked.

He said, "I didn't think anyone could be that mad." I didn't say anything. He went over to his desk. "You don't want to go on any more, do you?"

"No."

"Suppose I told you you want to quit because you're right on the very edge of finding out what you want to know?"

"Why don't you tell me and see what I do?"

He just shook his head. "I'm not telling you anything. Go on, leave if you want to. I'll give you back your change."

"How many people quit just when they're on top of the answer?"

"Quite a few."

"Well, I ain't going to." I lay down.

He didn't laugh and he didn't say, "Good," and he didn't make any fuss about it. He just picked up his phone and said, "Cancel everything for this afternoon," and went back to his chair, up there out of my sight.

It was very quiet in there. He had the place sound-proofed.

I said, "Why do you suppose Lone let me live there so long when I couldn't do any of the things that the other kids could?"

"Maybe you could."

"Oh, no," I said positively. "I used to try. I was strong for a kid my age and I knew how to keep my mouth shut, but aside from those two things I don't think I was any different from any kid. I don't think I'm any different right now, except what difference there might be from living with Lone and his bunch."

"Has this anything to do with 'Baby is three'?"

I looked up at the gray ceiling. "Baby is three. Baby is three. I went up to a big house with a winding drive that ran under a sort of theater-marquee thing. Baby is three. Baby . . ."

"How old are you?"

"Thirty-three," I said, and the next thing you know I was up off that couch like it was hot and heading for the door.

Stern grabbed me. "Don't be foolish. Want me to waste a whole afternoon?"

"What's that to me? I'm paying for it."

"All right, it's up to you."

I went back. "I don't like any part of this," I said.

"Good. We're getting warm then."

"What made me say 'Thirty-three'? I ain't thirty-three. I'm fifteen. And another thing . . ."

"Yes?"

"It's about that 'Baby is three.' It's me saying it, all right. But when I think about it—it's not my voice."

"Like thirty-three's not your age?"

"Yeah," I whispered.

"Gerry," he said warmly, "there's nothing to be afraid of."

I realized I was breathing too hard. I pulled myself together. I said, "I don't like remembering saying things in somebody else's voice."

"Look," he told me. "This head-shrinking business, as you called it a while back, isn't what most people think. When I go with you into the world of your mind—or when you go yourself, for that matter—what we find isn't so very different from the so-called real world. It seems so at first, because the patient comes out with all sorts of fantasies and irrationalities and weird experiences. But everyone lives in that kind of world. When one of the ancients coined the phrase 'truth is stranger than fiction,' he was talking about that.

"Everywhere we go, everything we do, we're surrounded by symbols, by things so familiar we don't ever look at them or don't see them if we do look. If anyone ever could report to you exactly what we saw and thought while walking ten feet down the street, you'd get the most twisted, clouded, partial picture you ever ran across. And nobody ever looks at what's around him with any kind of attention until he gets into a place like this. The fact that he's looking at past events doesn't matter; what counts is that he's seeing clearer than he ever could before, just because, for once, he's trying.

"Now—about this 'thirty-three' business. I don't think a man could get a nastier shock than to find he has some one else's memories. The ego is too important to let slide that way. But consider: all your thinking is done in code and you have the key to only about a tenth of it. So you run into a stretch of code which is abhorrent to you. Can't you see that the only way you'll find the key to it is to stop avoiding it?"

"You mean I'd started to remember with . . . with somebody else's mind?"

"It looked like that to you for a while, which means something. Let's try to find out what."

"All right." I felt sick. I felt tired. And I suddenly realized that being sick and being tired was a way of trying to get out of it.

"Baby is three," he said.

Baby is maybe. Me, three, thirty-three, me, you Kew you.

"Kew!" I yelled. Stern didn't say anything. "Look, I don't know why, but I think I know how to get to this, and this isn't the way. Do you mind if I try something else?"

"You're the doctor," he said.

I had to laugh. Then I closed my eyes.

There, through the edges of the hedges, the ledges and wedges of windows were shouldering up to the sky. The lawns were sprayed-on green, neat and clean, and all the flowers looked as if they were afraid to let their petals break and be untidy.

I walked up the drive in my shoes. I'd had to wear shoes and my feet couldn't breathe. I didn't want to go to the house, but I had to.

I went up the steps between the big white columns and looked at the door. I wished I could see through it, but it was too white and thick. There was a window the shape of a fan over it, too high up though, and a window on each side of it, but they were all crudded up with colored glass. I hit on the door with my hand and left dirt on it.

Nothing happened so I hit it again. It got snatched open and a tall, thin colored woman stood there. "What you want?"

I said I had to see Miss Kew.

"Well, Miss Kew don't want to see the likes of you," she said. She talked too loud. "You got a dirty face."

I started to get mad then. I was already pretty sore about having to come here, walking around near people in the daytime and all. I said, "My face ain't got nothin' to do with it. Where's Miss Kew? Go on, find her for me."

She gasped. "You can't speak to me like that!"

I said, "I didn't want to speak to you like any way. Let me in." I started wishing for Janie. Janie could of moved her. But I had to handle it by myself. I wasn't doing so hot, either. She slammed the door before I could so much as curse at her.

So I started kicking on the door. For that, shoes are great. After a while, she snatched the door open again so sudden I almost went on my can. She had a broom with her. She screamed at me, "You get away from here, you trash, or I'll call the police!" She pushed me and I fell.

I got up off the porch floor and went for her. She stepped back and whupped me one with the broom as I went past, but anyhow I was inside now. The woman was making little shrieking noises and coming for me. I took the broom away from her and then somebody said "Miriam!" in a voice like a grown goose.

I froze and the woman went into hysterics. "Oh, Miss Alicia, look out! He'll kill us all. Get the police. Get the—"

"Miriam!" came the honk, and Miriam dried up.

There at the top of the stairs was this prune-faced woman with a dress on that had lace on it. She looked a lot older than she was, maybe because she held her mouth so tight. I guess she was about thirty-three—*thirty-three*. She had mean eyes and a small nose.

I asked, "Are you Miss Kew?"

"I am. What is the meaning of this invasion?"

"I got to talk to you, Miss Kew?"

"Don't say 'got to.' Stand up straight and speak out."

The maid said, "I'll get the police."

Miss Kew turned on her. "There's time enough for that, Miriam. Now, you dirty little boy, what do you want?"

"I got to speak to you by yourself," I told her.

"Don't you let him do it, Miss Alicia," cried the maid.

"Be quiet, Miriam. Little boy, I told you not to say 'got to.' You may say whatever you have to say in front of Miriam."

"Like hell." They both gasped. I said, "Lone told me not to."

"Miss Alicia, are you goin' to let him—"

"Be quiet, Miriam! Young man, you will keep a civil—" Then her eyes popped up real round. "*Who* did you say . . ."

"Lone said so."

"Lone." She stood there on the stairs looking at her hands. Then she said, "Miriam, that will be all." And you wouldn't know it was the same woman, the way she said it.

The maid opened her mouth, but Miss Kew stuck out a finger that might as well of had rifle-sight on the end of it. The maid beat it.

"Hey," I said, "here's your broom." I was just going to throw it, but Miss Kew got to me and took it out of my hand.

"In there," she said.

She made me go ahead of her into a room as big as our swimming hole. It had books all over and leather on top of the tables, with gold flowers drawn into the corners."

She pointed to a chair. "Sit there. No, wait a moment." She went to the fireplace and got a newspaper out of a box and brought it over and unfolded it on the seat of the chair. "Now sit down."

I sat on the paper and she dragged up another chair, but didn't put no paper on it.

"What is it? Where is Lone?"

"He died," I said.

She pulled in her breath and went white. She stared at me until her eyes started to water.

"You sick?" I asked her. "Go ahead, throw up. It'll make you feel better."

"Dead? Lone is dead?"

"Yeah. There was a flash flood last week and when he went out the next night in that big wind, he walked under a old oak tree that got gullied under by the flood. The tree come down on him."

"*Came* down on him," she whispered. "Oh, no . . . it's not true."

"It's true, all right. We planted him this morning. We couldn't keep him around no more. He was beginning to st—"

"Stop!" She covered her face with her hands.

"What's the matter?"

"I'll be all right in a moment," she said in a low voice. She went and stood in front of the fireplace with her back to me. I took off one of my shoes while I was waiting for her to come back. But instead she talked from where she was. "Are you Lone's little boy?"

"Yeah. He told me to come to you."

"Oh, my dear child!" She came running back and I thought for a second she was going to pick me up or something, but she stopped short and wrinkled up her nose a little bit. "Wh-what's your name?"

"Gerry," I told her.

"Well, Gerry, how would you like to live with me in this nice big house and—and have new clean clothes—and everything?"

"Well, that's the whole idea. Lone told me to come to you. He said you got more dough than you know what to do with, and he said you owed him a favor."

"A favor?" That seemed to bother her.

"Well," I tried to tell her, "he said he done something for you once and you said some day you'd pay him back for it if you ever could. This is it."

"What did he tell you about that?" She'd got her honk back by then.

"Not a damn thing."

"Please don't use that word," she said, with her eyes closed. Then she opened them and nodded her head. "I promised and I'll do it. You live here from now on. If—if you want to."

"That's got nothin' to do with it. Lone *told* me to."

"You'll be happy here," she said. She gave me an up-and-down. "I'll see to that."

"Okay. Shall I go get the other kids?"

"*Other* kids—children?"

"Yeah. This ain't for just me. For all of us—the whole gang."

"Don't say 'ain't.' " She leaned back in her chair, took out a silly little handkerchief and dabbed her lips with it, looking at me the whole time. "Now tell me about these—these other children."

"Well, there's Janie, she's eleven like me. And Bonnie and Beanie are eight, they're twins, and Baby. Baby is three."

I screamed. Stern was kneeling beside the couch in a flash, holding his palms against my cheeks to hold my head still; I'd been whipping it back and forth.

"Good boy," he said. "You found it. You haven't found out *what* it is, but now you know *where* it is."

"But for sure," I said hoarsely. "Got water?"

He poured me some water out of a Thermos flask. It was so cold it hurt. I lay back and rested, like I'd climbed a cliff. I said, "I can't take anything like that again."

"You want to call it quits for today?"

"What about you?"

"I'll go on as long as you want me to."

I thought about it. "I'd like to go on, but I don't want no thumping around. Not for a while yet."

"If you want another of those inaccurate analogies," Stern said, "psychiatry is like a road map. There are always a lot of different ways to get from one place to another place."

"I'll go around by the long way," I told him. "The eight-lane highway. Not that track over the hill. My clutch is slipping. Where do I turn off?"

He chuckled. I liked the sound of it. "Just past that gravel driveway."

"I been there. There's a bridge washed out."

"You've been on this whole road before," he told me. "Start at the other side of the bridge."

"I never thought of that. I figured I had to do the whole thing, every inch."

"Maybe you won't have to, maybe you will, but the bridge will be easy to cross when you've covered everything else. Maybe there's nothing of value on the bridge and maybe there is, but you can't get near it till you've looked everywhere else."

"Let's go." I was real eager, somehow.

"Mind a suggestion?"

"No."

"Just talk," he said. "Don't try to get too far into what you're saying. That first stretch, when you were eight—you really lived it. The second one, all about the kids, you just talked about. Then, the visit when you were eleven, you felt that. Now just talk again."

"All right."

He waited, then said quietly, "In the library. You told her about the other kids."

I told her about . . . and then she said . . . and something happened, and I screamed. She comforted me and I cussed at her.

But we're not thinking about that now. We're going on.

In the library. The leather, the table, and whether I'm able to do with Miss Kew what Lone said.

What Lone said was, "There's a woman lives up on the top of the hill in the Heights section, name of Kew. She'll have to take care of you. You got to get her to do that. Do everything she tells you, only stay together. Don't you ever let any one of you get away from the others, hear? Aside from that, just you keep Miss Kew happy and she'll keep you happy. Now you do what I say." That's what Lone said. Between every word there was a link like steel cable, and the whole thing made something that couldn't be broken. Not by me it couldn't.

Miss Kew said, "Where are your sisters and the baby?"

"I'll bring 'em."

"Is it near here?"

"Near enough." She didn't say anything to that, so I got up. "I'll be back soon."

"Wait," she said. "I—really, I haven't had time to think. I mean—I've got to get things ready, you know."

I said, "You don't need to think and you are ready. So long." From the door I heard her saying, louder and louder as I walked away, "Young man, if you're to live in this house, you'll learn to be a good deal better-mannered—" and a lot more of the same.

I yelled back at her, "Okay, *okay!*" and went out.

The sun was warm and the sky was good, and pretty soon I got back to Lone's house. The fire was out and Baby stunk. Janie had knocked over her easel and was sitting on the floor by the door with her head in her hands. Bonnie and Beanie were on a stool with their arms around each other, pulled up together as close as they could get, as if it was cold in there, although it wasn't.

I hit Janie in the arm to snap her out of it. She raised her head. She had gray eyes—or maybe it was more a kind of green—but now they had a funny look about them, like water in a glass that had some milk left in the bottom of it.

I said, "What's the matter around here?"

"What's the matter with what?" she wanted to know.

"All of yez," I said.

She said, "We don't give a damn, that's all."

"Well, all right," I said, "but we got to do what Lone said. Come on."

"No." I looked at the twins. They turned their backs on me. Janie said, "They're hungry."

"Well, why not give 'em something?"

She just shrugged. I sat down. What did Lone have to go get himself squashed for?

"We can't blesh no more," said Janie. It seemed to explain everything.

"Look," I said, "I've got to be Lone now."

Janie thought about that and Baby kicked his feet. Janie looked at him. "You can't," she said.

"I know where to get the heavy food and the turpentine," I said. "I can find that springy moss to stuff in the logs, and cut wood, and all."

But I couldn't call Bonnie and Beanie from miles away to unlock doors. I couldn't just say a word to Janie and make her get water and blow up the fire and fix the battery. I couldn't make us blesh.

We all stayed like that for a long time. Then I heard the bassinet creak. I looked up. Janie was staring into it.

"All right," she said. "Let's go."

"Who says so?"

"Baby."

"Who's running things now?" I said, mad. "Me or Baby?"

"Baby," Janie said.

I got up and went over to bust her one in the mouth, and then I stopped. If Baby could make them do what Lone wanted, then it would get done. If I started pushing them all around, it wouldn't. So I didn't say anything. Janie got up and walked out the door. The twins watched her go. Then Bonnie disappeared. Beanie picked up Bonnie's clothes and walked out. I got Baby out of the bassinet and draped him over my shoulders.

It was better when we were all outside. It was getting late in the day and the air was warm. The twins flitted in and out of the trees like a couple of flying squirrels, and Janie and I walked along like we were going swimming or something. Baby started to kick, and Janie looked at him a while and got him fed, and he was quiet again.

When we came close to town, I wanted to get everybody close together, but I was afraid to say anything. Baby must of said it instead. The twins came back to us and Janie gave them their clothes and they walked ahead of us, good as you please. I don't know how Baby did it. They sure hated to travel that way.

We didn't have no trouble except one guy we met on the street near Miss Kew's place. He stopped in his tracks and gaped at us, and Janie looked at him and made his hat go so far down over his eyes that he like to pull his neck apart getting it back up again.

What do you know, when we got to the house somebody had washed off all the dirt I put on the door. I had one hand on Baby's arm and one on his ankle and him draped over my neck, so I kicked the door and left some more dirt.

"There's a woman here name of Miriam," I told Janie. "She says anything, tell her to go to hell."

The door opened and there was Miriam. She took one look and jumped back six feet. We all trailed inside. Miriam got her wind and screamed, "Miss Kew! Miss Kew!"

"Go to hell," said Janie, and looked at me. I didn't know what to do. It was the first time Janie ever did anything I told her to.

Miss Kew came down the stairs. She was wearing a different dress, but it was just as stupid and had just as much lace. She opened her mouth and nothing came out, so she just left it open until something happened. Finally she said, "Dear gentle Lord preserve us!"

The twins lined up and gawked at her. Miriam sidled over to the wall and sort of slid along it, keeping away from us, until she could get to the door and close it. She said, "Miss Kew, if those are the children you said were going to live here, I quit."

Janie said, "Go to hell."

Just then Bonnie squatted down on the rug. Miriam squawked and jumped at her. She grabbed hold of Bonnie's arm and went to snatch her up. Bonnie disappeared, leaving Miriam with one small dress and the damnedest expression on her face. Beanie grinned enough to split her head in two and started to wave like mad. I looked where she was waving, and there was Bonnie, naked as a jaybird, up on the banister at the top of the stairs.

Miss Kew turned around and saw her and sat down plump on the steps. Miriam went down, too, like she'd been slugged. Beanie picked up Bonnie's dress and walked up the steps past Miss Kew and handed it over. Bonnie put it on. Miss Kew sort of lolled around and looked up. Bonnie and Beanie came back down the stairs hand in hand to where I was. Then they lined up and gaped at Miss Kew.

"What's the matter with her?" Janie asked me.

"She gets sick every once in a while."

"Let's go back home."

"No," I told her.

Miss Kew grabbed the banister and pulled herself up. She stood there hanging on to it for a while with her eyes closed. All of a sudden she stiffened herself. She looked about four inches taller. She came marching over to us.

"Gerard" she honked.

I think she was going to say something different. But she sort of checked herself and pointed. "What in heaven's name is *that?*" And she aimed her finger at me.

I didn't get it right away, so I turned around to look behind me. "What?"

"That! That!"

"Oh!" I said. "That's Baby."

I slung him down off my back and held him up for her to look at. She made a sort of moaning noise and jumped over and took him away from me. She held him out in front of her and moaned again and called him a poor little thing, and ran and put him down on a long bench, with cushions under the colored-glass window. She bent over him and put her knuckle in her mouth and bit on it and moaned some more. Then she turned to me.

"How long has he been like this?"

I looked at Janie and she looked at me. I said, "He's always been like he is."

She made a sort of cough and ran to where Miriam was lying flaked out on the floor. She slapped Miriam's face a couple of times back and forth. Miriam sat up and looked us over. She closed her eyes and shivered and sort of climbed up Miss Kew hand over hand until she was on her feet.

"Pull yourself together," said Miss Kew between her teeth. "Get a basin with some hot water and soap. Wash-cloth. Towels. Hurry!" She gave Miriam a big push. Miriam staggered and grabbed at the wall, and then ran out.

Miss Kew went back to Baby and hung over him, titchtitching with her lips all tight.

"Don't mess with him," I said. "There's nothin' wrong with him. We're hungry."

She gave me a look like I'd punched her. "Don't speak to me!"

"Look," I said, "we don't like this any more'n you do. If Lone hadn't told us to, we wouldn't never have come. We were doing all right where we were."

"Don't say 'wouldn't never,' " said Miss Kew. She looked at all of us, one by one. Then she took that silly little hunk of handkerchief and pushed it against her mouth.

"See?" I said to Janie. "All the time gettin' sick."

"Ho-ho," said Bonnie.

Miss Kew gave her a long look. "Gerard," she said in a choked sort of voice, "I understood you to say that these children were your sisters."

"Well?"

She looked at me as if I was real stupid. "We don't have little colored girls for sisters, Gerard."

Janie said, "*We* do."

Miss Kew walked up and back, real fast. "We have a great deal to do," she said, talking to herself.

Miriam came in with a big oval pan and towels and stuff on her arm. She put it down on the bench thing and Miss Kew stuck the back of her hand in the water, then picked up Baby and dunked him right in it. Baby started to kick.

I stepped forward and said, "Wait a minute. Hold on now. What do you think you're doing?"

Janie said, "Shut up, Gerry. He says it's all right."

"All right? She'll drown him."

"No, she won't. Just shut up."

Working up a froth with the soap, Miss Kew smeared it on Baby and turned him over a couple of times and scrubbed at his head and like to smothered him in a big white towel. Miriam stood gawking while Miss Kew lashed up a dishcloth around him so it come out pants. When she was done, you wouldn't of known it was the same baby. And by the time Miss Kew finished with the job, she seemed to have a better hold on herself. She was breathing hard and her mouth was even tighter. She held out the baby to Miriam.

"Take this poor thing," she said, "and put him—"

But Miriam backed away. "I'm sorry, Miss Kew, but I am leaving here and I don't care."

Miss Kew got her honk out. "You can't leave me in a predicament like this! These children need help. Can't you see that for yourself?"

Miriam looked me and Janie over. She was trembling. "You ain't safe, Miss Alicia. They ain't just dirty. They're crazy!"

"They're victims of neglect, and probably no worse than you or I would be if we'd been neglected. And don't say 'ain't.' Gerard!"

"What?"

"Don't say—oh, dear, we have so much to do. Gerard, if you and your—these other children are going to live here, you shall have to make a great many changes. You cannot live under this roof and behave as you have so far. Do you understand that?"

"Oh, sure. Lone said we was to do whatever you say and keep you happy."

"Will you do whatever I say?"

"That's what I just said, isn't it?"

"Gerard, you shall have to learn not to speak to me in that tone. Now, young man, if I told you to do what Miriam says, too, would you do it?"

I said to Janie, "What about that?"

"I'll ask Baby." Janie looked at Baby and Baby wobbled his hands and drooled some. She said, "It's okay."

Miss Kew said, "Gerard, I asked you a question."

"Keep your pants on," I said. "I got to find out, don't I? Yes, if that's what you want, we'll listen to Miriam too."

Miss Kew turned to Miriam. "You hear that, Miriam?"

Miriam looked at Miss Kew and at us and shook her head. Then she held out her hands a bit to Bonnie and Beanie.

They went right to her. Each one took hold of a hand. They looked up at her and grinned. They were probably planning some sort of hellishness, but I guess they looked sort of cute. Miriam's mouth twitched and I thought for a second she was going to look human. She said, "All right, Miss Alicia."

Miss Kew walked over and handed her the baby and she started upstairs with him. Miss Kew herded us along after Miriam. We all went upstairs.

They went to work on us then and for three years they never stopped.

"That was hell," I said to Stern.

"They had their work cut out."

"Yeah, I s'pose they did. So did we. Look, we were going to do exactly what Lone said. Nothing on earth could of stopped us from doing it. We were tied and bound to doing every last little thing Miss Kew said to do. But she and Miriam never seemed to understand that. I guess they felt they had to push every inch of the way. All they had to do was make us understand what they wanted, and we'd of done it. That's okay when it's something like telling me not to climb into bed with Janie. Miss Kew raised holy hell over that. You'd of thought I'd robbed the Crown Jewels, the way she acted.

"But when it's something like, 'You must behave like little ladies and gentlemen,' it just doesn't mean a thing. And two out of three orders she gave us were like that. 'Ah-ah!' she'd say. 'Language, language!' For the longest time I didn't dig that at all. I finally asked her what the hell she meant, and then she finally come out with it. But you see what I mean."

"I certainly do," Stern said. "Did it get easier as time went on?"

"We only had real trouble twice, once about the twins and once about Baby. That one was real bad."

"What happened?"

"About the twins? Well, when we'd been there about a week or so we began to notice something that sort of stunk. Janie and me, I mean. We began to notice that we almost never got to see Bonnie and Beanie. It was like the house was two houses, one part for Miss Kew and Janie and me, and the other part for Miriam and the twins. I guess we'd have noticed it sooner if things hadn't been such a hassel at first, getting us into new clothes and making us sleep all the time at night, and all that. But here was the thing: We'd all get turned out in the side yard to play, and then along comes lunch, and the twins got herded off to eat with Miriam while we ate with Miss Kew. So Janie said, 'Why don't the twins eat with us?'

" 'Miriam's taking care of them, dear,' Miss Kew says.

"Janie looked at her with those eyes. 'I know that. Let 'em eat here and I'll take care of 'em.'

"Miss Kew's mouth got all tight again and she said, 'They're little colored girls, Jane. Now eat your lunch.'

"But that didn't explain anything to Janie or me, either. I said, 'I want 'em to eat with us. Lone said we should stay together.'

" 'But you *are* together,' she says. 'We all live in the same house. We all eat the same food. Now let us not discuss the matter.'

"I looked at Janie and she looked at me and she said, 'So why can't we all do this livin' and eatin' right here?'

"Miss Kew put down her fork and looked hard. 'I have explained it to you and I have said that there will be no further discussion.'

"Well, I thought that was real nowhere. So I just rocked back my head and bellowed, 'Bonnie! Bonnie!' and *bing*, there they were.

"So all hell broke loose. Miss Kew ordered them out and they wouldn't go, and Miriam come steaming in with their clothes, and she couldn't catch them, and Miss Kew got to honking at them and finally at me. She said this was too much. Well, maybe she'd had a hard week, but so had we. So Miss Kew ordered us to leave.

"I went and got Baby and started out, and along came Janie and the twins. Miss Kew waited till we were all out the door and next thing you know she ran out after us. She passed us and got in front of me and made me stop. So we all stopped.

" 'Is this how you follow Lone's wishes?' she asked.

"I told her yes. She said she understood Lone wanted us to stay with her. And I said, 'Yeah, but he wanted us to stay together more.'

"She said come back in, we'd have a talk. Janie asked Baby and Baby said okay, so we went back. We had a compromise. We didn't eat in the dining room no more. There was a side porch, a sort of verandah thing with glass windows, with a door to the dining room and a door to the kitchen, and we all ate out there after that. Miss Kew ate by herself.

"But something funny happened because of that whole cockeyed hassel."

"What was that?" Stern asked me.

I laughed. "Miriam. She looked and sounded like always but she started slipping us cookies between meals. You know, it took me years to figure out what all that was about. I mean it. From what I've learned about people, there seems to be two armies fightin' about race. One's fightin' to keep 'em apart, and one's fightin' to get 'em together. But I don't see why both sides are so *worried* about it! Why don't they just forget it?"

"They can't. You see, Gerry, it's necessary for people to believe they are superior in some fashion. You and Lone and the kids—you were a pretty tight unit. Didn't you feel you were a little better than all the rest of the world?"

"Better? How could we be better?"

"Different, then."

"Well, I suppose so, but we didn't think about it. Different, yes. Better, no."

"You're a unique case," Stern said. "Now go on and tell me about the other trouble you had. About Baby."

"Baby. Yeah. Well, that was a couple of months after we moved to Miss Kew's. Things were already getting real smooth, even then. We'd learned all the 'yes, ma'am, no, ma'am' routines by then and she'd got us catching up with school—regular periods morning and afternoon, five days a week. Janie had long ago quit taking care of

Baby, and the twins walked to wherever they went. That was funny. They could pop from one place to another right in front of Miss Kew's eyes and she wouldn't believe what she saw. She was too upset about them suddenly showing up bare. They quit doing it and she was happy about it. She was happy about a lot of things. It had been years since she'd seen anybody—years. She'd even had the meters put outside the house so no one would ever have to come in. But with us there, she began to liven up. She quit wearing those old-lady dresses and began to look halfway human. She ate with us sometimes, even.

"But one fine day I woke up feeling real weird. It was like somebody had stolen something from me when I was asleep, only I didn't know what. I crawled out of my window and along the ledge into Janie's room, which I wasn't supposed to do. She was in bed. I went and woke her up. I can still see her eyes, the way they opened a little slit, still asleep, and then popped up wide. I didn't have to tell her something was wrong. She knew, and she knew what it was.

" 'Baby's gone!' she said.

"We didn't care then who woke up. We pounded out of her room and down the hall and into the little room at the end where Baby slept. You wouldn't believe it. The fancy crib he had and the white chest of drawers and all that mess of rattles and so on, they were gone, and there was just a writing desk there. I mean it was as if Baby had never been there at all.

"We didn't say anything. We just spun around and busted into Miss Kew's bedroom. I'd never been in there but once and Janie only a few times. But forbidden or not, this was different. Miss Kew was in bed, with her hair braided. She was wide awake before we could get across the room. She pushed herself back and up until she was sitting against the headboard. She gave the two of us the cold eye.

" 'What is the meaning of this?' she wanted to know.

" 'Where's Baby?' I yelled at her.

" 'Gerard,' she says, 'there is no need to shout.'

"Janie was a real quiet kid, but she said, 'You better tell us where he is, Miss Kew,' and it would of scared you to look at her when she said it.

"So all of a sudden Miss Kew took off the stone face and held out her hands to us. 'Children,' she said, 'I'm sorry. I really am sorry. But I've just done what is best. I've sent Baby away. He's gone to live with some children like him. We could never make him really happy here. You know that.'

"Janie said, 'He never told us he wasn't happy.'

"Miss Kew brought out a hollow kind of laugh. 'As if he could talk, the poor little thing.'

" 'You better get him back here,' I said. 'You don't know what you're fooling with. I told you we wasn't ever to break up.'

"She was getting mad, but she held on to herself. 'I'll try to explain it to you, dear,' she said. 'You and Jane here and even the twins are all normal, healthy children and you'll grow up to be fine men and women. But poor Baby's—different. He's not going to grow very much more, and he'll never walk and play like other children.'

" 'That doesn't matter,' Janie said. 'You had no call to send him away.'

"And I said, 'Yeah. You better bring him back, but quick.'

"Then she started to jump salty. 'Among the many things I have taught you is, I am sure, not to dictate to your elders. Now then, you run along and get dressed for breakfast, and we'll say no more about this.'

"I told her, nice as I could, 'Miss Kew, you're going to wish you brought him back right now. But you're going to bring him back soon. Or else.'

"So then she got up out of her bed and ran us out of the room."

I was quiet a while, and Stern asked, "What happened?"

"Oh," I said, "she brought him back." I laughed suddenly. "I guess it's funny now, when you come to think of it. Nearly three months of us getting bossed around, and her ruling the roost, and then all of a sudden we lay down the law. We'd tried our best to be good according to her ideas, but, by God, that time she went too far. She got the treatment from the second she slammed her door on us. She had a big china pot under her bed, and it rose up in the air and smashed through her dresser mirror. Then one of the drawers in the dresser slid open and a glove come out of it and smacked her face.

"She went to jump back on the bed and a whole section of plaster fell off the ceiling onto the bed. The water turned on in her little bathroom and the plug went in, and just about the time it began to overflow, all her clothes fell off their hooks. She went to run out of the room, but the door was stuck, and when she yanked on the handle it opened real quick and she spread out on the floor. The door slammed shut again and more plaster come down on her. Then we went back in and stood looking at her. She was crying. I hadn't known till then that she could.

" 'You going to get Baby back here?' I asked her.

"She just lay there and cried. After a while she looked up at us. It was real pathetic. We helped her up and got her to a chair. She just looked at us for a while, and at the mirror, and at the busted ceiling, and then whispered, 'What happened? What happened?'

" 'You took Baby away,' I said. 'That's what.'

"So she jumped up and said real low, real scared, but real strong: 'Something struck the house. An airplane. Perhaps there was an earthquake. We'll talk about Baby after breakfast.'

"I said, 'Give her more, Janie.'

"A big gob of water hit her on the face and chest and made her nightgown stick to her, which was the kind of thing that upset her most. Her braids stood straight up in the air, more and more, till they dragged her standing straight up. She opened her mouth to yell and the powder puff off the dresser rammed into it. She clawed it out.

" 'What are you doing? What are you doing?' she says, crying again.

"Janie just looked at her and put her hands behind her, real smug. 'We haven't done anything,' she said.

"And I said, 'Not yet we haven't. You going to get Baby back?'

"And she screamed at us, 'Stop it! Stop it! Stop talking about that mongoloid idiot! It's no good to anyone, not even itself! How could I ever make believe it's mine?'

"I said, 'Get rats, Janie.'

"There was a scuttling sound along the baseboard. Miss Kew covered her face with her hands and sank down on the chair. 'Not rats,' she said. 'There are no rats here.' Then something squeaked and she went all to pieces. Did you ever see anyone really go to pieces?"

"Yes," Stern said.

"I was about as mad as I could get," I said, "but that was almost too much for me. Still, she shouldn't have sent Baby away. It took a couple of hours for her to get straightened out enough so she could use the phone, but we had Baby back before lunch time." I laughed.

"What's funny?"

"She never seemed able to rightly remember what had happened to her. About three weeks later I heard her talking to Miriam about it. She said it was the house settling suddenly. She said it was a good thing she'd sent Baby out for that medical checkup—the poor little thing might have been hurt. She really believed it, I think."

"She probably did. That's fairly common. We don't believe anything we don't want to believe."

"How much of this do you believe?" I asked him suddenly.

"I told you before—it doesn't matter. I don't want to believe or disbelieve it."

"You haven't asked me how much of it I believe."

"I don't have to. You'll make up your own mind about that."

"Are you a *good* psychotherapist?"

"I think so," he said. "Whom did you kill?"

The question caught me absolutely off guard. "Miss Kew," I said. Then I started to cuss and swear. "I didn't mean to tell you that."

"Don't worry about it," he said. "What did you do it for?"

"That's what I came here to find out."

"You must have really hated her."

I started to cry. Fifteen years old and crying like that!

He gave me time to get it all out. The first part of it came out in noises, grunts and squeaks that hurt my throat. Much more than you'd think came out when my nose started to run. And finally—words.

"Do you know where I came from? The earliest thing I can remember is a punch in the mouth. I can still see it coming, a fist as big as my head. Because I was crying. I been afraid to cry ever since. I was crying because I was hungry. Cold, maybe. Both. After that, big dormitories, and whoever could steal the most got the most. Get the hell kicked out of you if you're bad, get a big reward if you're good. Big reward: they let you alone. Try to live like that. Try to live so the biggest, most wonderful thing in the whole damn world is just to have 'em let you alone!

"So a spell with Lone and the kids. Something wonderful: you belong. It never happened before. Two yellow bulbs and a fireplace and they light up the world. It's all there is and all there ever has to be.

"Then the big change: clean clothes, cooked food, five hours a day school; Columbus and King Arthur and a 1925 book on Civics that explains about septic tanks. Over it all a great big square-cut lump of ice, and you watch it melting and the corners curve, and you know it's because of you, Miss Kew . . . hell, she had too much control over herself ever to slobber over us, but it was there, that feeling. Lone took care of us because it was part of the way he lived. Miss Kew took care of us and none of it was the way she lived. It was something she wanted to do.

"She had a weird idea of 'right' and a wrong idea of 'wrong,' but she stuck to them, tried to make her ideas do us good. When she couldn't understand, she figured it was her own failure . . . and there was an almighty lot she didn't understand and never could. What went right was our success. What went wrong was her mistake. That last year, that was . . . oh, good."

"So?"

"So I killed her. Listen," I said. I felt I had to talk fast. I wasn't short of time, but I had to get rid of it. "I'll tell you all I know about it. The day before I killed her. I woke up in the morning and the sheets crackly clean under me, the sunlight coming in through white curtains and bright red-and-blue drapes. There's a closet full of my clothes—mine, you see; I never had anything that was really mine before—and downstairs Miriam clinking around with breakfast and the twins laughing. Laughing with *her*, mind you, not just with each other like they always did before.

"In the next room, Janie moving around, singing, and when I see her, I know her face will shine inside and out. I get up. There's *hot* hot water and the toothpaste bites my tongue. The clothes fit me and I go downstairs and they're all there and I'm glad to see them and they're glad to see me, and we no sooner get set around the table when Miss Kew comes down and everyone calls out to her at once.

"And the morning goes by like that, school with a recess, there in the big long living room. The twins with the ends of their tongues stuck out, drawing the alphabet instead of writing it, and then Janie, when it's time, painting a picture, a real picture of a cow with trees and a yellow fence that goes off into the distance. Here I am lost between the two parts of a quadratic equation, and Miss Kew bending close to help me, and I smell the sachet she has on her clothes. I hold up my head to smell it better, and far away I hear the shuffle and klunk of filled pots going on the stove back in the kitchen.

"And the afternoon goes by like that, more school and some study and boiling out into the yard, laughing. The twins chasing each other, running on their two feet to get where they want to go; Janie dappling the leaves in her picture, trying to get it just the way Miss Kew says it ought to be. And Baby, he's got a big play-pen. He don't move around much any more, he just watches and dribbles some, and gets packed full of food and kept as clean as a new sheet of tinfoil.

"And supper, and the evening, and Miss Kew reading to us, changing her voice every time someone else talks in the story, reading fast and whispery when it embarrasses her, but reading every word all the same.

"And I had to go and kill her. And that's all."

"You haven't said why," Stern said.

"What are you—stupid?" I yelled.

Stern didn't say anything. I turned on my belly on the couch and propped up my chin in my hands and looked at him. You never could tell what was going on with him, but I got the idea that he was puzzled.

"I said why," I told him.

"Not to me."

I suddenly understood that I was asking too much of him. I said slowly, "We all woke up at the same time. We all did what somebody else wanted. We lived through a day someone else's way, thinking someone else's thoughts, saying other people's words. Jane painted someone else's pictures, Baby didn't talk to anyone, and we were all happy with it. Now do you see?"

"Not yet."

"God!" I said. I thought for a while. "We didn't blesh."

"Blesh? Oh. But you didn't after Lone died, either."

"That was different. That was like a car running out of gas, but the car's there—there's nothing wrong with it. It's just waiting. But after Miss Kew got done with us, the car was taken all to pieces, see?"

It was his turn to think a while. Finally he said, "The mind makes us do funny things. Some of them seem completely reasonless, wrong, insane. But the cornerstone of the work we're doing is this: there's a chain of solid, unassailable logic in the things we do. Dig deep enough and you find cause and effect as clearly in this field as you do in any other. I said *logic*, mind; I didn't say 'correctness' or 'rightness' or 'justice' or anything of the sort. Logic and truth are two very different things, but they often look the same to the mind that's performing the logic.

"When that mind is submerged, working at cross-purposes with the surface mind, then you're all confused. Now in your case, I can see the thing you're pointing at—that in order to preserve or to rebuild that peculiar bond between you kids, you had to get rid of Miss Kew. But I don't see the logic. I don't see that regaining that 'bleshing' was worth destroying this new-found security which you admit was enjoyable."

I said desperately, "Maybe it wasn't worth destroying it."

Stern leaned forward and pointed his pipe at me. "It *was* because it made you do what you did. After the fact, maybe things look different. But when you were moved to do it, the important thing was to destroy Miss Kew and regain this thing you'd had before. I don't see why and neither do you."

"How are we going to find out?"

"Well, let's get to the most unpleasant part, if you're up to it."

I lay down. "I'm ready."

"All right. Tell me everything that happened just before you killed her."

I fumbled through that last day, trying to taste the food, hear the voices. A thing came and went and came again: it was the crisp feeling of the sheets. I thrust it away because it was at the beginning of that day, but it came back again, and I realized it was at the end, instead.

I said, "What I just told you, all that about the children doing things other people's way instead of their own, and Baby not talking, and everyone happy about it, and finally that I had to kill Miss Kew. It took a long time to get to that, and a long time to start doing it. I guess I lay in bed and thought for four hours before I got up again. It was dark and quiet. I went out of the room and down the hall and into Miss Kew's bedroom and killed her."

"How?"

"That's all there is!" I shouted, as loud as I could. Then I quieted down. "It was awful dark . . . it still is. I don't know. I don't want to know. She did love us. I know she did. But I had to kill her."

"All right, all right," Stern said "I guess there's no need to get too gruesome about this. You're—"

"What?"

"You're quite strong for your age, aren't you, Gerard?"

"I guess so. Strong enough, anyway."

"Yes," he said.

"I still don't see that logic you were talking about." I began to hammer on the couch with my fist, hard, once for each word: "Why—did—I—have—to—go—and—do—that?"

"Cut that out," he said. "You'll hurt yourself."

"I ought to get hurt," I said.

"Ah?" said Stern.

I got up and went to the desk and got some water. "What am I going to do?"

"Tell me what you did after you killed her, right up until the time you came here."

"Not much," I said. "It was only last night. I took her checkbook. I went back to my room, sort of numb. I put all my clothes on except my shoes. I carried them. I went out. Walked a long time, trying to think, went to the bank when it opened. Cashed a check for eleven hundred bucks. Got the idea of getting some help from a psychiatrist, spent most of the day looking for one, came here. That's all."

"Didn't you have any trouble cashing the check?"

"I never have any trouble making people do what I want them to do."

He gave a surprised grunt.

"I know what you're thinking—I couldn't make Miss Kew do what I wanted."

"That's part of it," he admitted.

"If I had of done that," I told him, "she wouldn't of been Miss Kew any more. Now the banker—all I made him do was be a banker."

I looked at him and suddenly realized why he fooled with the pipe all the time. It was so he could look down at it and you wouldn't be able to see his eyes.

"You killed her," he said—and I knew he was changing the subject—"and destroyed something that was valuable to you. It must have been less valuable to you than the chance to rebuild this thing you used to have with the other kids. And you're not sure of the value of that." He looked up. "Does that describe your main trouble?"

"Just about."

"You know the single thing that makes people kill?" When I didn't answer, he said, "Survival. To save the self or something which identifies with the self. And in this case that doesn't apply, because your setup with Miss Kew had far more survival value for you, singly and as a group, than the other."

"So maybe I just didn't have a good enough reason to kill her."

"You had, because you did it. We just haven't located it yet. I mean we have the reason, but we don't know why it was important enough. The answer is somewhere in you."

"Where?"

He got up and walked some. "We have a pretty consecutive lifestory here. There's fantasy mixed with the fact, of course, and there are areas in which we have no detailed information, but we have a beginning and a middle and an end. Now I can't say for sure, but the answer may be in that bridge you refused to cross a while back. Remember?"

I remembered all right. I said, "Why that? Why can't we try something else?"

He quietly pointed out, "Because you just said it. Why are you shying away from it?"

"Don't go making big ones out of little ones," I said. Sometimes the guy annoyed me. "That bothers me. I don't know why, but it does."

"Something's lying hidden in there and you're bothering *it* so it's fighting back. Anything that fights to stay concealed is very possibly the thing we're after. Your trouble is concealed, isn't it?"

"Well, yes," I said, and I felt that sickness and faintness again, and again I pushed it away. Suddenly I wasn't going to be stopped any more. "Let's go get it." I lay down.

He let me watch the ceiling and listen to silence for a while, and then he said, "You're in the library. You've just met Miss Kew. She's talking to you; you're telling her about the children."

I lay very still. Nothing happened. Yes, it did; I got tense inside all over, from the bones out, more and more. When it got as bad as it could, still nothing happened.

I heard him get up and cross the room to the desk. He fumbled there for a while; things clicked and hummed. Suddenly I heard my own voice:

"Well, there's Janie, she's eleven like me. And Bonnie and Beanie are eight, they're twins, and Baby. Baby is three."

And the sound of my own scream—

And nothingness.

Sputtering out of the darkness. I came up flailing with my fists. Strong hands caught my wrists. They didn't check my arms; they just grabbed and rode. I opened my eyes. I was soaking wet. The Thermos lay on its side on the rug. Stern was crouched beside me, holding my wrists. I quit struggling.

"What happened?"

He let me go and stood back watchfully. "Lord," he said, "what a charge!"

I held my head and moaned. He threw me a hand-towel and I used it. "What hit me?"

"I've had you on tape the whole time," he explained. "When you wouldn't get into the recollection, I tried to nudge you into it by using your own voice as you recounted it before. It works wonders sometimes."

"It worked wonders this time," I growled. "I think I blew a fuse."

"In effect, you did. You were on the trembling verge of going into the thing you don't want to remember, and you let yourself go unconscious rather than do it."

"What are you so pleased about?"

"Last-ditch defense," he said tersely. "We've got it now. Just one more try."

"Now hold on. The last-ditch defense is that I drop dead."

"You won't. You've contained this episode in your subconscious mind for a long time and it hasn't hurt you."

"Hasn't it?"

"Not in terms of killing you."

"How do you know it won't when we drag it out?"

"You'll see."

I looked up at him sideways. Somehow he struck me as knowing what he was doing.

"You know a lot more about yourself now than you did at the time," he explained softly. "You can apply insight. You can evaluate it as it comes up. Maybe not completely, but enough to protect yourself. Don't worry. Trust me. I can stop it if it gets too bad. Now just relax. Look at the ceiling. Be aware of your toes. Don't look at your toes. Look straight up. Your toes, your big toes. Don't move your toes, but feel them. Count outward from your big toes, one count for each toe. One, two, three. Feel that third toe. Feel the toe, feel it, feel it go limp, go limp, go limp. The toe next to it on both sides gets limp. So limp because your toes are limp, all of your toes are limp—"

"What are you doing?" I shouted at him.

He said in the same silky voice, "You trust me and so do your toes trust me. They're all limp because you trust me. You—"

"You're trying to hypnotize me. I'm not going to let you do that."

"You're going to hypnotize yourself. You do everything yourself. I just point the way. I point your toes to the path. Just point your toes. No one can make you go anywhere you don't want to go, but you want to go where your toes are pointed where your toes are limp where your . . ."

On and on and on. And where was the dangling gold ornament, the light in the eyes, the mystic passes? He wasn't even sitting where I could see him. Where was the talk about how sleepy I was supposed to be? Well, he knew I wasn't sleepy and didn't want to be sleepy. I just wanted to be toes. I just wanted to be limp, just a limp toe. No brains in a toe, a toe to go, go, go eleven times, eleven, I'm eleven . . .

I split in two, and it was all right, the part that watched the part that went back to the library, and Miss Kew leaning toward me, but not too near, me with the newspaper crackling under me on the library chair, me with one shoe off and my limp toes dangling . . . and I felt a mild surprise at this. For this was hypnosis, but I was quite conscious, quite altogether there on the couch with Stern droning away at me, quite able to roll over and sit up and talk to him and walk out if I wanted to, but I just didn't want to. Oh, if this was what hypnosis was like, I was all for it. I'd work at this. This was all right.

There on the table I'm able to see that the gold will unfold on the leather, and whether I'm able to stay by the table with you, with Miss Kew, with Miss Kew . . .

". . . and Bonnie and Beanie are eight, they're twins, and Baby. Baby is three."

"Baby is three," she said.

There was a pressure, a stretching apart, and a . . . a breakage. And with a tearing agony and a burst of triumph that drowned the pain, it was done.

And this is what was inside. All in one flash, but all this.

Baby is three? My baby would be three if there were a baby, which there never was . . .

Lone, I'm open to you. Open, is this open enough?

His irises like wheels. I'm sure they spin, but I never catch them at it. The probe that passes invisibly from his brain, through his eyes, into mine. Does he know what it means to me? Does he care? He doesn't care, he doesn't know; he empties me and I fill as he directs me to; he drinks and waits and drinks again and never looks at the cup.

When I saw him first, I was dancing in the wind, in the wood, in the wild, and I spun about and he stood there in the leafy shadows, watching me. I hated him for it. It was not my wood, not my gold-spangled fern-tangled glen. But it was my dancing that he took, freezing it forever by being there. I hated him for it, hated the way he looked, the way he stood, ankle-deep in the kind wet ferns, looking like a tree with roots for feet and clothes the color of earth. As I stopped he moved, and then he was just a man, a great ape-shouldered, dirty animal of a man, and all my hate was fear suddenly and I was just as frozen.

He knew what he had done and he didn't care. Dancing . . . never to dance again, because never would I know the woods were free of eyes, free of tall, uncaring, dirty animalmen. Summer days with the clothes choking me, winter nights with the precious decencies round and about me like a shroud, and never to dance again, never to remember dancing without remembering the shock of knowing he had seen me. How I hated him! Oh, how I hated him!

To dance alone where no one knew, that was the single thing I hid to myself when I was known as Miss Kew, that Victorian, older than her years, later than her time; correct and starched, lace and linen and lonely. Now indeed I would be all they said, through and through, forever and ever, because he had robbed me of the one thing I dared to keep secret.

He came out into the sun and walked to me, holding his great head a little on one side. I stood where I was, frozen inwardly and outwardly and altogether by the core of anger and the layer of fear. My arm was still out, my waist still bent from my dance, and when he stopped, I breathed again because by then I had to.

He said, "You read books?"

I couldn't bear to have him near me, but I couldn't move. He put out his hard hand and touched my jaw, turned my head up until I had to look into his face. I cringed away from him, but my face would not leave his hand, though he was not holding it, just lifting it. "You got to read some books for me. I got no time to find them."

I asked him, "Who are you?"

"Lone," he said. "You going to read books for me?"

"No. Let me go, let me go!" He wasn't holding me.

"What books?" I cried.

He thumped my face, not very hard. It made me look up a bit more. He dropped his hand away. His eyes, the irises were going to spin. . . .

"Open up in there," he said. "Open way up and let me see."

There were books in my head, and he was looking at the titles . . . he was not looking at the titles, for he couldn't read. He was looking at what I knew of the books. I suddenly felt terribly useless, because I had only a fraction of what he wanted.

"What's that?" he barked.

I knew what he meant. He'd gotten it from inside my head. I didn't know it was in there, even, but he found it.

"Telekinesis," I said.

"How is it done?"

"Nobody knows if it can be done. Moving physical objects with the mind!"

"It can be done," he said. "This one?"

"Teleportation. That's the same thing—well, almost. Moving your own body with mind power."

"Yeah, yeah, I see it," he said gruffly.

"Molecular interpenetration. Telepathy and clairvoyance. I don't know anything about them. I think they're silly."

"Read about 'em. It don't matter if you understand or not. What's this?"

It was there in my brain, on my lips. "Gestalt."

"What's that?"

"Group. Like a cure for a lot of diseases with one kind of treatment. Like a lot of thoughts expressed in one phrase. The whole is greater than the sum of the parts."

"Read about that, too. Read a whole lot about that. That's the *most* you got to read about. That's important."

He turned away, and when his eyes came away from mine it was like something breaking, so that I staggered and fell to one knee. He went off into the woods without looking back. I got my things and ran home. There was anger, and it struck me like a storm. There was fear, and it struck me like a wind. I knew I would read the books, I knew I would come back, I knew I would never dance again.

So I read the books and I came back. Sometimes it was every day for three or four days, and sometimes, because I couldn't find a certain book, I might not come back for ten. He was always there in the little glen, waiting, standing in the shadows, and he took what he wanted of the books and nothing of me. He never mentioned the next meeting. If he came there every day to wait for me, or if he only came when I did, I have no way of knowing.

He made me read books that contained nothing for me, books on evolution, on social and cultural organization, on mythology, and ever so much on symbiosis. What I had with him were not conversations; sometimes nothing audible would pass between us but his grunt of surprise or small, short hum of interest.

He tore the books out of me the way he would tear berries from a bush, all at once; he smelled of sweat and earth and the green juices his heavy body crushed when he moved through the wood.

If he learned anything from the books, it made no difference in him.

There came a day when he sat by me and puzzled something out.

He said, "What book has something like this?" Then he waited for a long time, thinking. "The way a termite can't digest wood, you know, and microbes in the termite's belly can, and what the termite eats is what the microbe leaves behind. What's that?"

"Symbiosis," I remembered. I remembered the words. Lone tore the content from words and threw the words away. "Two kinds of life depending upon one another for existence."

"Yeah. Well, is there a book about four-five kinds doing that?"

"I don't know."

Then he asked, "What about this? You got a radio station, you got four-five receivers, each receiver is fixed up to make something different happen, like one digs and one flies and one makes noise, but each one takes orders from the one place. And each one has its own power and its own thing to do, but they are all apart. Now: is there life like that, instead of radio?"

"Where each organism is a part of the whole, but separated? I don't think so . . . unless you mean social organizations, like a team, or perhaps a gang of men working, all taking orders from the same boss."

"No," he said immediately, "not like that. Like one single animal." He made a gesture with his cupped hand which I understood.

I asked, "You mean a *gestalt* life-form? It's fantastic."

"No book has about that, huh?"

"None I ever heard of."

"I got to know about that," he said heavily. "There is such a thing. I want to know if it ever happened before."

"I can't see how anything of the sort could exist."

"It does. A part that fetches, a part that figures, a part that finds out, and a part that talks."

"Talks? Only humans talk."

"I know," he said, and got up and went away.

I looked and looked for such a book but found nothing remotely like it. I came back and told him so. He was still a very long time, looking off to the blue-on-blue line of the hilly horizon. Then he drove those about-to-spin irises at me and searched.

"You learn, but you don't think," he said, and looked again at the hills.

"This all happens with humans," he said eventually. "It happens piece by piece right under folks' noses, and they don't see it. You got mind-readers. You got people can move things with their mind. You got people can move themselves with their mind. You got people can figure anything out if you just think to ask them. What you ain't got is the one kind of person who can pull 'em all together, like a brain pulls together the parts that press and pull and feel heat and walk and think and all the other things.

"I'm one," he finished suddenly. Then he sat still for so long I thought he had forgotten me.

"Lone," I said, "what do you do here in the woods?"

"I wait," he said. "I ain't finished yet." He looked at my eyes and snorted in irritation. "I don't mean 'finished' like you're thinking. I mean I ain't—completed yet. You know about a worm when it's cut, growin' whole again? Well, forget about the cut. Suppose it just grew that way, for the first time, see? I'm getting parts. I ain't finished. I want a book about that kind of animal that is me when I'm finished."

"I don't know of such a book. Can you tell me more? Maybe if you could, I'd think of the right book or a place to find it."

He broke a stick between his huge hands, put the two pieces side by side and broke them together with one strong twist.

"All I know is I got to do what I'm doing like a bird's got to nest when it's time. And I know that when I'm done I won't be anything to brag about. I'll be like a body stronger and faster than anything there ever was, without the right kind of head on it. But maybe that's because I'm one of the first. That picture you had, the cave-man . . ."

"Neanderthal."

"Yeah. Come to think of it, he was not great shakes. An early try at something new. That's what I'm going to be. But maybe the right kind of head'll come along after I'm all organized. Then it'll be something."

He grunted with satisfaction and went away.

I tried, for days I tried, but I couldn't find what he wanted. I found a magazine which stated that the next important evolutionary step in man would be in a psychic rather than a physical direction, but it said nothing about a—shall I call it a *gestalt* organism? There was something about slime molds, but they seem to be more a hive activity of amoebae than even a symbiosis.

To my own unscientific, personally uninterested mind, there was nothing like what he wanted except possibly a band marching together, everyone playing different instruments with different techniques and different notes, to make a single thing move along together. But he hadn't meant anything like that.

So I went back to him in the cool of an early fall evening, and he took what little I had in my eyes, and turned from me angrily with a gross word I shall not permit myself to remember.

"You can't find it," he told me. "Don't come back."

He got up and went to a tattered birch and leaned against it, looking out and down into the wind-tossed crackling shadows. I think he had forgotten me already. I know he leaped like a frightened animal when I spoke to him from so near. He must have been completely immersed in whatever strange thoughts he was having, for I'm sure he didn't hear me coming.

I said, "Lone, don't blame me for not finding it. I tried."

He controlled his startlement and brought those eyes down on me. "Blame? Who's blamin' anybody?"

"I failed you," I told him, "and you're angry."

He looked at me so long I became uncomfortable.

"I don't know what you're talkin' about," he said.

I wouldn't let him turn away from me. He would have. He would have left me forever with not another thought; he didn't *care!* It wasn't cruelty or thoughtlessness as I have been taught to know those things. He was as uncaring as a cat is of the bursting of a tulip bud.

I took him by the upper arms and shook him, it was like trying to shake the front of my house. "You *can* know!" I screamed at him. "You know what I read. You must know what I think!"

He shook his head.

"I'm a person, a woman," I raved at him. "You've used me and used me and you've given me nothing. You've made me break a lifetime of habits—reading until all hours, coming to you in the rain and on Sunday—you don't talk to me, you don't look at me, you don't know anything about me and you don't care. You put some sort of a spell on me that I couldn't break. And when you're finished, you say, 'Don't come back.'"

"Do I have to give something back because I took something?"

"People do."

He gave that short, interested hum. "What do you want me to give you? I ain't got anything."

I moved away from him. I felt . . . I don't know what I felt. After a time I said, "I don't know."

He shrugged and turned. I fairly leaped at him, dragging him back. "I want you to—"

"Well, damn it, what?"

I couldn't look at him; I could hardly speak. "I don't know. There's something, but I don't know what it is. It's something that— I couldn't say if I knew it." When he began to shake his head, I took his arms again. "You've read the books out of me; can't you read the . . . the *me* out of me?"

"I ain't never tried." He held my face up and stepped close. "Here," he said.

His eyes projected their strange probe at me and I screamed. I tried to twist away. I hadn't wanted this, I was sure I hadn't. I struggled terribly. I think he lifted me right off the ground with his big hands. He held me until he was finished, and then let me drop. I huddled to the ground, sobbing. He sat down beside me. He didn't try to touch me. He didn't try to go away. I quieted at last and crouched there, waiting.

He said, "I ain't going to do much of that no more."

I sat up and tucked my shirt close around me and laid my cheek on my updrawn knees so I could see his face. "What happened?"

He cursed. "Damn mishmash inside you. Thirty-three years old—what you want to live like that for?"

"I live very comfortably," I said with some pique.

"Yeah," he said. "All by yourself for ten years now 'cept for someone to do your work. Nobody else."

"Men are animals, and women . . ."

"You really hate women. They all know something you don't."

"I don't want to know. I'm quite happy the way I am."

"Hell you are."

I said nothing to that. I despise that kind of language.

"Two things you want from me. Neither makes no sense." He looked at me with the first real expression I have ever seen in his face: a profound wonderment. "You want to know all about me, where I came from, how I got to be what I am."

"Yes, I do want that. What's the other thing I want that you know and I don't?"

"I was born some place and growed like a weed somehow," he said, ignoring me. "Folks who didn't give even enough of a damn to try the orphanage routine. So I just ran loose, sort of in training to be the village idiot. I'da made it, but I took to the woods instead."

"Why?"

He wondered why, and finally said, "I guess because the way people lived didn't make no sense to me. Out here I can grow like I want."

"How is that?" I asked over one of those vast distances that built and receded between him and me so constantly.

"What I wanted to get from your books."

"You never told me."

For the second time he said, "You learn, but you don't think. There's a kind of—well, *person*. It's all made of separate parts, but it's all one person. It has like hands, it has like legs, it has like a talking mouth, and it has like a brain. That's me, a brain for that person. Damn feeble, too, but the best I know of."

"You're mad."

"No, I ain't," he said, unoffended and completely certain. "I already got the part that's like hands. I can move 'em anywhere and they do what I want, though they're too young yet to do much good. I got the part that talks. That one's real good."

"I don't think you talk very well at all," I said. I cannot stand incorrect English.

He was surprised. "I'm not talking about me! She's back yonder with the others."

"She?"

"The one that talks. Now I need one that thinks, one that can take anything and add it to anything else and come up with a right answer. And once they're all together, and all the parts get used together often enough, I'll be that new kind of thing I told you about. See? Only—I wish it had a better head on it than me."

My own head was swimming. "What made you start doing this?"

He considered me gravely. "What made you start growing hair in your armpits?" he asked me. "You don't figure a thing like that. It just happens."

"What is that . . . that thing you do when you look in my eyes?"

"You want a name for it? I ain't got one. I don't know how I do it. I know I can get anyone I want to do anything. Like you're going to forget about me."

I said in a choked voice, "I don't want to forget about you."

"You will." I didn't know then whether he meant I'd forget, or I'd *want* to forget. "You'll hate me, and then after a long time you'll be grateful. Maybe you'll be able to do something for me some time. You'll be that grateful that you'll be glad to do it. But you'll forget, all right, everything but a sort of . . . feeling. And my name, maybe."

I don't know what moved me to ask him, but I did, for-lornly.

"And no one will ever know about you and me?"

"Can't," he said. "Unless . . . well, unless it was the head of the animal, like me, or a better one." He heaved himself up.

"Oh, wait, wait!" I cried. He mustn't go yet, he mustn't. He was a tall, dirty beast of a man, yet he had enthralled me in some dreadful way. "You haven't given me the other . . . whatever it was."

"Oh," he said. "Yeah, that."

He moved like a flash. There was a pressure, a stretching apart, and a . . . a breakage. And with a tearing agony and a burst of triumph that drowned the pain, it was done.

I came up out of it, through two distinct levels:

I am eleven, breathless from shock from a transferred agony of that incredible entrance into the ego of another. And:

I am fifteen, lying on the couch while Stern drones on, ". . . quietly, quietly limp, your ankles and legs as limp as your toes, your belly goes soft, the back of your neck is as limp as your belly, it's quiet and easy and all gone soft and limper than limp. . . ."

I sat up and swung my legs to the floor. "Okay," I said.

Stern looked a little annoyed. "This is going to work," he said, "but it can only work if you cooperate. Just lie—"

"It did work," I said.

"What?"

"The whole thing. A to Z." I snapped my fingers. "Like that."

He looked at me piercingly. "What do you mean?"

"It was right there, where you said. In the library. When I was eleven. When she said, 'Baby is three.' It knocked loose something that had been boiling around in her for three years, and it all came blasting out. I got it, full force; just a kid, no warning, no defenses. It had such a—a pain in it, like I never knew could be."

"Go on," said Stern.

"That's really all. I mean that's not what was in it; it's what it did to me. What it was, a sort of hunk of her own self. A whole lot of things that happened over about four months, every bit of it. She knew Lone."

"You mean a whole *series* of episodes?"

"That's it."

"You got a series all at once? In a split second?"

"That's right. Look, for that split second I *was* her, don't you see? I was her, everything she'd ever done, everything she'd ever thought and heard and felt. Everything, everything, all in the right order if I wanted to bring it out like that. Any part of it if I wanted it by itself. If I'm going to tell you about what I had for lunch, do I have to tell you everything else I've ever done since I was born? No. I tell you I *was* her, and then and forever after I can remember anything she could remember up to that point. In just that one flash."

"A *gestalt*," he murmured.

"Aha!" I said, and thought about that. I thought about a whole lot of things. I put them aside for a moment and said, "Why didn't I know all this before?"

"You had a powerful block against recalling it."

I got up excitedly. "I don't see why. I don't see that at all."

"Just natural revulsion," he guessed. "How about this? You had a distaste for assuming a female ego, even for a second."

"You told me yourself, right at the beginning, that I didn't have that kind of a problem."

"Well, how does this sound to you? You say you felt pain in that episode. So—you wouldn't go back into it for fear of re-experiencing the pain."

"Let me think, let me think. Yeah, yeah, that's part of it—that thing of going into someone's mind. She opened up to me because I reminded her of Lone. I went in. I wasn't ready; I'd never done it before, except maybe a little, against resistance. I went all the way in and it was too much; it frightened me away from trying it for years. And there it lay, wrapped up, locked away. But as I grew older, the power to do that with my mind got stronger and stronger, and still I was afraid to use it. And the more I grew, the more I felt, down deep, that Miss Kew had to be killed before she killed the . . . what I am. My God!" I shouted. "Do you know what I am?"

"No," he said. "Like to tell me about it?"

"I'd like to," I said. "Oh, yes, I'd like that."

He had that professional open-minded expression on his face, not believing or disbelieving, just taking it all in. I had to tell him, and I suddenly realized that I didn't have enough words. I knew the things, but not the names for them.

Lone took the meanings and threw the words away.

Further back: *"You read books. Read books for me."*

The look of his eyes. That—"opening up" thing.

I went over to Stern. He looked up at me, I bent close. First he was startled, then he controlled it, then he came even closer to me.

"My God," he murmured. "I didn't look at those eyes before. I could have sworn those irises spun like wheels. . . ."

Stern read books. He'd read more books than I ever imagined had been written. I slipped in there, looking for what I wanted.

I can't say exactly what it was like. It was like walking in a tunnel, and in this tunnel, all over the roof and walls, wooden arms stuck out at you, like the thing at the carnival, the merry-go-round, the thing you snatch the brass rings from. There's a brass ring on the end of each of these arms, and you can take any one of them you want to.

Now imagine you make up your mind which rings you want, and the arms hold only those. Now picture yourself with a thousand hands to grab the rings off with. Now just suppose the tunnel is a zillion miles long, and you can go from one end of it to the other, grabbing rings, in just the time it takes you to blink once. Well, it was like that, only easier.

It was easier for me to do than it had been for Lone.

Straightening up, I got away from Stern. He looked sick and frightened.

"It's all right," I said.

"What did you do to me?"

"I needed some words. Come on, come on. Get professional."

I had to admire him. He put his pipe in his pocket and gouged the tips of his fingers hard against his forehead and cheeks. Then he sat up and he was okay again.

"I know," I said. "That's how Miss Kew felt when Lone did it to her."

"What *are* you?"

"I'll tell you. I'm the central ganglion of a complex organism which is composed of Baby, a computer; Bonnie and Beanie, teleports; Janie, telekineticist; and myself, telepath and central control. There isn't a single thing about any of us that hasn't been documented: the teleportation of the Yogi, the telekinetics of some gamblers, the idiosavant mathematicians, and most of all, the so-called poltergeist, the moving about of household goods through the instrumentation of a young girl. Only in this case every one of my parts delivers at peak performance.

"Lone organized it, or it formed around him; it doesn't matter which. I replaced Lone, but I was too underdeveloped when he died, and on top of that I got an occlusion from that blast from Miss Kew. To that extent you were right when you said the blast made me subconsciously afraid to discover what was in it. But there was another good reason for my not being able to get in under that 'Baby is three' barrier.

"We ran into the problem of what it was I valued more than the security Miss Kew gave us. Can't you see now what it was? My *gestalt* organism was at the point of death from that security. I figured she had to be killed or it—*I*—would be. Oh, the parts would live on: two little colored girls with a speech impediment, one introspective girl with an artistic bent, one mongoloid idiot, and me—ninety per cent short-circuited potentials and ten per cent juvenile delinquent." I laughed. "Sure, she had to be killed. It was self-preservation for the *gestalt*."

Stern bobbled around with his mouth and finally got out: "I don't—"

"You don't need to," I laughed. "This is wonderful. You're good—real good. Now I want to tell you this, because you can appreciate a fine point in your specialty. You talk about occlusions! I couldn't get past the 'Baby is three' thing because in it lay the clues to what I really am. I couldn't find that out because I was afraid to remember that I was two things—Miss Kew's little boy, and something a hell of a lot bigger. I couldn't be both, and I wouldn't release either one."

He said, with his eyes on his pipe, "Now you can?"

"I have."

"And what now?"

"What do you mean?"

Stern leaned back against the corner of his desk. "Did it occur to you that maybe this—*gestalt* organism of yours is already dead?"

"It isn't."

"How do you know?"

"How does your head know your arm works?"

He touched his face. "So . . . now what?"

I shrugged. "Did the Pekin man look at Homo Sap walking erect and say, 'Now what?' We'll live, that's all, like a man, like a tree, like anything else that lives. We'll feed and grow and experiment and breed. We'll defend ourselves." I spread my hands. "We'll just do what comes naturally."

"But what can you do?"

"What can an electric motor do? It depends on where we apply ourselves."

Stern was very pale. "Just what do you—*want* to do?"

I thought about that. He waited until I was quite finished thinking and didn't say anything. "Know what?" I said at last. "Ever since I was born, people been kicking me around, right up until Miss Kew took over. And what happened with her? She damn near killed me."

I thought some more, and said, "Everybody's had fun but me. The kind of fun everybody has is kicking someone around, someone small who can't fight back. Or they do you favors until they own you, or kill you." I looked at him and grinned. "I'm just going to have fun, that's all."

He turned his back. I think he was going to pace the floor, but right away he turned again. I knew then he would keep an eye on me. He said, "You've come a long way since you walked in here."

I nodded. "You're a *good* head-shrinker."

"Thanks," he said bitterly. "And you figure you're all cured now, all adjusted and ready to roll."

"Well sure. Don't you?"

He shook his head. "All you've found out is what you are. You have a lot more to learn."

I was willing to be patient. "Like?"

"Like finding out what happens to people who have to live with guilt like yours. You're different, Gerry, but you're not that different."

"I should feel guilty about saving my life?"

He ignored that. "One other thing: You said a while back that you'd been mad at everybody all your life—that's the way you lived. Have you ever wondered why?"

"Can't say I have."

"One reason is that you were so alone. That's why being with the other kids, and then with Miss Kew, came to mean so much."

"So? I've still got the kids."

He shook his head slowly. "You *and* the kids are a single creature. Unique. Unprecedented." He pointed the pipestem at me. "*Alone.*"

The blood started to pound in my ears.

"Shut up," I said.

"Just think about it," he said softly. "You can do practically anything. You can have practically everything. And none of it will keep you from being alone."

"Shut up, shut up . . . Everybody's alone."

He nodded. "But some people learn how to live with it."

"How?"

He said, after a time, "Because of something you don't know anything about. It wouldn't mean anything to you if I told you."

"Tell me and see."

He gave me the strangest look. "It's sometimes called morality."

"I guess you're right. I don't know what you're talking about." I pulled myself together. I didn't have to listen to this. "You're afraid," I said. "You're afraid of *Homo Gestalt.*"

He made a wonderful effort and smiled. "That's bastard terminology."

"We're a bastard breed," I said. I pointed. "Sit down over there."

He crossed the quiet room and sat at the desk. I leaned close to him and he went to sleep with his eyes open. I straightened up and looked around the room. Then I got the Thermos flask and filled it and put it on the desk. I fixed the corner of the rug and put a clean towel at the head of the couch. I went to the side of the desk and opened it and looked at the tape recorder.

Like reaching out a hand, I got Beanie. She stood by the desk, wide-eyed.

"Look here," I told her. "Look good, now. What I want to do is erase all this tape. Go ask Baby how."

She blinked at me and sort of shook herself, and then leaned over the recorder. She was there—and gone—and back, just like that. She pushed past me and turned two knobs, moved a pointer until it clicked twice. The tape raced backward past the head swiftly, whining.

"All right," I said, "beat it."

She vanished.

I got my jacket and went to the door. Stern was still sitting at the desk, staring.

"A *good* head-shrinker," I murmured. I felt fine.

Outside I waited, then turned and went back in again.

Stern looked up at me. "Sit over there, Sonny."

"Gee," I said. "Sorry, sir. I got in the wrong office."

"That's all right," he said.

I went out and closed the door. All the way down to the police station I grinned. They'd take my report on Miss Kew and like it. And sometimes I laughed, thinking about this Stern, how he'd figure the loss of an afternoon and the gain of a thousand bucks. Much funnier than thinking about him being dead.

What the hell is morality, anyway?

PART THREE
Morality

"WHAT'S he to you, Miss Gerald?" demanded the sheriff.

"Gerard," she corrected. She had gray-green eyes and a strange mouth. "He's my cousin."

"All Adam's chillun are cousins, one way or the other. You'll have to tell me a little more than that."

"He was in the Air Force seven years ago," she said. "There was some—trouble. He was discharged. Medical."

The sheriff thumbed through the file on the desk before him. "Remember the doctor's name?"

"Thompson first, then Bromfield. Dr. Bromfield signed the discharge."

"Guess you do know something about him at that. What was he before he did his hitch in the Air Force?"

"An engineer. I mean, he would have been if he'd finished school."

"Why didn't he?"

She shrugged. "He just disappeared."

"So how do you know he's here?"

"I'd recognize him anywhere," she said. "I saw . . . I saw it happen."

"Did you now." The sheriff grunted, lifted the file, let it drop. "Look, Miss Gerald, it's not my business to go advising people. But you seem like a nice respectable girl. Why don't you just forget him?"

"I'd like to see him, if I may," she said quietly.

"He's crazy. Did you know that?"

"I don't think so."

"Slammin' his fist through a plate glass window. For nothing."

She waited. He tried again. "He's dirty. He don't know his own name, hardly."

"May I see him?"

The sheriff uttered a wordless growl and stood up. "Them Air Force psychos had any sense, they'd've put him where he would never even get near a jail. This way."

The walls were steel plates like a ship's bulkhead, studded with rivets, painted a faded cream above and mustard color below. Their footsteps echoed. The sheriff unlocked a heavy door with one small high grating and slid it aside. They stepped through and he closed and locked it. He motioned her ahead of him and they came into a barnlike area, concrete on walls and ceiling. Built around it was a sort of balcony; under and over this were the cells, steel walled, fronted by close-set bars. There were perhaps twenty cells. Only a half dozen were occupied. It was a cold, unhappy place.

"Well, what did you expect?" demanded the sheriff, reading her expression. "The Waldorf Plaza or something?"

"Where is he?" she asked.

They walked to a cell on the lower tier. "Snap out of it, Barrows. Lady to see you."

"Hip! Oh, Hip!"

The prisoner did not move. He lay half on, half off a padded steel bunk, one foot on the mattress, one on the floor. His left arm was in a dirty sling.

"See! Nary a word out of him. Satisfied, Miss?"

"Let me in," she breathed. "Let me talk to him."

He shrugged and reluctantly unlocked the door. She stepped in, turned. "May I speak to him alone?"

"Liable to get hurt," he warned.

She gazed at him. Her mouth was extraordinarily expressive. "Well," he said at length, "I'll stay in the area here. You yell if you need help. S'help me I'll put a slug through your neck, Barrows, if you try anything." He locked the barred door behind the girl.

She waited until he stepped away and then went to the prisoner. "Hip," she murmured. "Hip Barrows."

His dull eyes slid in their sockets until they approximated her direction. The eyes closed and opened in a slow, numb blink.

She knelt beside him. "Mr. Barrows," she whispered, "you don't know me. I told them I was your cousin. I want to help you."

He was silent.

She said, "I'm going to get you out of here. Don't you want to get out?"

For a long moment he watched her face. Then his eyes went to the locked door and back to her face again.

She touched his forehead, his cheek. She pointed at the dirty sling. "Does it hurt much?"

His eyes lingered, withdrew from her face, found the bandage. With effort, they came up again. She asked, "Aren't you going to say anything? Don't you want me to help?"

He was silent for so long that she rose. "I'd better go. Don't forget me. I'll help you." She turned to the door.

He said, "Why?"

She returned to him. "Because you're dirty and beaten and don't care—and because none of that can hide what you are."

"You're crazy," he muttered tiredly.

She smiled. "That's what they say about you. So we have something in common."

He swore, foully.

Unperturbed, she said, "You can't hide behind that either. Now listen to me. Two men will come to see you this afternoon. One is a doctor. The other is a lawyer. We'll have you out of here this evening."

He raised his head and for the first time something came into his lethargic face. Whatever it was was not pretty. His voice came from deep in his chest. He growled, "What type doctor?"

"For your arm," she said evenly. "Not a psychiatrist. You'll never have to go through that again."

He let his head drop back. His features slowly lost their expression. She waited and when he had nothing else to offer, she turned and called the sheriff.

* * *

It was not too difficult. The sentence was sixty days for malicious mischief. There had been no alternative fine offered. The lawyer rapidly proved that there should have been, and the fine was paid. In his clean new bandages and his filthy clothes, Barrows was led out past the glowering sheriff, ignoring him and his threat as to what the dirty bum could expect if he ever showed up in town again.

The girl was waiting outside. He stood stupidly at the top of the jailhouse steps while she spoke to the lawyer. Then the lawyer was gone and she touched his elbow. "Come on, Hip."

He followed like a wound-up toy, walking whither his feet had been pointed. They turned two corners and walked five blocks and then up the stone steps of a clean, dried spinster of a house with a bay window and colored glass set into the main door. The girl opened the main door with one key and a door in the hallway with another. He found himself in the room with the bay window. It was high ceilinged, airy, clean.

For the first time he moved of his own volition. He turned around, slowly, looking at one wall after another. He put out his hand and lifted the corner of a dresser scarf, and let it fall. "Your room?"

"Yours," she said. She came to him and put two keys on the dresser. "Your keys." She opened the top drawer. "Your socks and handkerchiefs." With her knuckles she rapped on each drawer in turn. "Shirts. Underclothes." She pointed to a door. "Two suits in there; I think they'll fit. A robe. Slippers, shoes." She pointed to another door. "Bathroom. Lots of towels, lots of soap. A razor."

"Razor?"

"Anyone who can have keys can have a razor," she said gently. "Get presentable, will you? I'll be back in fifteen minutes. Do you know how long it is since you've eaten anything?"

He shook his head.

"Four days. 'Bye now."

She slipped through the door and was gone, even as he fumbled for something to say to her. He looked at the door for a long time. Then he swore and fell limply back on the bed.

He scratched his nose and his hand slid down to his jaw. It was ragged, itchy. He half rose, muttered, "Damn if I will," and lay back. And then, somehow, he was in the bathroom, peering at himself in the mirror. He wet his hands, splashed water on his face, wiped the dirt off onto a towel and peered again. He grunted and reached for the soap.

He found the razor, he found the underclothes, the slacks, socks, slippers, shirt, jacket. When he looked into the mirror he wished he had a comb. When she elbowed the door open she put her packages on the top of the dresser and then she was smiling up at him, her hand out, the comb in it. He took it wordlessly and went and wet his head and combed it.

"Come on, it's all ready," she called from the other room. He emerged. She had taken the lamp off the night table and had spread out a thick oval platter on which was a lean, rare steak, a bottle of ale, a smaller bottle of stout, a split Idaho potato with butter melting in it, hot rolls in a napkin, a tossed salad in a small wooden bowl.

"I don't want nothing," he said, and abruptly fell to. There was nothing in the world then but the good food filling his mouth and throat, the tingle of ale and the indescribable magic of the charcoal crust.

When the plate was empty, it and the table suddenly wanted to fly upward at his head. He toppled forward, caught the sides of the table and held it away from him. He trembled violently. She spoke from behind him, "All right. It's all right," and put her hands on his shoulders, pressed him back into his chair. He tried to raise his hand and failed. She wiped his clammy forehead and upper lip with the napkin.

In time, his eyes opened. He looked round for her, found her sitting on the edge of the bed, watching him silently. He grinned sheepishly. *"Whew!"*

She rose. "You'll be all right now. You'd better turn in. Good night!"

She was in the room, she was out of it. She had been with him, he was alone. It made a change which was too important to tolerate and too large to understand. He looked from the door to the bed and said "Good night," only because they were the last words she had said, and they hung shimmering in the silence.

He put his hands on the chair arms and forced his legs to cooperate. He could stand but that was all. He fell forward and sidewise, curling up to miss the table as he went down. He lay across the counterpane and blackness came.

* * *

"Good morning."

He lay still. His knees were drawn up and the heels of his hands were tight on his cheekbones. He closed his eyes tighter than sleep to shut out the light. He closed his kinesthetic sense to shut out the slight tilting of the mattress which indicated where she sat on the bed. He disconnected his hearing lest she speak again. His nostrils betrayed him; he had not expected there to be coffee in the room and he was wanting it, wanting it badly, before he thought to shut it out.

Fuzzily he lay thinking, thinking something about her. If she spoke again, he thought, he'd show her. He'd lie there till she spoke again and when she spoke he'd ignore her and lie still some more.

He waited.

Well, if she wasn't going to speak again, he couldn't ignore her, could he?

He opened his eyes. They blazed, round and angry. She sat near the foot of the bed. Her body was still, her face was still, her mouth and her eyes were alive.

He coughed suddenly, violently. It closed his eyes and when he opened them he was no longer looking at her. He fumbled vaguely at his chest, then looked down at himself.

"Slep' in my clothes all night," he said.

"Drink your coffee."

He looked at her. She still had not moved, and did not. She was wearing a burgundy jacket with a gray-green scarf. She had long, level, gray-green eyes, the kind which in profile are deep clear triangles. He looked away from her, farther and farther away, until he saw the coffee. A big pot, a thick hot cup, already poured. Black and strong and good. "Whoo," he said, holding it, smelling it. He drank. "Whoo."

He looked at the sunlight now. Good. The turn and fall and turn again of the breeze-lifted marquisette at the window, in and out of a sunbeam. Good. The luminous oval, a shadow of the sunlight itself, where the sun glanced off the round mirror on one wall to the clean paint on the adjoining one. Good. He drank more good coffee.

He set the cup down and fumbled at his shirt buttons. He was wrinkled and sweaty. "Shower," he said.

"Go ahead," said the girl. She rose and went to the dresser where there was a cardboard box and some paper sacks. She opened the box and took out an electric hot plate. He got three buttons undone and somehow the fourth and fifth came off with little explosive tearing sounds. He got the rest of his clothes off somehow. The girl paid him no attention, neither looking at him nor away, just calmly doing things with the hot plate. He went into the bathroom and fussed for a long time with the shower handles, getting the water just right. He got in and let the water run on the nape of his neck. He found soap in the dish, so he let the water run on his head and then rubbed it furiously with the cake of soap until he was mantled in warm, kind, crawling lather. *God*, the thought came from somewhere, *I'm thin as a xylophone. Got to put some beef back on or I'll get sick and . . .* The same thought looped back to him, interrupting itself: *Not supposed to get well. Get good and sick, stay sick. Get sicker.* Angrily he demanded, "Who says I got to get sick?" but there was no answer except a quick echo off the tiles.

He shut off the water and stepped out and took an oversized towel from the rack. He started one end of it on his scalp, worked it on his hair from one end to the other. He threw it on the floor, in the corner, and took another towel and rubbed himself pink. He threw that one down too and came out into the room. The robe lay over the arm of an easy chair by the door so he put it on.

The girl was spooning fragrant bacon grease over and over three perfect eggs in a pan. When he sat down on the edge of the bed she slid the eggs deftly onto a plate, leaving all the grease behind in the pan. They were perfect, the whites completely firm, the yolks unbroken, liquid, faintly filmed over. There was bacon, four brief seconds less than crisp, paper dried and aromatic. There was toast, golden outside, soft and white inside, with butter melting quickly, running to find and fill the welcoming caves and crevices; two slices with butter, one with marmalade. And these lay in some sunlight, giving off a color possible only to marmalade and to stained glass.

He ate and drank coffee; ate more and drank coffee and more coffee. All the while she sat in the easy chair with his shirt in her lap and her hands like dancers, while the buttons grew back onto the material under their swift and delicate paces.

He watched her and when she was finished he came to her and put out his hand for the shirt, but she shook her head and pointed. "A clean one."

He found a knitted pullover polo shirt. While he dressed she washed his dishes and the frying pan and straightened out the bed. He lay back in the easy chair and she knelt before him and worked the soggy dressing off his left hand, inspected the cuts and bound them up again. The bandage was firm and comforting. "You can do without the sling now," she said, pleased. She got up and went to the bed. She sat there facing him, still again except for her eyes, except for her mouth.

Outside an oriole made a long slender note, broke it, and let the fragments fall through the shining air. A stake-bed truck idled past, busily shaking the string of cowbells on its back, while one hoarse man and one with a viola voice flanked it afoot, chanting. In one window came a spherical sound with a fly at its heart and at the other appeared a white kitten. Out by the kitten went the fly and the kitten reared up and batted at it, twisted and sprang down out of sight as if it had meant all along to leave; only a fool would have thought it had lost its balance.

And in the room was quiet and a watchfulness which was without demand, except perhaps a guarding against leaving anything un-watched. The girl sat with her hands aslumber and her eyes awake, while a pipe-cleaner man called Healing was born in all his cores, all his marrow, taking the pose of his relaxed body, resting and growing a little and resting again and growing.

Later, she rose. Without consultation, but merely because it seemed time to do so, she picked up a small handbag and went to the door where she waited. He stirred, rose, went to her. They went out.

They walked slowly to a place where there was smooth rolling land, mowed and tended. Down in the hollow some boys played softball. They stood for a while, watching. She studied his face and when she saw reflected in it only the moving figures and not the consecutive interest of the game itself, she touched his elbow and moved on. They found a pond where there were ducks and straight cinder paths with flower beds. She picked a primrose and put it in his lapel. They found a bench. A man pushed a bright clean wagon up to them. She bought a frankfurter and a bottle of soda and handed them to him. He ate and drank silently.

It was a quiet time they had together.

When it began to grow dark, she brought him back to the room. She left him alone for half an hour and returned to find him sitting just where she had left him. She opened packages and cooked chops and mixed a salad, and while he was eating, made more coffee. After dinner he yawned. She was on her feet immediately. "Good night," she said, and was gone.

He turned slowly and looked at the closed door. After a time he said, "Good night." He undressed and got into bed and turned out the light.

The next day was the day they rode on a bus and lunched in a restaurant.

The day after that was the one they stayed out a little later to see a band concert.

Then there was the afternoon when it rained and they went to a movie which he watched wordlessly, not smiling, not frowning, not stirring to the musical parts.

"Your coffee." "Let's get these to the laundry." "Come." "Good night." These were the things she said to him. Otherwise she watched his face and, undemandingly, she waited.

He awoke, and it was too dark. He did not know where he was. The face was there, wide-browed, sallow, with its thick lenses and its pointed chin. Wordlessly, he roared at it and it smiled at him. When he realized that the face was in his mind and not in the room, it disappeared . . . no; it was simply that he knew it was not there. He was filled with fury that it was not there; his brain was fairly melting with rage. *Yes, but who is he?* he asked, and answered, "I don't know, I don't know, I don't know . . ." and his voice became a moan, softer and softer and softer until it was gone. He inhaled deeply and then something inside him slipped and fell apart and he began to cry. Someone took his hand, took his other hand, held them together; it was the girl; she'd heard him, she'd come. He was not alone.

Not alone . . . it made him cry harder, bitterly. He held her wrists as she bent over him, looked up through darkness at her face and her hair and he wept.

She stayed with him until he was finished and for as long afterward as he held her hand. When he released it he was asleep, and she drew the blanket up to his chin and tiptoed out.

In the morning he sat on the edge of the bed, watching the steam from his coffee spread and fade in the sunlight, and when she put the eggs before him he looked up at her. His mouth quivered. She stood before him, waiting.

At last he said, "Have you had your breakfast yet?"

Something was kindled in her eyes. She shook her head.

He looked down at the plate, puzzling something out. Finally he pushed it away from him a fraction of an inch and stood up. "You have this," he said. "I'll fix some more."

He had seen her smile but he had not noticed it before. Now, it was as if the warmth of all of them was put together for this one. She sat down and ate. He fried his eggs, not as well as she had done, and they were cooked before he thought of toast and the toast burned while he was eating the eggs. She did not attempt to help him in any way, even when he stared blankly at the little table, frowned and scratched his jaw. In his own time he found what he was looking for—the other cup on top of the dresser. He poured fresh coffee for her and took the other which she had not touched, for himself, and she smiled again.

"What's your name?" he asked her, for the very first time.

"Janie Gerard."

"Oh."

She considered him carefully, then stretched down to the footpost of the bed where her handbag hung by its strap. She drew it toward her, opened it, and took out a short piece of metal. At first glance, it was a piece of aluminum tubing, perhaps eight inches long and oval in cross-section. But it was flexible—woven of tiny strands rather than extruded. She turned his right hand palm up, where it lay beside his coffee cup, and put the tubing into it.

He must have seen it for he was staring down into the cup. He did not close his fingers on it. His expression did not change. At length he took a slice of toast. The piece of tubing fell, rolled over, hung on the edge of a table and dropped to the floor. He buttered his toast.

After that first shared meal there was a difference. There were many differences. Never again did he undress before her or ignore the fact that she was not eating. He began to pay for little things—bus fares, lunches, and, later, to let her precede him through doorways, to take her elbow when they crossed streets. He went to the market with her and carried the packages.

He remembered his name; he even remembered that the "Hip"

was for "Hippocrates." He was, however, unable to remember how he came by the name, or where he had been born, or anything else about himself. She did not urge him, ask him. She simply spent her days with him, waiting. And she kept the piece of aluminum webbing in sight.

It was beside his breakfast plate almost every morning. It would be in the bathroom, with the handle of his toothbrush thrust into it. Once he found it in his side jacket pocket where the small roll of bills appeared regularly; this one time the bills were tucked into the tubing. He pulled them out and absently let the tubing fall and Janie had to pick it up. She put it in his shoe once and when he tried to put the shoe on and could not, he tipped it out onto the floor and let it lie there. It was as if it were transparent or even invisible to him; when, as in the case of finding his money in it, he had to handle it, he did so clumsily, with inattention, rid himself of it and apparently forgot it. Janie never mentioned it. She just quietly put in his path, time and time again, patient as a pendulum.

His afternoons began to possess a morning and his days, a yesterday. He began to remember a bench they had used, a theater they had attended, and he would lead the way back. She relinquished her guidance as fast as he would take it up until it was he who planned their days.

Since he had no memory to draw on except his time with her, they were days of discovery. They had picnics and rode learningly on buses. They found another theater and a place with swans as well as ducks.

There was another kind of discovery too. One day he stood in the middle of the room and turned, looking at one wall after another, at the windows and the bed. "I was sick, wasn't I?"

And one day he stopped on the street, stared at the grim building on the other side. "I was in there."

And it was several days after that when he slowed, frowned, and stood gazing into a men's furnishing shop. No—not into it. At it. At the window.

Beside him Janie waited, watching his face.

He raised his left hand slowly, flexed it, looked down at the curled scar on the back of his hand, the two straight ones, one long, one short, on his wrist.

"Here," she said. She pressed the piece of tubing into his hand.

Without looking at it he closed his fingers, made a fist. Surprise flickered across his features and then a flash of sheer terror and something like anger. He swayed on his feet.

"It's all right," said Janie softly.

He grunted questioningly, looked at her as if she were a stranger and seemed slowly to recognize her. He opened his hand and looked carefully at the piece of metal. He tossed it, caught it. "That's mine," he said.

She nodded.

He said, "I broke that window." He looked at it, tossed the piece of metal again, and put it in his pocket and began to walk again. He was quiet for a long time and just as they mounted the steps of their house he said, "I broke the window and they put me in that jail. And you got me out and I was sick and you brought me here till I was well again."

He took out his keys and opened the door, stood back to let her pass in. "What did you want to do that for?"

"Just wanted to," she said.

He was restless. He went to the closet and turned out the pockets of his two suit jackets and his sport coat. He crossed the room and pawed aimlessly at the dresser scarf and opened and shut drawers.

"What is it?"

"That thing," he said vaguely. He wandered into and out of the bathroom. "You know, that piece of pipe, like."

"Oh," she said.

"I had it," he muttered unhappily. He took another turn around the room and then shouldered past Janie where she sat on the bed, and reached to the night table. "Here it is!"

He looked at it, flexed it, and sat down in the easy chair. "Hate to lose that," he said relievedly. "Had it a long time."

"It was in the envelope they were holding for you while you were in jail," Janie told him.

"Yuh. Yuh." He twisted it between his hands, then raised it and shook it at her like some bright, thick, admonishing forefinger. "This thing—"

She waited.

He shook his head. "Had it a long time," he said again. He rose, paced, sat down again. "I was looking for a guy who . . . *Ah!*" he growled, "I can't remember."

"It's all right," she said gently.

He put his head in his hands. "Damn near almost found him too," he said in a muffled voice. "Been looking for him a long time. I've *always* been looking for him."

"Always?"

"Well, ever since . . . Janie, I can't remember again."

"All right."

"All right, all right, it isn't all right!" He straightened and looked at her. "I'm sorry, Janie. I didn't mean to yell at you."

She smiled at him. He said, "Where was that cave?"

"Cave?" she echoed.

He waved his arms up, around. "Sort of a cave. Half cave, half log house. In the woods. Where was it?"

"Was I there with you?"

"No," he said immediately. "That was before, I guess. I don't remember."

"Don't worry about it."

"I *do* worry about it!" he said excitedly. "I can worry about it, can't I?" As soon as the words were out, he looked to her for forgiveness and found it. "You got to understand," he said more quietly, "this is something I—I got to—Look," he said, returning to exasperation, "can something be more important than anything else in the world, and you can't even remember what it is?"

"It happens."

"It's happened to me," he said glumly. "I don't like it either."

"You're getting yourself all worked up," said Janie.

"Well, sure!" he exploded. He looked around him, shook his head violently. "What is this? What am I doing here? Who are you, anyway, Janie? What are you getting out of this?"

"I like seeing you get well."

"Yeah, get well," he growled. "I should get well! I ought to be sick. Be sick and get sicker."

"Who told you that?" she rapped.

"Thompson," he barked and then slumped back, looking at her with stupid amazement on his face. In the high, cracking voice of an adolescent he whimpered, "Thompson? Who's Thompson?"

She shrugged and said, matter-of-factly, "The one who told you you ought to be sick, I suppose."

"Yeah," he whispered, and again, in a soft-focused flood of enlightenment, "yeah-h-h-h . . ." He wagged the piece of mesh tubing at her. "I saw him. Thompson." The tubing caught his eye then and he held it still, staring at it. He shook his head, closed his eyes. "I was looking for . . ." His voice trailed off.

"Thompson?"

"Nah!" he grunted. "I never wanted to see *him*! Yes I did," he amended. "I wanted to beat his brains out."

"You did?"

"Yeah. You see, he—he was—aw, what's the matter with my *head*?" he cried.

"Sh-h-h," she soothed.

"I can't remember, I can't," he said brokenly. "It's like . . . you see something rising up off the ground, you got to grab it, you jump so hard you can feel your kneebones crack, you stretch up and get your fingers on it, just the tips of your fingers. . . ." His chest swelled and sank. "Hang there, like forever, your fingers on it, knowing you'll never make it, never get a grip. And then you fall, and you watch it going up and up away from you, getting smaller and smaller, and you'll never—" He leaned back and closed his eyes. He was panting. He breathed, barely audible, "And you'll never . . ."

He clenched his fists. One of them still held the tubing and again he went through the discovery, the wonder, the puzzlement. "Had this a long time," he said, looking, at it. "Crazy. This must sound crazy to you, Janie.'

"Oh, no."

"You still think I'm crazy?"

"*No.*"

"I'm sick," he whimpered.

Startlingly, she laughed. She came to him and pulled him to his feet. She drew him to the bathroom and reached in and switched on the light. She pushed him inside, against the washbasin, and rapped the mirror with her knuckles. "Who's sick?"

He looked at the firm-fleshed, well-boned face that stared out at him, at its glossy hair and clear eyes. He turned to Janie, genuinely astonished. "I haven't looked this good in years! Not since I was in the . . . Janie, was I in the Army?"

"Were you?"

He looked into the mirror again. "Sure don't *look* sick," he said, as if to himself. He touched his cheek. "Who keeps telling me I'm sick?"

He heard Janie's footsteps receding. He switched off the light and joined her. "I'd like to break that Thompson's back," he said. "Throw him right through a—"

"What is it?"

"Funny thing," he said, "was going to say, through a brick wall. I was thinking it so hard I could see it, me throwing him."

"Perhaps you did."

He shook his head. "It wasn't a wall. It was a plate glass window. I know!" he shouted. "I saw him and I was going to hit him. I saw him standing right there on the street looking at me and I yelled and jumped him and . . . and . . ." He looked down at his scarred hand. He said, amazed, "I turned right around and hauled off and hit the window instead. God."

He sat down weakly. "That's what the jail was for and it was all over. Just lie there in that rotten jail, sick. Don't eat, don't move, get sick and sicker and it's all over."

"Well, it isn't all over, is it?"

He looked at her. "No. No, it isn't. Thanks to you." He looked at her eyes, her mouth. "What about you, Janie? What are you after, anyway?"

She dropped her eyes.

"Oh, I'm sorry, I'm sorry. That must've sounded . . ." He put out a hand to her, dropped it without touching her. "I don't know what's gotten into me today. It's just that . . . I don't figure you, Janie. What did I ever do for you?"

She smiled quickly. "Get better."

"It's not enough," he said devoutly. "Where do you live?"

She pointed. "Right across the hall."

"Oh," he said. He remembered the night he had cried, and pushed the picture away in embarrassment. He turned away, hunting for a change of subject, any change. "Let's go out."

"All right." Was that relief he detected in her voice?

They rode on a roller coaster and ate cotton candy and danced in an outdoor pavilion. He wondered aloud where he had ever learned to dance, but that was the only mention he made of the things which were troubling him until late in the evening. It was the first time he had consciously enjoyed being with Janie; it was an Occasion, rather than a way of life. He had never known her to laugh so easily, to be so eager to ride this and taste that and go yonder to see what was there. At dusk they stood side by side, leaning on a railing which overlooked the lake, watching the bathers. There were lovers on the beach, here and there. Hip smiled at the sight, turned to speak to Janie about it and was arrested by the strange wistfulness which softened her taut features. A surge of emotion, indefinable and delicate, made him turn away quickly. It was in part a recognition of the rarity of her introspection and an unwillingness to interrupt it for her; and partly a flash of understanding that her complete preoccupation with him was not necessarily all she wanted of life. Life had begun for him, to all intents and purposes, on the day she came to his cell. It had never occurred to him before that her quarter of a century without him was not the clean slate that his was.

Why had she rescued him? Why him, if she must rescue someone? And—why?

What could she want from him? Was there something in his lost life that he might give her? If there was, he vowed silently, it was hers, whatever it might be; it was inconceivable that anything, anything at all she might gain from him would be of greater value than his own discovery of the life which produced it.

But what could it be?

He found his gaze on the beach and its small galaxy of lovers, each couple its own world, self-contained but in harmony with all the others adrift in the luminous dusk. Lovers . . . he had felt the tuggings of love . . . back somewhere in the mists, he couldn't quite remember where, with whom . . . but it was there, and with it his old, old reflex, *not until I've hunted him down and*— But again he lost the thought. Whatever it was, it had been more important to him than love or marriage or a job or a colonelcy. (Colonelcy? Had he ever wanted to be a colonel?)

Well, then maybe it was a conquest. Janie loved him. She'd seen him and the lightning had struck and she wanted him, so she was going about it in her own way. Well, then! If that's what she wanted . . .

He closed his eyes, seeing her face, the tilt of her head in that waiting, attentive silence; her slim strong arms and lithe body, her magic hungry mouth. He saw a quick sequence of pictures taken by the camera of his good male mind, but filed under "inactive" in his troubled, partial one: Janie's legs silhouetted against the window, seen through the polychrome cloud of her liberty silk skirt. Janie in a peasant blouse, with a straight spear of morning sunlight bent and molded to her bare shoulder and the soft upper curve of her breast. Janie dancing, bending away and cleaving to him as if he and she were the gold leaves of an electroscope. (*Where had he seen . . . worked with . . . an electroscope. . Oh, of course! In the . . .* But it was gone.) Janie barely visible in the deep churning dark, palely glowing through a mist of nylon and the flickering acid of his tears, strongly holding his hands until he quieted.

But this was no seduction, this close intimacy of meals and walks and long shared silences, with never a touch, never a wooing word. Lovemaking, even the suppressed and silent kind, is a demanding thing, a thirsty and yearning thing. Janie demanded nothing. She only . . . she only waited. If her interest lay in his obscured history she was taking a completely passive attitude, merely placing herself to receive what he might unearth. If something he had been, something he had done, was what she was after, wouldn't she question and goad, probe and pry the way Thompson and Bromfield had done? (*Bromfield? Who's he?*) But she never had, never.

No, it must be this other, this thing which made her look at lovers with such contained sadness, with an expression on her face like that of an armless man spell-bound by violin music. . . .

Picture of Janie's mouth, bright, still, waiting. Picture of Janie's clever hands. Picture of Janie's body, surely as smooth as her shoulder, as firm as her forearm, warm and wild and willing—

They turned to each other, he the driving, she the driven gear. Their breath left them, hung as a symbol and a promise between them, alive and merged. For two heavy heartbeats they had their single planet in the lovers' spangled cosmos; and then Janie's face twisted in a spasm of concentration, bent not toward a ponderous control, but rather to some exquisite accuracy of adjustment.

A thing happened to him, as if a small sphere of the hardest vacuum had appeared deep within him. He breathed again and the magic about them gathered itself and whipped in with the breath to fill the vacuum which swallowed and killed it, all of it, in a tick of time. Except for the brief spastic change in her face, neither had moved; they still stood in the sunset, close together, her face turned up to his, here gloried, here tinted, there self-shining in its own shadow. But the magic was gone, the melding; they were two, not one, and this was Janie quiet, Janie patient, Janie not damped, but unkindled. But no—the real difference was in him. His hands were lifted to go round her and no longer cared to and his lips lost their grip on the unborn kiss and let it fall away and be lost. He stepped back. "Shall we go?"

A swift ripple of regret came and went across Janie's face. It was a thing like many other things coming now to plague him: smooth and textured things forever presenting themselves to his fingertips and never to his grasp. He almost understood her regret, it was there for him, it was there—and gone, altogether gone, dwindling high away from him.

They walked silently back to the midway and the lights, their pitiable thousands of candlepower; and to the amusement rides, their balky pretense at motion. Behind them in the growing dark they left all real radiance, all significant movement. All of it; there was not enough left for any particular reaction. With the compressed air guns which fired tennis balls at wooden battleships; the cranks they turned to make the top greyhounds race up a slope; the darts they threw at balloons—with these they buried something now so negligible it left no mound.

At an elaborate stand were a couple of war surplus servomechanisms rigged to simulate radar gun directors. There was a miniature anti-aircraft gun to be aimed by hand, its slightest movement followed briskly by the huge servo-powered gun at the back. Aircraft silhouettes were flashed across the domed half ceiling. All in all, it was a fine conglomeration of gadgetry and dazzle, a truly high-level catch-penny.

Hip went first, amused, then intrigued, then enthralled as his small movements were so obediently duplicated by the whip and weave of the massive gun twenty feet away. He missed the first "plane" and the second; after that he had the fixed error of the gun calculated precisely and he banged away at every target as fast as they could throw them and knocked out every one. Janie clapped her hands like a child and the attendant awarded them a blurred and glittering clay statue of a police dog worth all of a fifth of the admission price. Hip took it proudly, and waved Janie up to the trigger. She worked the aiming mechanism diffidently and laughed as the big gun nodded and shook itself. His cheeks flushed, his eyes expertly anticipating the appearance-point of each target. Hip said out of the corner of his mouth, "Up forty or better on your right quadrant, corp'r'l, or the pixies'll degauss your fuses."

Janie's eyes narrowed a trifle and perhaps that was to help her aiming. She did not answer him. She knocked out the first target that appeared before it showed fully over the artificial horizon, and the second, and the third. Hip swatted his hands together and called her name joyfully. She seemed for a moment to be pulling herself together, the odd, effortful gesture of a preoccupied man forcing himself back into a conversation. She then let one go by and missed four in a row. She hit two, one low, one high, and missed the last by half a mile. "Not very good," she said tremulously.

"Good enough," he said gallantly. "You don't have to hit 'em these days, you know."

"You don't?"

"Nah. Just get near. Your fuses take over from there. This is the world's most diabetic dog."

She looked down from his face to the statuette and giggled. "I'll keep it always," she said. "Hip, you're getting that nasty sparkle stuff all over your jacket. Let's give it away."

They marched up and across and down and around the tinsel stands in search of a suitable beneficiary, and found him at last—a solemn urchin of seven or so, who methodically sucked the memory of butter and juice from a wellworn corncob. "This is for *you*," caroled Janie. The child ignored the extended gift and kept his frighteningly adult eyes on her face.

Hip laughed. "No sale!" He squatted beside the boy. "I'll make a deal with you. Will you haul it away for a dollar?"

No response. The boy sucked his corncob and kept watching Janie.

"Tough customer," grinned Hip.

Suddenly Janie shuddered. "Oh, let's leave him alone," she said, her merriment gone.

"He can't outbid *me*," said Hip cheerfully. He set the statue down by the boy's scuffed shoes and pushed a dollar bill into the rip which looked most like a pocket. "Pleasure to do business with you, sir," he said and followed Janie, who had already moved off.

"Regular chatterbox," laughed Hip as he caught up with her. He looked back. Half a block away, the child still stared at Janie. "Looks like you've made a lifetime impress—*Janie!*"

Janie had stopped dead, eyes wide and straight ahead, mouth a triangle of shocked astonishment. "The little *devil!*" she breathed. "At his age!" She whirled and looked back.

Hip's eyes obviously deceived him for he saw the corncob leave the grubby little hands, turn ninety degrees and thump the urchin smartly on the cheekbone. It dropped to the ground; the child backed away four paces, shrilled an unchivalrous presumption and an unprintable suggestion at them and disappeared into an alley.

"Whew!" said Hip, awed. "You're so right!" He looked at her admiringly. "What clever ears you have, grandma," he said, not very successfully covering an almost prissy embarrassment with badinage. "I didn't hear a thing until the second broadside he threw."

"Didn't you?" she said. For the first time he detected annoyance in her voice. At the same time he sensed that he was not the subject of it. He took her arm. "Don't let it bother you. Come on, let's eat some food."

She smiled and everything was all right again.

Succulent pizza and cold bear in a booth painted a too-bright, edge-worn green. A happy-weary walk through the darkening booths to the late bus which waited, breathing. A sense of membership because of the fitting of the spine to the calculated average of the bus seats. A shared doze, a shared smile, at sixty miles an hour through the flickering night, and at last the familiar depot on the familiar street, echoing and empty but *my* street in *my* town.

They woke a taxi driver and gave him their address. "Can I be more alive than this?" he murmured from his corner and then realized she had heard him. "I mean," he amended, "it's as if my whole world, everywhere I lived, was once in a little place inside my head, so deep I couldn't see out. And then you made it as big as a room and then as big as a town and tonight as big as . . . well, a lot bigger," he finished weakly.

A lonely passing streetlight passed her answering smile over to him. He said, "So I was wondering how much bigger it can get."

"Much bigger," she said.

He pressed back sleepily into the cushions. "I feel fine," he murmured. "I feel . . . Janie," he said in a strange voice, "I feel sick."

"You know what that is," she said calmly.

A tension came and went within him and he laughed softly. "Him again. He's wrong. He's wrong. He'll never make me sick again. *Driver!*"

His voice was like soft wood tearing. Startled, the driver slammed on his brakes. His surged forward out of his seat and caught the back of the driver under his armpit. "Go back," he said excitedly.

"Goddlemighty," the driver muttered. He began to turn the cab around. Hip turned to Janie, an answer, some sort of answer, half formed, but she had no question. She sat quietly and waited. To the driver Hip said, "Just the next block. Yeah, here. Left. Turn left."

He sank back then, his cheek to the window glass, his eyes raking the shadowed houses and black lawns. After a time he said, "There. The house with the driveway, there where the big hedge is."

"Want I should drive in?"

"No," Hip said. "Pull over. A little further . . . there, where I can see in."

When the cab stopped, the driver turned around and peered back. "Gettin' out here? That's a dollar 'n—"

"*Shh!*" The sound came so explosively that the driver sat stunned. Then he shook his head wearily and turned to face forward. He shrugged and waited.

Hip stared through the driveway's gap in the hedge at the faintly gleaming white house, its stately porch and porte-cochefe, its neat shutters and fanlit door.

"Take us home," he said after a time.

Nothing was said until they got there. Hip sat with one hand pressing his temples, covering his eyes. Janie's corner of the cab was dark and silent.

When the machine stopped Hip slid out and absently handed Janie to the walk. He gave the driver a bill, accepting the change, pawed out a tip and handed it back. The cab drove off.

Hip stood looking down at the money in his hand, sliding it around on his palm with his fingers. "Janie?"

"Yes, Hip."

He looked at her. He could hardly see her in the darkness. "Let's go inside."

They went in. He switched on the lights. She took off her hat and hung her bag on the bedpost and sat down on the bed, her hands on her lap. Waiting.

He seemed blind, so deep was his introspection. He came awake slowly, his gaze fixed on the money in his hand. For a moment it seemed without meaning to him; then slowly, visibly, he recognized it and brought it into his thoughts, into his expression. He closed his hand on it, shook it, brought it to her and spread it out on the night table—three crumpled bills, some silver. "It isn't mine," he said.

"Of course it is!"

He shook his head tiredly. "No it isn't. None of it's been mine. Not the roller coaster money or the shopping money or coffee in the mornings or . . . I suppose there's rent here."

She was silent.

"That house," he said detachedly. "The instant I saw it I knew I'd been there before. I was there just before I got arrested. I didn't have any money then. I remember. I knocked on the door and I was dirty and crazy and they told me to go around the back if I wanted something to eat. I didn't have any money; I remember that so well. All I had was . . ."

Out of his pocket came the woven metal tube. He caught lamp-light on its side, flicked it off again, squeezed it, then pointed with it at the night table. "Now, ever since I came here, I have money. In my left jacket pocket every day. I never wondered about it. It's your money, isn't it, Janie?"

"It's yours. Forget about it, Hip. It's not important."

"What do you mean it's mine?" he barked. "Mine because you give it to me?" He probed her silence with a bright beam of anger and nodded. "Thought so."

"Hip!"

He shook his head, suddenly, violently, the only expression he could find at the moment for the great tearing wind which swept through him. It was anger, it was humiliation, it was a deep futility and a raging attack on the curtains which shrouded his self-knowledge. He slumped down into the easy chair and put his hands over his face.

He sensed her nearness, then her hand was on his shoulder. "Hip . . ." she whispered. He shrugged the shoulder and the hand was gone. He heard the faint sound of springs as she sat down again on the bed.

He brought his hands down slowly. His face was twisted, hurt. "You've got to understand, I'm not mad at you, I haven't forgotten what you've done, it isn't that," he blurted. "I'm all mixed up again," he said hoarsely. "Doing things, don't know why. Things I *got* to do, I don't know what. Like . . . ." He stopped to think, to sort the thousand scraps that whirled and danced in the wind which blew through him, "Like knowing this is wrong; I shouldn't be here, getting fed, spending money, but I don't know who ever said I shouldn't, where I learned it. And . . . and like what I told you, this thing about finding somebody and I don't know who it is and I don't know why. I said tonight . . . ." He paused and for a long moment filled the room with the hiss of breath between his teeth, his tense-curled lips. "I said tonight, my world . . . the place I live, it's getting bigger all the time. It just now got big enough to take in that house where we stopped. We passed that corner and I knew the house was there and I had to look at it. I knew I'd been there before, dirty and all excited . . . knocked . . . they told me to go around back . . . I yelled at them somebody else came. I asked them, I wanted to know about some—"

The silence, again the hissing breath.

"—children who lived there, and no children lived there. And I shouted again, everybody was afraid, I straightened out a little. I told them just tell me what I wanted to know. I'd go away, I didn't want to frighten anybody. I said all right, no children, then tell me where is Alicia Kew, just let me talk to Alicia Kew."

He straightened up, his eyes alight, and pointed the piece of tubing at Janie. "You see? I remember, I remember her name, Alicia Kew!" He sank back. "And they said, 'Alicia Kew is dead.' And then they said, oh *her* children! And they told me where to go to find them. They wrote it down someplace, I've got it here some-where. . . ." He began to fumble through his pockets, stopped sud-denly and glared at Janie. "It was the old clothes, *you* have it, *you've* hidden it!"

If she had explained, if she had answered, it would have been all right but she only watched him.

"All right," he gritted. "I remembered one thing, I can remember another. Or I can go back there and ask again. I don't need you."

Her expression did not change but, watching it, he knew suddenly that she was holding it still and that it was a terrible effort to her.

He said gently, "I did need you. I'd've died without you. You've been . . . ." He had no word for what she had been to him so he stopped searching for one and went on, "It's just that I've got so I don't need you that way any more. I have some things to find out but I have to do it myself."

At last she spoke: "You have done it yourself, Hip. Every bit of it. All I've done is to put you where you could do it. I—want to go on with that."

"You don't need to," he reassured her. "I'm a big boy now. I've come a long way; I've come alive. There can't be much more to find out."

"There's a lot more," she said sadly.

He shook his head positively. "I tell you, I *know!* Finding out about those children, about this Alicia Kew, and then the address where they'd moved—that was right at the end; that was the place where I got my fingertips on the—whatever it was I was trying to grab. Just that one more place, that address where the children are; that's all I need. That's where he'll be."

"He?"

"The one, you know, the one I've been looking for. His name is—" He leapt to his feet. "His name's—"

He brought his fist into his palm, a murderous blow. "I forgot," he whispered.

He put his stinging hand to the short hair at the back of his head, screwed up his eyes in concentration. Then he relaxed. "It's all right," he said. "I'll find out, now."

"Sit down," she said. "Go on, Hip. Sit down and listen to me."

Reluctantly he did; resentfully he looked at her. His head was full of almost-understood pictures and phrases. He thought, *Can't she let me alone? Can't she let me think a while?* But because she . . . Because she was Janie, he waited.

'You're right, you can do it," she said. She spoke slowly and with extreme care. "You can go to the house tomorrow, if you like, and get the address and find what you've been looking for. And it will mean absolutely—*nothing*—to you. Hip, I *know!*"

He glared at her.

"Believe me, Hip; believe me!"

He charged across the room, grabbed her wrists, pulled her up, thrust his face to hers. "You know!" he shouted. "I *bet* you know. You know every damn thing, don't you? You have all along. Here I am going half out of my head wanting to know and you sit there and watch me squirm!"

"Hip! Hip, my arms—"

He squeezed them tighter, shook her. "You *do* know, don't you? All about me?"

"Let me go. Please let me go. Oh, Hip, you don't know what you're doing!"

He flung her back on the bed. She drew up her legs, turned on her side, propped up on one elbow and, through tears, incredible tears, tears which didn't belong to any Janie he had yet seen, she looked up at him. She held her bruised forearm, flexed her free hand. "You don't know," she choked, "what you're . . ." And then she was quiet, panting, sending, through those impossible tears, some great, tortured, thwarted message which he could not read.

Slowly he knelt beside the bed. "Ah, Janie. Janie."

Her lips twitched. It could hardly have been a smile but it wanted to be. She touched his hair. "It's all right," she breathed.

She let her head fall to the pillow and closed her eyes. He curled his legs under him, sat on the floor, put his arms on the bed and rested his cheek on them.

She said, with her eyes closed, "I understand, Hip; I do understand. I want to help, I want to go on helping."

"No you don't," he said, not bitterly, but from the depths of an emotion something like grief.

He could tell—perhaps it was her breath—that he had started the tears again. He said, "You know about me. You know everything I'm looking for." It sounded like an accusation and he was sorry. He meant it only to express his reasoning. But there wasn't any other way to say it. "Don't you?"

Still keeping her eyes closed, she nodded.

"Well then."

He got up heavily and went back to his chair. *When she wants something out of me*, he thought viciously, *she just sits and waits for it.* He slumped into the chair and looked at her. She had not moved. He made a conscious effort and wrung the bitterness from his thought, leaving only the content, the advice. He waited.

She sighed then and sat up. At sight of her rumpled hair and flushed cheeks, he felt a surge of tenderness. Sternly he put it down.

She said, "You have to take my word. You'll have to trust me, Hip."

Slowly he shook his head. She dropped her eyes, put her hands together. She raised one, touched her eye with the back of her wrist.

She said, "That piece of cable."

The tubing lay on the floor where he had dropped it. He picked it up. "What about it?"

"When was the first time you remembered you had it—remembered it was yours?"

He thought. "The house. When I went to the house, asking."

"No," she said, "I don't mean that. I mean, after you were sick."

"Oh." He closed his eyes briefly, frowned. "The window. The time I remembered the window, breaking it. I remembered that and then it . . . oh!" he said abruptly. "You put it in my hand."

"That's right. And for eight days I'd been putting it in your hand. I put it in your shoe, once. On your plate. In the soap dish. Once I stuck your toothbrush inside it. Every day, half a dozen times a day—eight days, Hip!"

"I don't—"

"You don't understand! Oh, I can't blame you."

"I wasn't going to say that. I was going to say, I don't believe you."

At last she looked at him; when she did he realized how rare it was for him to be with her without her eyes on his face. "Truly," she said intensely. "Truly, Hip. That's the way it was."

He nodded reluctantly. "All right. So that's the way it was. What has that to do with—"

"Wait," she begged. "You'll see . . . now, every time you touched the bit of cable, you refused to admit it existed. You'd let it roll right out of your hand and you wouldn't see it fall to the floor. You'd step on it with your bare feet and not even feel it. Once it was in your food, Hip; you picked it up with a forkful of lima beans, you put the end of it in your mouth, and then just let it slip away; you didn't know it was there!"

"Oc—" he said with an effort, then, "occlusion. That's what Bromfield called it." *Who was Bromfield?* But it escaped him; Janie was talking.

"That's right. Now listen carefully. When the time came for the occlusion to vanish, it did; and there you stood with the cable in your hand, knowing it was real. But nothing I could do beforehand could make that happen until it was ready to happen!"

He thought about it. "So—what made it ready to happen?"

"You went back."

"To the store, the plate glass window?"

"Yes," she said and immediately, "No. What I mean is this: You came alive in this room, and you—well, you said it yourself: the world got bigger for you, big enough to let there be a room, then big enough for a street, then a town. But the same thing was happening with your memory. Your memory got big enough to include yesterday, and last week, and then the jail, and then the thing that got you into jail. Now look: At that moment, the cable meant something to you, something terribly important. But when it happened, for all the time after it happened, the cable meant nothing. It didn't mean anything until the second your memory could go back that far. Then it was real again."

"Oh," he said.

She dropped her eyes. "I knew about the cable. I could have explained it to you. I tried and tried to bring it to your attention but you couldn't see it until you were ready. All right—I know a lot more about you. But don't you see that if I told you, *you wouldn't be able to hear me?*"

He shook his head, not in denial but dazedly. He said, "But I'm not—sick any more!"

He read the response in her expressive face. He said faintly, "Am I?" and then anger curled and kicked inside him. "Come on now," he growled, "you don't mean to tell me I'd suddenly get deaf if you told me where I went to high school."

"Of course not," she said impatiently. "It's just that it wouldn't mean anything to you. It wouldn't relate." She bit her lip in concentration. "Here's one: You've mentioned Bromfield a half dozen times."

"Who? Bromfield? I have not."

She looked at him narrowly. "Hip—you have. You mentioned him not ten minutes ago."

"Did I?" He thought. He thought hard. Then he opened his eyes wide. "By God, I did!"

"All right. Who is he? What was he to you?"

"Who?"

"Hip!" she said sharply.

"I'm sorry," he said. "I guess I'm a little mixed up." He thought again, hard, trying to recall the entire sequence, every word. At last, "B-bromfield," he said with difficulty.

"It will hardly stay with you. Well, it's a flash from a long way back. It won't mean anything to you until you go back that far and get it."

"Go back? Go back how?"

"Haven't you been going back and back—from being sick here to being in jail to getting arrested, and just before that, to your visit to that house? Think about that, Hip. Think about why you went to the house."

He made an impatient gesture. "I don't need to. Can't you see? I went to that house because I was searching for something—what was it? Oh, children; some children who could tell me where the halfwit was." He leapt up, laughed. "You see? The halfwit—I remembered. I'll remember it all, you'll see. The halfwit . . . I'd been looking for him for years, forever. I . . . forget why, but," he said, his voice strengthening, "that doesn't matter any more now. What I'm trying to tell you is that I don't have to go all the way back; I've done all I need to do. I'm back on the path. Tomorrow I'm going to that house and get that address and then I'll go to wherever that is and finish what I started out to do in the first place when I lost the—"

He faltered, looked around bemusedly, spied the tubing lying on the chair arm, snatched it up. "This," he said triumphantly. "It's part of the—the—oh, *damn* it!"

She waited until he had calmed down enough to hear her. She said, "You see?"

"See what?" he asked brokenly, uncaring, miserable.

"If you go out there tomorrow, you'll walk into a situation you don't understand, for reasons you can't remember, asking for some-one you can't place, in order to go find out something you can't conceive of. But," she admitted, "you are right, Hip—you *can* do it."

"If I did," he said, "it would all come back."

She shook her head. He said harshly, "You know everything, don't you?"

"Yes, Hip."

"Well, I don't care. I'm going to do it anyway."

She took one deep breath. "You'll be killed."

"*What?*"

"If you go out there you will be killed," she said distinctly. "Oh, Hip, haven't I been right so far? Haven't I? Haven't you gotten back a lot already—really gotten it back, so it doesn't slip away from you?"

Agonized, he said, "You tell me I can walk out of here tomorrow and find whatever it is I've been looking—Looking? *Living* for . . . and you tell me it'll kill me if I do. What do you want from me? What are you trying to tell me to do?"

"Just keep on," she pleaded. "Just keep on with what you've been doing."

"For what?" he raged. "Go back and back, go farther away from the thing I want? What good will—"

"Stop it!" she said sharply. To his own astonishment he stopped. "You'll be biting holes in the rug in a minute," she said gently and with a gleam of amusement. "That won't help."

He fought against her amusement but it was irresistible. He let it touch him and thrust it away; but it had touched him. He spoke more quietly: "You're telling me I mustn't *ever* find the—the halfwit and the . . . whatever it is?"

"Oh," she said, her whole heart in her reflection, "oh, *no!* Hip, you'll find it, truly you will. But you have to know what it is; you have to know why."

"How long will it take?"

She shook her head soberly. "I don't know."

"I can't wait. Tomorrow—" He jabbed a finger at the window. The dark was silvering, the sun was near, pressing it away. *"Today,* you see? *Today* I could go there . . . I've got to; you understand how much it means, how long I've been . . ." His voice trailed off; then he whirled on her. "You say I'll be killed; I'd rather be killed, there with it in my hands; it's what I've been living for anyway!"

She looked up at him tragically. "Hip—"

"No!" he snapped. "You can't talk me out of it."

She started to speak, stopped, bent her head. Down she bent, to hide her face on the bed.

He strode furiously up and down the room, then stood over her. His face softened. "Janie," he said, "help me. . . ."

She lay very still. He knew she was listening. He said, "If there's danger . . . if something is going to try to kill me . . . tell me what. At least let me know what to look for."

She turned her head, faced the wall, so he could hear her but not see her. In a labored voice she said, "I didn't say anything will try to kill you. I said you *would* be killed."

He stood over her for a long time. Then he growled, "All right. I will. Thanks for everything, Janie. You better go home."

She crawled off the bed slowly, weakly, as if she had been flogged. She turned to him with such a look of pity and sorrow in her face that his heart was squeezed. But he set his jaw, looked toward the door, moved his head toward it.

She went, not looking back, dragging her feet. It was more than he could bear. But he let her go.

The bedspread was lightly rumpled. He crossed the room slowly and looked down at it. He put out his hand, then fell forward and plunged his face into it. It was still warm from her body and for an instant so brief as to be indefinable, he felt a thing about mingled breaths, two spellbound souls turning one to the other and about to be one. But then it was gone, everything was gone and he lay exhausted.

Go on, get sick. Curl up and die. "All right," he whispered.

Might as well. What the difference anyway? Die or get killed, who cares?

Not Janie.

He closed his eyes and saw a mouth. He thought it was Janie's, but the chin was too pointed. The mouth said, *"Just lie down and die, that's all,"* and smiled. The smile made light glance off the thick glasses which must mean he was seeing the whole face. And then there was a pain so sharp and swift that he threw up his head and grunted. His hand, his hand was cut. He looked down at it, saw the scars which had made the sudden, restimulative pain. "Thompson, I'm gonna kill that Thompson."

Who was Thompson who was Bromfield who was the halfwit in the cave . . . cave, where is the cave where the children . . . children . . . no, it was *children's* . . . where the children's . . . *clothes*, that's it! Clothes, old, torn, rags; but that's how he . . .

Janie . . . You will be killed. *Just lie down and die.*

His eyeballs rolled up, his tensions left him in a creeping lethargy. It was not a good thing but it was more welcome than feeling. Someone said, "Up forty or better on your right quadrant, corp'r'l, or the pixies'll degauss your fuses." What said that?

He, Hip Barrows. He said it.

Who'd he say it to?

Janie with her clever hand on the ack-ack prototype.

He snorted faintly. Janie wasn't a corporal. "Reality isn't the most pleasant of atmospheres, Lieutenant. But we like to think we're engineered for it. It's a pretty fine piece of engineering, the kind an engineer can respect. Drag in an obsession and reality can't tolerate it. Something has to give; if reality goes, your fine piece of engineering is left with nothing to operate on. Nothing it was designed to operate on. So it operates badly. So kick the obsession out; start functioning the way you were designed to function."

Who said that? Oh—Bromfield. The jerk! He should know better than to try to talk engineering to an engineer. "Cap'n Bromfield" (tiredly, the twenty damn thousandth time), "if I wasn't an engineer I wouldn't've found it, I wouldn't've recognized it and I wouldn't give a damn now." Ah, it doesn't matter.

It doesn't matter. Just curl up and as long as Thompson don't show his face. *Just curl up and . . .* "No, by God," roared Hip Barrows. He sprang off the bed, stood quaking in the middle of the room. He clapped his hands over his eyes and rocked like a storm-blown sapling. He might be all mixed up, Bromfield's voice, Thompson's face, a cave full of children's clothes, Janie who wanted him killed; but there was one thing he was sure of, one thing he *knew*: Thompson wasn't going to make him curl up and die. Janie had rid him of *that* one!

He whimpered as he rocked, "Janie . . . ?"

Janie didn't want him to die.

Janie didn't want him killed; what's the matter here? Janie just wants . . . go back. Take time.

He looked at the brightening window.

Take time? Why, maybe today he could get that address and see those children and find the halfwit and . . . well, find him anyway; that's what he wanted, wasn't it? *Today*. Then by God he'd show Bromfield who had an obsession!

If he lived, he'd show Bromfield.

But no; what Janie wanted was to go the other way, go back. For how long? More hungry years, nobody believes you, no one helps, you hunt and hunt, starve and freeze, for a little clue and another to fit it: the address that came from the house with the porte-cochère which came from the piece of paper in the children's clothes which were . . . in the . . .

"Cave," he said aloud. He stopped rocking, straightened.

He had found the cave. And in the cave were children's clothes, and among them was the dirty little scrawled-up piece of paper and that had led him to the porte-cochère house, right here in town.

Another step backward, a big one too; he was deeply certain of that. Because it was the discovery in the cave that had really proved he had seen what Bromfield claimed he had not seen; he had a piece of it! He snatched it up and bent it and squeezed it: silvery, light, curiously woven—the piece of tubing. Of course, of *course!* The piece of tubing had come from the cave too. Now he had it.

A deep excitement began to grow within him. She'd said "Go back," and he had said no, it takes too long. How long for this step, this rediscovery of the cave and its treasures?

He glanced at the window. It couldn't have been more than thirty minutes—forty at the outside. Yes, and while he was all messed up, exhausted, angry, guilty, hurt. Suppose he tried this going-back business head-on, rested, fed with all his wits about him, with—with Janie to help?

He ran to the door, threw it open, bounded across the hall, shoved the opposite door open. "Janie, listen," he said, wildly excited. "Oh, Janie—" and his voice was cut off in a sharp gasp. He skidded to a stop six feet into the room, his feet scurrying and slipping, trying to get him back out into the hall again, shut the door. "I beg your— excuse *me*," he bleated out of the shock which filled him. His back struck the door, slammed it; he turned hysterically, pawed it open, and dove outside. God, he thought, I wish she'd *told* me. He stumbled across the hall to his own room, feeling like a gong which had just been struck. He closed and locked his door and leaned against it. Somewhere he found a creaky burst of embarrassed laughter which helped. He half turned to look at the panels of his locked door, drawn to them against his will. He tried to prevent his mind's eye from going back across the hall and through the other door; he failed; he saw the picture of it again, vividly, and again he laughed, hot-faced and uncomfortable. "She should've told me," he muttered.

His bit of tubing caught his eye and he picked it up and sat down in the big chair. It drove the embarrassing moment away; brought back the greater urgency. He had to see Janie. Talk with her. Maybe it was crazy but she'd know: maybe they could do the going-back thing fast, really fast, so fast that he could go find that halfwit today after all. Ah . . . it was probably hopeless; but Janie, Janie'd know. Wait then. She'd come when she was ready; she had to.

He lay back, shoved his feet as far out as they would go, tilted his head back until the back of the chair snugged into the nape of his neck. Fatigue drifted and grew within him like a fragrant smoke, clouding his eyes and filling his nostrils.

His hands went limp, his eyes closed. Once he laughed, a small foolish snicker; but the picture didn't come clear enough or stay long enough to divert him from his deep healthy plunge into sleep.

Bup-bup-bup-bup-bup-bup-bup-bup.

(Fifties, he thought, way off in the hills. Lifelong ambition of every red-blooded boy; get a machine gun and make like a garden hose with it.)

Wham-wham-wham-wham!

(Oerlikons! Where'd they dredge those things up from? Is this an ack-ack station or is it a museum?)

"Hip! Hip Barrows!"

(For Pete's sake, when is that corporal going to learn to say "Lieutenant"? Not that I have a whistle, one way or another, but one of these days he'll do it in front of some teenage Air Force Colonel and get us both bounced for it.)

Wham! Wham! "Oh . . . Hip!"

He sat up palming his eyes, and the guns were knuckles on a door and the corporal was Janie, calling somewhere, and the anti-aircraft base shattered and misted and blew away to the dream factory.

"Hip!"

"Come on," he croaked. "Come on in."

"It's locked."

He grunted and got numbly to his feet. Sunlight poured in through the curtains. He reeled to the door and opened it. His eyes wouldn't track and his teeth felt like a row of cigar butts.

"Oh, Hip!"

Over her shoulder he saw the other door and he remembered. He drew her inside and shut his door. "Listen, I'm awful sorry about what happened. I feel like a damn fool."

"Hip—don't," she said softly. "It doesn't matter, you know that. Are you all right?"

"A little churned up," he admitted and was annoyed by the reappearance of his embarrassed laugh. "Wait till I put some cold water on my face and wake up some." From the bathroom he called, "Where you been?"

"Walking. I had to think. Then . . . I waited outside. I was afraid you might—you know. I wanted to follow you, be with you. I thought I might help. . . . You really are all right?"

"Oh sure. And I'm not going anywhere without talking to you first. But about the other thing—I hope *she's* all right."

"What?"

"I guess she got a worse shock than I did. I wish you'd told me you had somebody in there with you. I wouldn't've barged—"

"Hip, what are you talking about? What happened?"

"Oh!" he said. "Omigosh. You came straight here—you haven't been in your room yet."

"No. What on *earth* are you—"

He said, actually blushing, "I wish she'd told you about it rather than me. Well, I suddenly had to see you, but *bad*. So I steamed across the hall and charged in, never dreaming there would be anyone but you there, and here I am halfway across the room before I could even stop, and there stood this friend of yours."

"Who? Hip, for heaven's sake—"

"The woman. Had to be someone you know, Janie. Burglars aren't likely to prance around naked."

Janie put a slow hand up to her mouth.

"A colored woman. Girl. Young."

"Did she . . . what did she . . . "

"I don't know what she did. I didn't get but a flash glimpse of her—if that's any comfort to her. I hightailed right out of there. Aw, Janie, I'm sorry. I know it's sort of embarrassing, but it can't be *that* bad. Janie!" he cried in alarm.

"He's found us . . . We've got to get out of here," she whispered. Her lips were nearly white; she was shaking. "Come on, oh, come *on!*"

"Now wait! Janie, I got to talk to you. I—"

She whirled on him like a fighting animal. She spoke with such intensity that her words blurred. "Don't talk! Don't ask me. I can't tell you; you wouldn't understand. Just get out of here, get away." With astonishing power her hand closed on his arm and pulled. He took two running steps or he would have been flat on the floor. She was at the door, opening it, as he took the second step, and she took the slack of his shirt in her free hand, pulled him through, pushed him down the hall toward the outer exit. He caught himself against the doorpost; surprise and anger exploded together within him and built an instant of mighty stubbornness. No single word she might have uttered could have moved him; braced and on guard as he was, not even her unexpected strength could have done anything but cause him to strike back. But she said nothing nor did she touch him; she ran past, white and whimpering in terror, and bounded down the steps outside.

He did the only thing his body would do, without analysis or conscious decision. He found himself outside, running a little behind her. "Janie . . ."

"Taxi!" she screamed.

The cab had barely begun to slow down when she had the door open. Hip fell in after her. "Go on," said Janie to the driver and knelt on the seat to peer through the rear window.

"Go where?" gasped the driver.

"Just go. Hurry."

Hip joined her at the window. All he could see was the dwindling house front, one or two gaping pedestrians. "What was it? What happened?"

She simply shook her head.

"What was it?" he insisted. "The place going to explode or something?"

Again she shook her head. She turned away from the window and cowered into the corner. Her white teeth scraped and scraped at the back of her hand. He reached out and gently put it down. She let him.

Twice more he spoke to her, but she would not answer except to acknowledge it, and that only by turning her face slightly away from him each time. He subsided at last, sat back and watched her.

Just outside of town where the highway forks, the driver asked timidly, "Which way?" and it was Hip who said, "Left." Janie came out of herself enough to give him a swift, grateful glance and sank out of sight behind her face.

At length there was a difference in her, in some inexplicable way, though she still sat numbly staring at nothing. He said quietly, "Better?"

She put her eyes on him and, appreciably later, her vision. A rueful smile plucked at the corners of her mouth. "Not worse anyway."

"Scared," he said.

She nodded. "Me too," he said, his face frozen. She put her hand on his arm. "Oh Hip, I'm sorry; I'm more sorry than I can say. I didn't expect this—not so soon. And I'm afraid there isn't anything I can do about it now."

"Why?"

"I can't tell you."

"You can't tell me? Or you can't tell me *yet?*"

She said, carefully, "I told you what you'd have to do—go back and back; find all the places you've been and the things that happened, right to the beginning. You can do it, given time." The terror was in her face again and turned to a sadness. "But there isn't any more time."

He laughed almost joyfully. "There is." He seized her hand. "This morning I found the cave. That's two years back, Janie! I know where it is, what I found there: some old clothes, children's clothes. An address, the house with the porte-cochère. And my piece of tubing, the one thing I ever saw that proved I was right in searching for . . . for . . . Well," he laughed, "that's the next step backward. The important thing is that I found the cave, the biggest step yet. I did it in thirty minutes or so and I did it without even trying. Now I'll *try.* You say we have no more time. Well, maybe not weeks, maybe not days; do we have a day, Janie? Half a day?"

Her face began to glow. "Perhaps we have," she said. "Perhaps . . . Driver! This will do."

It was she who paid the driver; he did not protest it. They stood at the town limits, a place of open, rolling fields barely penetrated by the cilia of the urban animal: here a fruit stand, there a gas station, and across the road, some too-new dwellings of varnished wood and obtrusive stucco. She pointed to the high meadows.

"We'll be found," she said flatly, "but up there we'll be alone . . . and if—anything comes, we can see it coming."

On a knoll in the foothills, in a green meadow where the regrowth barely cloaked the yellow stubble of a recent mowing, they sat facing one another, where each commanded half a horizon.

The sun grew high and hot and the wind blew and a cloud came and went. Hip Barrows worked; back and back he worked. And Janie listened, waited, and all the while she watched, her clear deep eyes flicking from side to side over the open land.

Back and back . . . dirty and mad, Hip Barrows had taken nearly two years to find the house with the porte-cochère. For the address had a number and it had a street; but no town, no city.

It took three years from the insane asylum to the cave. A year to find the insane asylum from the county clerk's office. Six months to find the county clerk from the day of his discharge. From the birth of his obsession until they threw him out of the Service, another six months.

Seven plodding years from starch and schedules, promise and laughter, to a dim guttering light in a jail cell. Seven years snatched away, seven years wingless and falling.

Back through the seven years he went until he knew what he had been before they started.

It was on the anti-aircraft range that he found an answer, a dream, and a disaster.

Still young, still brilliant as ever, but surrounded by puzzling rejection, Lieutenant Barrows found himself with too much spare time, and he hated it.

The range was small, in some respects merely a curiosity, a museum, for there was a good deal of obsolete equipment. The installation itself, for that matter, was obsolete in that it had been superseded years ago by larger and more efficient defense nets and was now part of no system. But it had a function in training gunners and their officers, radar men and technicians.

The Lieutenant, in one of his detested idle moments, went rummaging into some files and came up with some years-old research figures on the efficiency of proximity fuses, and some others on the minimum elevations at which these ingenious missiles, with their fist-sized radar transmitters, receivers and timing gear, might be fired. It would seem that ack-ack officers would much rather knock out a low-flying plane than have their sensitive shells pre-detonated by an intervening treetop of power pole.

Lieutenant Barrows' eye, however, was one of those which pick up mathematical discrepancies, however slight, with the accuracy of the Toscanini ear for pitch. A certain quadrant in a certain sector in the range contained a tiny area over which passed more dud shells than the law of averages should respectably allow. A high-dud barrage or two or three perhaps, over a year, might indicate bad quality control in the shells themselves; but when every flight of low-elevation "prox" shells over a certain point either exploded on contact or not at all, the revered law was being broken. The scientific mind recoils at law-breaking of this sort, and will pursue a guilty phenomenon as grimly as ever society hunted its delinquents.

What pleased the Lieutenant most was that he had here an exclusive. There had been little reason for anyone to throw great numbers of shells at low elevations anywhere. There had been less reason to do so over the area in question. Therefore it was not until Lieutenant Barrows hunted down and compared a hundred reports spread over a dozen years that anyone had had evidence enough to justify an investigation.

But it was going to be *his* investigation. If nothing came of it, nothing need be said. If on the other hand it turned out to be important, he could with immense modesty and impressive clarity bring the matter to the attention of the Colonel; and perhaps then the Colonel might be persuaded to revise his opinion of ROTC Lieutenants. So he made a field trip on his own time and discovered an area wherein to varying degrees his pocket voltmeter would not work properly. And it dawned on him that what he had found was something which inhibited magnetism. The rugged but sensitive coils and relays in the proximity fuses, to all intents and purposes, ceased to exist when they passed this particular hillside lower than forty yards. Permanent magnets were damped just as electromagnets.

Nothing in Barrows' brief but brilliant career had even approached this incredible phenomenon in potential. His accurate and imaginative mind drank and drank of it and he saw visions: the identification and analysis of the phenomenon (Barrows Effect, perhaps?) and then a laboratory effort—successful of course—to duplicate it. Then, application. A field generator which would throw up an invisible wall of the force; aircraft and their communications—even their intercoms—failing with the failure of their many magnets. Seeking gear on guided missiles, arming and blasting devices, and of course the disarming of proximity fuses . . . the perfect defensive weapon for the electromagnetic age . . . and how much else? No limit to it. Then there would be the demonstrations of course, the Colonel introducing him to renowned scientists and military men: *"This, gentlemen, is your ROTC man!"*

But first he had to find what was doing it, now that he knew where it was being done; and so he designed and built a detector. It was simple and ingenious and very carefully calibrated. While engaged in the work, his irrepressible mind wrought and twisted and admired and reworked the whole concept of "contramagnetism." He extrapolated a series of laws and derived effects just as a mathematical pastime and fired them off to the Institute of Electrical Engineers, who could appreciate them and did; for they were later published in the Journal. He even amused himself in gunnery practice by warning his men against low-elevation shelling over his area, because "the pixies would degauss (demagnetize) their proximity fuses." And this gave him a high delight, for he pictured himself telling them later that his fanciful remark had been nothing but the truth and that had they the wit God gave a goose they could have gone out and dug up the thing, whatever it was, for themselves.

At last he finished his detector. It involved a mercury switch and a solenoid and a variable power supply and would detect the very slightest changes in the field of its own magnet. It weighed about forty pounds but this mattered not at all since he did not intend to carry it. He got the best ordnance maps of the area that he could find, appointed as a volunteer the stupidest-looking Pfc he could find, and spent a long day of his furlough time out on the range, carefully zig-zagging the slope and checking the reading off on his map until he located the center of the degaussing effect.

It was in a field on an old abandoned farm. In the middle of the field was an ancient truck in the last stages of oxidation. Drought and drift, rain and thaw had all but buried the machine and the Lieutenant flogged himself and his patient soldier into a frenzy of explosive excavation. After sweaty hours, they had dug and scraped and brushed until what was left of the truck stood free and clear; and under it they found the source of the incredible field.

From each corner of the frame ran a gleaming silvery cable. They came together at the steering column and joined and thence a single cable ran upward to a small box. From the box protruded a level. There was no apparent power source but the thing was operating.

When Barrows pushed the lever forward, the twisted wreck groaned and sank noticeably into the soft ground. When he pulled the lever back, it crackled and creaked and lifted up to the limits of its broken springs and wanted to lift even more.

He returned the lever to neutral and stepped back.

This was everything he had hoped to find certainly and made practical the wildest of his dreams. It was the degaussing generator, awaiting only his dissection and analysis. But it was all these things as a by-product.

Lever forward, this device made the truck *heavier*. Lever back, *lighter*.

It was antigravity!

Antigravity: a fantasy, a dream. Antigravity, which would change the face of the earth in ways which would make the effects of steam, electricity, even nuclear power, mere sproutings of technology in the orchard this device would grow. Here was skyward architecture no artist had yet dared to paint; here was wingless flight and escape to the planets, to the stars, perhaps. Here was a new era in transportation, logistics, even the dance, even medicine. And oh, the research . . . and it was all his.

The soldier, the dull-witted Pfc, stepped forward and yanked the lever full back. He smiled and threw himself at Barrows' legs. Barrows kicked free, stood, sprang so his knees crackled. He stretched, reached, and the tips of his fingers touched the cool bright underside of one of the cables. The contact could not have lasted longer than a tenth of a second; but for years afterward, for all the years Barrows was to live, part of him seemed to stay there in the frozen instant, his fingertips on a miracle, his body adrift and free of earth.

He fell.

Nightmare.

First the breast-bursting time of pounding heart and forgotten breathing, the madness of an ancient ruin rising out of its element, faster and faster, smaller and smaller into the darkening sky, a patch, a spot, a speck, a hint of light where the high sunlight touched it. And then a numbness and pain when the breath came again.

From somewhere the pressure of laughter; from somewhere else, a fury to hate it and force it down.

A time of mad shouting arguments, words slurred into screams, the widening crescents of laughing eyes, and a scuttling shape escaping him, chuckling. *He did it . . . and he tripped me besides.*

And nothing to kill; racing into the growing dark and nothing there; pound-pound of feet and fire in the guts and flame in the mind. Falling, hammering the uncaring sod.

The lonely return to the empty, so empty, so very empty hole in the ground. Stand in it and yearn upward for the silver cables you will never see again.

A yellow-red eye staring. Bellow and kick; the detector rising too, but only so high, turning over and over, smashed, the eye blind.

The long way back to barracks, dragging an invisible man called Agony whose heavy hands were clamped upon a broken foot.

Fall down. Rest and rise. Splash through, wallow, rise and rest and then the camp.

HQ. Wooden steps, the door dark; hollow hammering; blood and mud and hammering. Footsteps, voices: astonishment, concern, annoyance, anger.

The white helmets and the brassards: MP. Tell them, bring the Colonel. No one else, only the Colonel.

Shut up, you'll wake the Colonel.

Colonel, it's anti-magnetron, to the satellite, and freight; no more jets!

Shut up, ROTC boy.

Fight them then and someone screamed when someone stepped on the broken foot.

The nightmare lifted and he was on a white cot in a white room with black bars on the windows and a big MP at the door.

"Where am I?"

"Hospital, prison ward, Lieutenant."

"God, what happened?"

"Search me, Sir. Mostly you seemed to want to kill some GI. Kept telling everybody what he looks like."

He put a forearm over his eyes. "The Pfc. Did you find him?"

"Lieutenant, there ain't such a man on the roster. Honest. Security's been through every file we got. You better take it easy, Sir."

A knock. The MP opened the door. Voices.

"Lieutenant, Major Thompson wants to talk to you. How you feel?"

"Lousy, Sergeant. Lousy. . . . I'll talk to him, if he wants."

"He's quiet now, Sir."

A new voice—*that* voice! Barrows pressed down on the forearm he held over his eyes until sparks shone. *Don't look; because if you're right, you'll kill him.*

The door. Footsteps. "Evening, Lieutenant. Ever talk to a psychiatrist before?"

Slowly, in terror of the explosion he knew must come, Barrows lowered his arm and opened his eyes. The clean, well-cup jacket with a Major's leaves and the Medical Corps insignia did not matter. The man's professionally solicitous manner, the words he spoke—these meant nothing. The only thing in the universe was the fact that the last time he had seen this face, it belonged to a Pfc, who had uncomplainingly and disinterestedly hauled his heavy detector around for a whole, hot day; who had shared his discovery; and who had suddenly smiled at him, pulled the lever, let a wrecked truck and a lifetime dream fall away upwards into the sky.

Barrows growled and leapt.

The nightmare closed down again.

They did everything they could to help him. They let him check the files himself and prove that there was no such Pfc. The "degaussing" effect? No observations of it. Of course, the Lieutenant himself admitted that he had taken all pertinent records to his quarters. No, they are not in the quarters. Yes, there was a hole in the ground out there and they'd found what he called his "detector," though it made no sense to anyone; it merely tested the field of its own magnet. As to Major Thompson, we have witnesses who can prove he was in the air on his way here when it happened. If the Lieutenant would only rid himself of the idea that Major Thompson is the missing Pfc, we'd get along much better; he isn't, you know; he couldn't be. But of course, Captain Bromfield might be better for you at that. . . .

I know what I did, I know what I saw. I'll find that device or whoever made it. And I'll kill that Thompson!

Bromfield was a good man and heaven knows he tried. But the combination in the patient of high observational talent and years of observational training would not accept the denial of its own data. When the demands for proof had been exhausted and the hysterical period was passed and the melancholia and finally the guarded, superficial equilibrium was reached, they tried facing him with the Major. He charged and it took five men to protect the Major.

These brilliant boys, you know. They crack.

So they kept him a while longer, satisfying themselves that Major Thompson was the only target. Then they wrote the Major a word of warning and they kicked the Lieutenant out. Too bad, they said.

The first six months was a bad dream. He was still full of Captain Bromfield's fatherly advice and he tried to get a job and stay with it until this "adjustment" the Captain talked about should arrive. It didn't.

He'd saved a little and he had his separation pay. He'd take a few months off and clear this thing out of his mind.

First, the farm. The device was on the truck and the truck obviously belonged to the farmer. Find him and there's your answer.

It took six months to find the town records (for the village had been preempted when the ack-ack range was added to the base) and to learn the names of the only two men who might tell him about the truck. A. Prodd, farmer. A halfwitted hired hand, name unknown, whereabouts unknown.

But he found Prodd, nearly a year later. Rumor took him to Pennsylvania and a hunch took him to the asylum. From Prodd, all but speechless in the last gasp of his latest dotage, he learned that the old man was waiting for his wife, that his son Jack had never been born, that old Lone maybe was an idiot, but nobody ever was a better hand at getting the truck out of the mud; that Lone was a good boy, that Lone lived in the woods with the animals, and that he, Prodd, had never missed a milking.

He was the happiest human being Hip had ever seen.

Barrows went into the woods with the animals. For three and a half years he combed those woods. He ate nuts and berries and trapped what he could; he got his pension check until he forgot about picking it up. He forgot engineering; he very nearly forgot his name. The only thing he cared to know was that to put such a device on such a truck was the act of an idiot, and that this Lone was a halfwit.

He found the cave, some children's clothes and a scrap of the silvery cable. An address.

He found the address. He learned where to find the children. But then he ran into Thompson—and Janie found him.

Seven years.

*   *   *

It was cool where he lay and under his head was a warm pillow and through his hair strayed a gentling touch. He was asleep, or he had been asleep. He was so completely exhausted, used, drained that sleeping and waking were synonymous anyway and it didn't matter. Nothing mattered. He knew who he was, who he had been. He knew what he wanted and where to find it; and find it he would when he had slept.

He stirred happily and the touch in his hair ceased and moved to his cheek where it patted him. In the morning, he thought comfortably, I'll go see my halfwit. But you know what, I think I'll take an hour off just remembering things. I won the sack race at the Sunday school picnic and they awarded me a khaki handkerchief. I caught three pike before breakfast at the Scout camp, trolling, paddling the canoe and holding the fishing line in my teeth; the biggest of the fish cut my mouth when he struck. I hate rice pudding. I love Bach and liverwurst and the last two weeks in May and deep clear eyes like . . .

"Janie?"

"I'm here."

He smiled and snuggled his head into the pillow and realized it was Janie's lap. He opened his eyes. Janie's head was a black cloud in a cloud of stars; a darker night in nighttime. "Nighttime?"

"Yes," she whispered. "Sleep well?"

He lay still, smiling, thinking of how well he had slept. "I didn't dream because I knew I could."

"I'm glad."

He sat up. She moved cautiously. He said, "You must be cramped up in knots."

"It's all right," she said. "I liked to see you sleep like that."

"Let's go back to town."

"Not yet. It's my turn. Hip. I have a lot to tell you."

He touched her. "You're cold. Won't it wait?"

"No—oh, no! You've got to know everything before he . . . before we're found."

"*He?* Who's he?"

She was quiet a long time. Hip almost spoke and then thought better of it. And when she did talk, she seemed so far from answering his question that he almost interrupted; but again he quelled it, letting her lead matters in her own way, in her own time.

She said, "You found something in a field; you had your hands on it just long enough to know what it was, what it could mean to you and to the world. And then the man who was with you, the soldier, made you lose it. Why do you suppose he did that?"

"He was a clumsy, brainless bastard."

She made no immediate comment but went on, "The medical officer then sent in to you, a Major, looked exactly like that Pfc to you."

"They proved otherwise."

He was close enough to her to feel the slight movement in the dark as she nodded. "Proof: the men who said they were with him in a plane all afternoon. Now, you had a sheaf of files which showed a perturbation of some sort which affected proximity fuses over a certain area. What happened to them?"

"I don't know. My room was locked, as far as I know, from the time I left that day until they went to search it."

"Did it ever occur to you that those three things—the missing Pfc, the missing files, and the resemblance of the Major to the Pfc—were the things which discredited you?"

"That goes without saying. I think if I could've straightened out any one or any two of those three things, I wouldn't have wound up with that obsession."

"All right. Now think about this. You stumbled and grubbed through seven years, working your way closer and closer to regaining what you had lost. You traced the man who built it and you were just about to find him. But something happened."

"My fault. I bumped into Thompson and went crazy."

She put her hand on his shoulder. "Suppose it wasn't carelessness that made that Pfc pull the lever. Suppose it was done on purpose."

He could not have been more shocked if she had fired a flashbulb in his face. The light was as sudden, as blinding, as that. When he could, he said, "Why didn't I ever think of that?"

"You weren't allowed to think of it," she said bitterly.

"What do you mean, I wasn't—"

"Please. Not yet," she said. "Now, just suppose for a moment that someone did this to you. Can you reason out who it was—why he did it—*how* he did it?"

"No," he said immediately. "Eliminating the world's first and only antigravitity generator makes no sense at all. Picking on me to persecute and doing it through such an elaborate method means even less. And as to method, why, he'd have to be able to reach into locked rooms, hypnotize witnesses and read minds!"

"He did," said Janie. "He can."

"Janie—*who?*"

"Who made the generator?"

He leaped to his feet and released a shout that went rolling down and across the dark field.

"Hip!"

"Don't mind me," he said, shaken. "I just realized that the only one who would dare to destroy that machine is someone who could make another if he wanted it. Which means that—oh, my *God!*—the soldier and the halfwit, and maybe Thompson—yes, Thompson: he's the one made me get jailed when I was just about to find him again—they're all the same!—Why didn't I ever think of that before?"

"I told you. You weren't allowed."

He sank down again. In the east, dawn hung over the hill like the loom of a hidden city. He looked at it, recognizing it as the day he had chosen to end his long, obsessive search and he thought of Janie's terror when he had determined to go headlong into the presence of this—this monster—without his sanity, without his memory, without arms or information.

"You'll have to tell me, Janie. All of it."

She told him—all of it. She told him of Lone, of Bonnie and Beanie and of herself; Miss Kew and Miriam, both dead now, and Gerry. She told how they had moved, after Miss Kew was killed, back into the woods, where the old Kew mansion hid and brooded, and how for a time they were very close. And then . . .

"Gerry got ambitious for awhile and decided to go through college, which he did. It was easy. Everything was easy. He's pretty unremarkable looking when he hides those eyes of his behind glasses, you know, people don't notice. He went through medical school too, and psych."

"You mean he really is a psychiatrist?" asked Hip.

"He is not. He just qualifies by the book. There's quite a difference. He hid in crowds; he falsified all sorts of records to get into school. He was never caught at it because all he had to do with anyone who was investigating him was to give them a small charge of that eye of his and they'd forget. He never failed any exam as long as there was a men's room he could go to."

"A what? Men's room?"

"That's right." She laughed. "There was hell to pay one time. See, he'd go in and lock himself in a booth and call Bonnie or Beanie. He'd tell them where he was stumped and they'd whip home and tell me and I'd get the answer from Baby and they'd flash back with the information, all in a few seconds. So one fine day another student heard Gerry talking and stood up in the next booth and peeked over. You can imagine! Bonnie and Beanie can't carry so much as a toothpick with them when they teleport, let alone clothes."

Hip clapped a hand to his forehead. "What happened?"

"Oh, Gerry caught up with the kid. He'd charged right out of there yelling that there was a naked girl in the john. Half of the student body dove in there; of course she was gone. And when Gerry caught up with the kid, he just naturally forgot all about it and wondered what all the yelling was about. They gave him a pretty bad time over it.

"Those were good times," she sighed. "Gerry was so interested in everything. He read all the time. He was at Baby all the time for information. He was interested in people and books and machines and history and art—everything. I got a lot from it. As I say, all the information cleared through me.

"But then Gerry began to . . . I was going to say, get sick, but that's not the way to say it." She bit her lip thoughtfully. "I'd say from what I know of people that only two kinds are really progressive—really dig down and learn and then use what they learn. A few are genuinely interested; they're just built that way. But the great majority want to prove something. They want to be better, richer. They want to be famous or powerful or respected. With Gerry the second operated for a while. He'd never had any real schooling and he'd always been a little afraid to compete. He had it pretty rough when he was a kid; ran away from an orphanage when he was seven and lived like a sewer rat until Lone picked him up. So it felt good to get honors in his classes and make money with a twist of his wrist any time he wanted it. And I think he was genuinely interested in some things for a little while: music and biology and one or two other things.

"But he soon came to realize that he didn't need to prove anything to anyone. He was smarter and stronger and more powerful than anybody. Proving it was just dull. He could have anything he wanted.

"He quit studying. He quit playing the oboe. He gradually quit everything. Finally he slowed down and practically stopped for a year. Who knows what went on in his head? He'd spend weeks lying around, not talking.

"Our *gestalt*, as we call it, was once an idiot, Hip, when it had Lone for a 'head.' Well, when Gerry took over it was a new, strong, growing thing. But when this happened to him, it was in retreat like what used to be called a manic-depressive."

"Uh!" Hip grunted. "A manic-depressive with enough power to run the world."

"He didn't want to run the world. He knew he could if he wanted to. He didn't see any reason why he should.

"Well, just like in his psych texts he retreated and soon he regressed. He got childish. And his kind of childishness was pretty vicious.

"I started to move around a little; I couldn't stand it around the house. I used to hunt around for things that might snap him out of it. One night in New York I dated a fellow I know who was one of the officers of the I.R.E."

"Institute of Radio Engineers," said Hip. "Swell outfit. I used to be a member."

"I know. This fellow told me about you."

"About *me?*"

"About what you called a 'mathematical recreation,' anyway. An extrapolation of the probable operating laws and attendant phenomena of magnetic flux in a gravity generator."

"God!"

She made a short and painful laugh. "Yes, Hip. I did it to you. I didn't know then of course. I just wanted to interest Gerry in something.

"He was interested all right. He asked Baby about it and got the answer pronto. You see, Lone built that thing before Gerry came to live with us. We'd forgotten about it pretty much."

"Forgotten! A thing like *that?*"

"Look, we don't think like other people."

"You don't," he said thoughtfully and, "Why should you?"

"Lone built it for the old farmer, Prodd. That was just like Lone. A gravity generator, to increase and decrease the weight of Prodd's old truck so he could use it as a tractor. All because Prodd's horse died and he couldn't afford another."

"No!"

"Yes. He was an idiot all right. Well, he asked Baby what effect it would have if this invention got out and Baby said plenty. He said it would turn the whole world upside down, worse than the industrial revolution. Worse than anything that ever happened. He said if things went one way we'd have such a war, you wouldn't believe it. If they went the other way, science would go too far, too fast. Seems that gravitics is the key to everything. It would lead to the addition of one more item to the Unified Field—what we now call psychic energy, or 'psionics.' "

"Matter, energy, space, time and psyche," he breathed, awed.

"Yup," Janie said casually, "all the same thing and this would lead to proof. There just wouldn't *be* any more secrets."

"That's the—the biggest thing I ever heard. So—Gerry decided us poor half-developed apes weren't worthy?"

"No Gerry! He doesn't care what happens to you apes! One thing he found out from Baby, though, was that whichever way it went the device would be traced to us. You should know. You did it by yourself. But Central Intelligence would've taken seven weeks instead of seven years.

"And that's what bothered Gerry. He was in retreat. He wanted to stew in his own juice in his hideout in the woods. He didn't want the Armed Forces of the United Nations hammering at him to come out and be patriotic. Oh sure, he could have taken care of 'em all in time, but only if he worked full time at it. Working full time was out of his field. He got mad. He got mad at Lone who was dead and he especially got mad at you."

"Whew. He could have killed me. Why didn't he?"

"Same reason he didn't just go out and confiscate the device before you saw it. I tell you, he was vicious and vengeful—childish. You'd bothered him. He was going to fix you for it.

"Now I must confess I didn't care much one way or the other, it did me so much good to see him moving around again. I went with him to the base.

"Now, here's something you just wouldn't remember. He walked right into your lab while you were calibrating your detector. He looked you once in the eye and walked out again with all the information you had, plus the fact that you meant to take it out and locate the device, and that you intended to—what was your phrase?—'appoint a volunteer.'"

"I was a hotshot in those days," said Hip ruefully.

She laughed. "You don't know. You just don't know. Well, out you came with that big heavy instrument on a strap. I saw you, Hip; I can still see you, your pretty tailored uniform, the sun on your hair . . . I was seventeen.

"Gerry told me to lift a Pfc shirt quick. I did, out of the barracks."

"I didn't know a seventeen-year-old could get in and out of a barracks with a whole skin. Not a female type seventeen-year-old."

"I didn't go in!" she said. Hip shouted in sheer surprise as his own shirt was wrenched and twisted. The tails flew up from under his belt and flapped wildly in the windless dawn. "Don't *do* that!" he gasped.

"Just making a point," she said, twinkling. "Gerry put on the shirt and leaned against the fence and waited for you. You marched right up to him and handed him the detector. 'Come on, soldier,' you said. 'You just volunteered for a picnic. You carry the lunch.'"

"What a little stinker I was!"

"I didn't think so. I was peeping out from behind the MP shack. I thought you were sort of wonderful. I did, Hip."

He half laughed. "Go on. Tell me the rest."

"You know the rest. Gerry flashed Bonnie to get the files out of your quarters. She found them and threw them down to me. I burned them. I'm sorry, Hip. I didn't know what Gerry was planning."

"Go on."

"Well, that's it. Gerry saw to it that you were discredited. Psychologically, it had to be that way. You claimed the existence of a Pfc no one had ever seen. You claimed he was the psychiatrist—a real danger sign, as any graduate medic knows. You claimed files, facts and figures to back you up and they couldn't be traced. You could prove that you'd dug something up, but there was nothing to show what it might have been. But most of all, you had a trained scientist's mind, in full possession of facts which the whole world could prove weren't so—and did. Something had to give."

"Cute," murmured Hip from deep in his chest.

"And just for good measure," said Janie with some difficulty, "he handed you a post-hypnotic command which made it impossible for you to relate him either as Major Thompson, psychiatrist, or as the Pfc, to the device.

"When I found out what he'd done I tried to make him help you. Just a little. He—he just laughed at me. I asked Baby what could be done. He said nothing. He said only that the command might be removed by a reverse abreaction."

"What in time is that?"

"Moving backward, mentally, to the incident itself. Abreaction is the process of reliving, in detail, an event. But you were blocked from doing that because you'd have to start from the administration of the command; that's where the incident started. And the only way would be to immobilize you completely, not tell you why, and unpeel all subsequent events one by one until you reached the command. It was a 'from now on' command like all such. It couldn't stop you when you were traveling in reverse.

"And how was I ever going to find you and immobilize you without letting you know why?"

"Holy smoke," Hip said boyishly. "This makes me feel kind of important. A guy like that taking all that trouble."

"Don't flatter yourself!" she said acidly, then: "I'm sorry, Hip. I didn't mean that the way it sounded. . . . It was no trouble for him. He swatted you like a beetle. He gave you a push and forgot all about you."

Hip grunted. "Thank you."

"He did it again!" she said furiously. "There you were, seven good youthful years shot, your good engineer's mind gone, with nothing left but a starved, dirty frame and a numb obsession that you were incapable of understanding or relieving. Yet, by heaven, you had enough of—whatever it is that makes you what you are—to drag through those seven years picking up the pieces until you were right at his doorstep. When he saw you coming—it was an accident, he happened to be in town—he knew immediately who you were and what you were after. When you charged him he diverted you into that plate glass window with just a blink of those . . . rotten . . . poison . . . eyes of his . . ."

"Hey," he said gently. "Hey, Janie, take it easy!"

"Makes me mad," she whispered, dashing her hand across her eyes. She tossed her hair back, squared her shoulders. "He sent you flying into the window and at the same time gave you that 'curl up and die' command. I saw it, I saw him do it. . . . S-so rotten. . . ."

She said, in a more controlled tone, "Maybe if it was the only one I could have forgotten it. I never could have approved it but I once had faith in him . . . you've got to understand, we're a part of something together, Gerry and I and the kids; something real and alive. Hating him is like hating your legs or your lungs."

"It says in the Good Book, 'If thine eye offend thee, pluck it out and cast it from thee. If thy right hand—' "

"Yes, your eye, your hand!" she cried. "Not your *head!*" She went on, "But yours wasn't the only case. Did you ever hear that rumor about the fusion of Element 83?"

"A fairy tale. Bismuth won't play those games. I remember vaguely . . . some crazy guy called Klackenhorst."

"A crazy guy called Klackenheimer," she corrected. "Gerry got into one of his bragging phases and let go with a differential he shouldn't have mentioned. Klack picked it up. He fusioned bismuth all right. And Gerry got worried; a thing like that would make too much of a splash and he was afraid he'd be bothered by a mob of people who might trace him. So he got rid of poor old Klack."

"Klackenheimer died of cancer!" snorted Hip.

She gave him a strange look. "I know," she said softly.

Hip beat his temples softly with his fists. Janie said, "There've been more. Not all big things like that. I dared him into wooing a girl once, strictly on his own, without using his talents. He lost out to someone else, an awfully sweet kid who sold washing machines door-to-door and was doing pretty well. The kid wound up with *acne rosacea.*"

"The nose like a beet. I've seen it."

"Like an extra-boiled, extra-swollen beet," she amended. "No job."

"No girl," he guessed.

She smiled and said, "She stuck by him. They have a little ceramics business now. He stays in the back."

He had a vague idea of where the business had come from. "Janie, I'll take your word for it. There were lots of 'em. But—why me? You went all out for me."

"Two good reasons. First, I saw him do that to you in town, make you charge his image in the glass, thinking it was him. It was the last piece of casual viciousness I ever wanted to see. Second, it was—well, it was *you*."

"I don't get you."

"Listen," she said passionately, "we're not a group of freaks. We're *Homo Gestalt*, you understand? We're a single entity, a new kind of human being. We weren't invented. We evolved. We're the next step up. We're alone; there are no more like us. We don't live in the kind of world you do, with systems of morals and codes of ethics to guide us. We're living on a desert island with a herd of goats!"

"I'm the goat."

"Yes, yes, you *are*, can't you see? But we were born on this island with no one like us to teach us, tell us how to behave. We can learn from the goats all the things that make a goat a good goat, but that will never change the fact that we're *not* a goat! You can't apply the same set of rules to us as you do to ordinary humans; we're just not the same thing!"

She waved him down as he was about to speak. "But listen, did you ever see one of those museum exhibits of skeletons of, say, horses, starting with the little Eohippus and coming right up the line, nineteen or twenty of them, to the skeleton of a Percheron? There's an awful lot of difference between number one and number nineteen. But what real difference is there between number fifteen and number sixteen? *Damn* little!" She stopped and panted.

"I hear you. But what's that to do with—"

"With you? Can't you see? *Homo Gestalt* is something new, something different, something superior. But the parts—the arms, the guts of it, the memory banks, just like the bones in those skeletons—they're the same as the step lower, or very little different. I'm *me*, I'm *Janie*. I saw him slap you down like that; you were like a squashed rabbit, you were mangy and not as young as you should be. But I recognized you. I saw you and then I saw you seven years ago, coming out into the yard with your detector and the sun on your hair. You were wide and tall and pressed and you walked like a big glossy stallion. You were the reason for the colors on a bantam rooster, you were a part of the thing that shakes the forest when the bull moose challenges; you were shining armor and a dipping pennant and my lady's girdle on your brow, you were, you were . . . I was *seventeen*, damn it, Barrows, whatever else I was. I was seventeen years old and all full of late spring and dreams that scared me."

Profoundly shaken, he whispered, "Janie . . . Janie . . ."

"Get away from me!" she spat. "Not what you think, not love at first sight. That's childish; love's a different sort of thing, hot enough to make you flow into something, interflow, cool and anneal and be a weld stronger than what you started with. I'm not talking about love. I'm talking about being seventeen and feeling . . . all . . ." She covered her face. He waited. Finally she put her hands down. Her eyes were closed and she was very still. ". . . all . . . *human*," she finished.

Then she said, matter-of-factly, "So that's why I helped you instead of anyone else."

He got up and walked into the fresh morning, bright now, new as the fright in a young girl's frightening dream. Again he recalled her total panic when he had reported Bonnie's first appearance; through her eyes he saw what it would be like if he, blind, numb, lacking weapons and insight, had walked again under that cruel careless heel.

He remembered the day he had emerged from the lab, stepped down into the compound, looking about for a slave. Arrogant, self-assured, shallow, looking for the dumbest Pfc in the place.

He thought more then about himself as he had been that day; not about what had happened with Gerry, for that was on the record, accomplished; susceptible to cure but not in fact to change. And the more he thought of himself as he had been the more he was suffused with a deep and choking humility.

He walked almost into Janie as she sat watching her hands sleeping in her lap as he had slept and he thought, surely they too must be full of pains and secrets and small magics too, to smile at.

He knelt beside her. "Janie," he said, and his voice was cracked, "you have to know what was inside that day you saw me. I don't want to spoil you-being-seventeen . . . I just want to tell you about the part of it that was me, some things that—weren't what you thought." He drew a deep breath. "I can remember it better than you because for you it's been seven years and for me it's only just before I went to sleep and dreamed that I went hunting for the halfwit. I'm awake again and the dream is gone, so I remember it all very well. . . .

"Janie, I had trouble when I was a child and the first thing I learned was that I was useless and the things I wanted were by definition worthless. I hardly questioned that until I broke away and found out that my new world had different values from my old one and in the new I was valuable. I was wanted, I belonged.

"And then I got into the Air Force and suddenly I wasn't a football hero and captain of the Debating Society. I was a bright fish with drying scales, and the mud-puppies had it all their way. I nearly died there, Janie.

"Yes, I found the degaussing field all by myself. But what I want you to know is that when I stepped out of the lab that day and you saw me, I wasn't the cockerel and the bull moose and those other things. I was going to discover something and bring it to humanity, not for humanity's sake, but so that they would . . ." he swallowed painfully, ". . . ask me to play the piano at the officers' club and slap me on the back and . . . look at me when I came in. That's all I wanted. When I found out that it was more than magnetic damping (which would make me famous) but antigravity (which would change the face of Earth) I felt only that it would be the President who asked me to play and generals who would slap my back; the things I wanted were the same."

He sank back on his haunches and they were quiet together for a long time. Finally she said, "What do you want now?"

"Not that any more," he whispered. He took her hands. "Not any more. Something different." Suddenly he laughed. "And you know what, Janie? *I don't know what it is!*"

She squeezed his hands and released them. "Perhaps you'll find out. Hip, we'd better go."

"All right. Where?"

She stood beside him, tall. "Home. *My* home."

"Thompson's?"

She nodded.

"Why, Janie?"

"He's got to learn something that a computer can't teach him. He's got to learn to be ashamed."

"Ashamed?"

"I don't know," she said, looking away from him, "how moral systems operate. I don't know how you get one started. All I know about morals is that if they're violated, you feel ashamed. I'll start him with that."

"What can I do?"

"Just come," she flashed. "I want him to see you—what you are, the way you think. I want him to remember what you were before, how much brilliance, how much promise you had, so he'll know how much he has cost you."

"Do you think any of that will really make a difference?"

She smiled; one could be afraid of someone who could smile like that. "It will," she said grimly. "He will have to face the fact that he is not omnipotent and that he can't kill something better than he is just because he's stronger."

"You want him to try to kill me?"

She smiled again and this time it was the smile of deep achievement. "He won't." She laughed, then turned to him quickly. "Don't worry about it, Hip. *I am his only link with Baby.* Do you think he'd perform a prefrontal lobotomy on himself? Do you think he'd risk cutting himself off from his memory? It isn't the kind of memory a man has, Hip. It's *Homo Gestalt's.* It's all the information it has ever absorbed, plus the computation of each fact against every other fact in every possible combination. He can get along without Bonnie and Beanie, he can get things done at a distance in other ways. He can get along without any of the other things I do for him. But he can't get along without Baby. He's had to ever since I began working with you. By this time he's frantic. He can touch Baby, lift him, talk to him. But he can't get a thing out of him unless he does it through me!"

"I'll come," he said quietly. Then he said, "You won't have to kill yourself."

They went first to their own house and Janie laughed and opened both locks without touching them. "I've wanted so to do that but I didn't dare," she laughed. She pirouetted into his room. "Look!" she sang. The lamp on the night table rose, sailed slowly through the air, settled to the floor by the bathroom. Its cord curled like a snake, sank into a baseboard outlet and the switch clicked. It lit. "Look!" she cried. The percolator hopped forward on the dresser-top, stopped. He heard water trickling and slowly condensed moisture formed on the outside as the pot filled up with ice water. "Look," she called, "look, look!" and the carpet grew a bulge which scuttled across and became nothing at the other side, the knives and forks and his razor and toothbrush and two neckties and a belt came showering around and down and lay on the floor in the shape of a heart with an arrow through it. He shouted with laughter and hugged her and spun her around. He said, "Why haven't I ever kissed you, Janie?"

Her face and body went quite still and in her eyes was an indescribable expression—tenderness, amusement and something else. She said, "I'm not going to tell you because you're wonderful and brave and clever and strong, but you're also just a little bit prissy." She spun away from him and the air was full of knives and forks and neckties, the lamp and the coffeepot, all going back to their places. At the door she said, "Hurry," and was gone.

He plunged after her and caught her in the hall. She was laughing.

He said, "I know why I never kissed you."

She kept her eyes down, but could not do the same with the corners of her mouth. "You do?"

"You can add water to a closed container. Or take it away." It was not a question.

"I can?"

"When we poor males start pawing the ground and horning the low branches off trees, it might be spring and it might be concreted idealism and it might be love. But it's always triggered by hydrostatic pressure in a little tiny series of reservoirs smaller than my little fingernail."

"It is?"

"So when the moisture content of these reservoirs is suddenly lowered, I—we—uh . . . well, breathing becomes easier and the moon has no significance."

"It hasn't?"

"And that's what you've been doing to me."

"I have?"

She pulled away from him, gave him her eyes and a swift, rich arpeggio of laughter. "You can't say it was an immoral thing to do," she said.

He gave her laughter back to her. "No *nice* girl would do a thing like that."

She wrinkled her nose at him and slipped into her room. He looked at her closed door and probably through it, and then turned away.

Smiling and shaking his head in delight and wonderment, encasing a small cold ball of terror inside him with a new kind of calm he had found; puzzled, enchanted, terrified and thoughtful, he turned the shower on and began to undress.

They stood in the road until after the taxi had gone and then Janie led the way into the woods. If they had ever been cut, one could not know it now. The path was faint and wandering but easy to follow, for the growth overhead was so thick that there was little underbrush.

They made their way toward a mossy cliff; and then Hip saw that it was not a cliff but a wall, stretching perhaps a hundred yards in each direction. In it was a massive iron door. It clicked as they approached and something heavy slid. He looked at Janie and knew that she was doing it.

The gate opened and closed behind them. Here the woods were just the same, the trees as large and as thick, but the path was of brick and took only two turns. The first made the wall invisible and the second, a quarter of a mile further, revealed the house.

It was too low and much too wide. Its roof was mounded rather than peaked or gabled. When they drew closer to it, he could see at each flank the heavy, gray-green wall, and he knew that this whole area was in prison.

"I don't, either," said Janie. He was glad she watched his face. *Gooble.*

Someone stood behind a great twisted oak near the house, peeping at them. "Wait, Hip." Janie walked quickly to the tree and spoke to someone. He heard her say, "You've *got* to. Do you want me dead?"

That seemed to settle the argument. As Janie returned he peered at the tree, but now there seemed to be no one there.

"It was Beanie," said Janie. "You'll meet her later. Come."

The door was ironbound, of heavy oak planks. It fitted with curious concealed hinges into the massive archway from which it took its shape. The only windows to be seen were high up in the mound-like gables and they were mere barred slits.

By itself—or at least, without a physical touch—the door swung back. It should have creaked, but it did not; it was silent as a cloud. They went in, and when the door closed there was a reverberation deep in the subsonic; he could feel it pounding on his belly.

On the floor was a reiteration of tiles, darkest yellow and a brownish gray, in hypnotic diamond shapes they were repeated in the wainscoting and in the upholstery of furniture either built-in or so heavy it had never been moved. The air was cool but too humid and the ceiling was too close. I am walking, he thought, in a great sick mouth.

From the entrance room they started down a corridor which seemed immensely long and was not at all, for the walls came in and the ceiling drew even lower while the floor rose slightly, giving a completely disturbing false perspective.

"It's all right," said Janie softly. He curled his lips at her, meaning to smile but quite unable to, and wiped cold water from his upper lip.

She stopped near the end door and touched the wall. A section of it swung back, revealing an anteroom with one other door in it. "Wait here, will you, Hip?" She was completely composed. He wished there were more light.

He hesitated. He pointed to the door at the end of the hall. "Is he in there?"

"Yes." She touched his shoulder. It was partly a salutation, partly an urging toward the little room. "I have to see him first," she said. "Trust me, Hip."

"I trust you all right. But are you—is he—"

"He won't do anything to me. Go on, Hip."

He stepped through. He had no chance to look back, for the door swung swiftly shut. It gave no more sign of its existence on this side than it had on the other. He touched it, pushed it. It might as well have been that great wall outside. There was no knob, no visible hinge or catch. The edges were hidden in the paneling; it simply had ceased to exist as a door.

He had one blinding moment of panic and then it receded. He went and sat down across from the other door which led, apparently, into the same room to which the corridor led.

There was not a sound.

He picked up an ottoman and placed it against the wall. He sat with his back tight against the paneling, watching the door with wide eyes.

Try that door, see if it's locked too.

He didn't dare, he realized. Not yet. He sensed vaguely what he would feel if he found it locked; he wanted no more just now than that chilling guess.

"Listen," he hissed to himself, furiously, "you'd better do something. Build something. Or maybe just *think*. But don't sit here like this."

Think. Think about that mystery in there, the pointed face with its thick lenses, which smiled and said, Go on, die.

Think about something else! Quick!

Janie. By herself, facing the pointed face with the—

Homo Gestalt, a girl, two tongued-tied Negroes, a mongoloid idiot and a man with a pointed face and—

Try that one again. *Homo Gestalt*, the next step upward. Well, sure, why not a psychic evolution instead of the physical?

Homo sapiens stood suddenly naked and unarmed but for the wrinkled jelly in his king-sized skull; he was as different as he could be from the beasts which bore him.

Yet he was the same, the same; to this day he was hungry to breed, hungry to own; he killed without compunction; if he was strong he took, if he was weak he ran; if he was weak and could not run, he died.

Homo sapiens was going to die.

The fear in him was a good fear. Fear is a survival instinct; fear in its way is a comfort for it means that somewhere hope is alive.

He began to think about survival.

Janie wanted *Homo Gestalt* to acquire a moral system so that such as Hip Barrows would not get crushed. But she wanted her *Gestalt* to thrive as well; she was a part of it. My hand wants me to survive, my tongue, my belly wants me to survive.

Morals: they're nothing but a coded survival instinct!

Aren't they? What about the societies in which it is immoral not to eat human flesh? What kind of survival is that?

Well, but those who adhere to morality survive within the group. If the group eats human flesh, you do too.

There must be a name for the code, the set of rules, by which an individual lives in such a way as to help his species—something over and above morals.

Let's define that as the ethos.

That's what *Homo Gestalt* needs: not morality, but an ethos. And shall I sit here, with my brains bubbling with fear, and devise a set of ethics for a superman?

I'll try. It's all I can do.

Define:

Morals: Society's code for individual survival. (That takes care of our righteous cannibal and the correctness of a naked man in a nudist group.)

Ethics: An individual's code for society's survival. (And that's your ethical reformer: he frees his slaves, he won't eat humans, he "turns the rascals out.")

Too pat, too slick; but let's work with 'em.

As a group, *Homo Gestalt* can solve his own problems. But as an entity:

He can't have a morality, because he is alone.

An ethic then. "An individual's code for society's survival." He has no society; yet he has. He has no species; he is his own species.

Could he—should he choose a code which would serve all of humanity?

With the thought, Hip Barrows had a sudden flash of insight, completely intrusive in terms of his immediate problem; yet with it, a load of hostility and blind madness lifted away from him and let him light and confident. It was this:

Who am I to make positive conclusions about morality, and codes to serve all of humanity?

Why—I am the son of a doctor, a man who chose to serve mankind, and who was positive that this was right. And he tried to make me serve in the same way, because it was the only rightness he was sure of. And for this I have hated him all my life . . . I see now, Dad, I see!

He laughed as the weight of old fury left him forever, laughed in purest pleasure. And it was as if the focus was sharper, the light brighter, in all the world, and as his mind turned back to his immediate problem, his thought seemed to place its fingers better on the rising undersurface, slide upward toward the beginnings of a grip.

The door opened. Janie said, "Hip—"

He rose slowly. His thought reeled on and on, close to something. If he could get a grip, get his fingers curled over it . . . "Coming."

He stepped through the door and gasped. It was like a giant greenhouse, fifty yards wide, forty deep; the huge panes overhead curved down and down and met the open lawn—it was more a park—at the side away from the house. After the closeness and darkness of what he had already seen it was shocking but it built in him a great exhilaration. It rose up and up and up rose his thought with it, pressing its fingertips just a bit higher. . . .

He saw the man coming. He stepped quickly forward, not so much to meet him as to be away from Janie if there should be an explosion. There was going to be an explosion; he knew that.

"Well, Lieutenant. I've been warned, but I can still say—this *is* a surprise."

"Not to me," said Hip. He quelled a surprise of a different nature; he had been convinced that his voice would fail him and it had not. "I've known for seven years that I'd find you."

"By God," said Thompson in amazement and delight. It was not a good delight. Over Hip's shoulder he said, "I apologize, Janie. I really didn't believe you until now." To Hip he said, "You show remarkable powers of recovery."

"Homo sap's a hardy beast," said Hip.

Thompson took off his glasses. He had wide round eyes, just the color and luminescence of a black-and-white television screen. The irises showed the whites all the way around; they were perfectly round and they looked as if they were just about to spin.

Once, someone had said, *Keep away from the eyes and you'll be all right.*

Behind him Janie said sharply, "Gerry!"

Hip turned. Janie put up her hand and left a small glass cylinder, smaller than a cigarette, hanging between her lips. She said, "I warned you, Gerry. You know what this is. Touch him and I bite down on it—and then you can live out the rest of your life with Baby and the twins like a monkey in a cage of squirrels."

The thought, the thought—"I'd like to meet Baby."

Thompson thawed; he had been standing, absolutely motionless, staring at Janie. Now he swung his glasses around in a single bright circle. "You wouldn't like him."

"I want to ask him a question."

"Nobody asks him questions but me. I suppose you expect an answer too?"

"Yes."

Thompson laughed. "Nobody gets answers these days."

Janie said quietly, "This way, Hip."

Hip turned toward her. He distinctly felt a crawling tension be-hind him, in the air, close to his flesh. He wondered if the Gorgon's head had affected men that way, even the ones who did not look at her.

He followed her down to a niche in the house wall, the one which was not curved glass. In it was a crib the size of a bathtub.

He had not known that Baby was so fat.

"Go ahead," said Janie. The cylinder bobbed once for each of her syllables.

"Yes, go ahead." Thompson's voice was so close behind him that he started. He had not heard the man following him at all and he felt boyish and foolish. He swallowed and said to Janie, "What do I do?"

"Just think your question. He'll probably catch it. Far as I know he receives everybody."

Hip leaned over the crib. Eyes gleaming dully like the uppers of dusty black shoes caught and held him. He thought, *Once this Gestalt had another head. It can get other telekines, teleports. Baby: Can you be replaced?*

"He says yes," said Janie. "That nasty little telepath with the corncob—remember?"

Thompson said bitterly, "I didn't think you'd commit such an enormity, Janie. I could kill you for that."

"You know how," said Janie pleasantly.

Hip turned slowly to Janie. The thought came closer, or he went high and faster than it was going. It was as if his fingers actually rounded a curve, got a barest of purchases.

If Baby, the heart and core, the ego, the repository of all this new being had ever been or done or thought—if Baby could be replaced, then *Homo Gestalt* was *immortal!*

And with a rush, he had it. He had it all.

He said evenly, "I asked Baby if he could be replaced; if his memory banks and computing ability could be transferred."

"Don't tell him that!" Janie screamed.

Thompson had slipped into his complete, unnatural stillness. At last he said, "Baby said yes. I already know that. Janie, you knew that all along, didn't you?"

She made a sound like a gasp or a small cough.

Thompson said, "And you never told me. But of course, you wouldn't. Baby can't talk to me; the next one might. I can get the whole thing from the Lieutenant, right now. So go ahead with the dramatics. I don't need you, Janie."

"Hip! Run! Run!"

Thompson's eyes fixed on Hip's. "No," he said mildly, "Don't run."

They were going to spin; they were going to spin like wheels, like fans, like . . . like . . .

Hip heard Janie scream and scream again and there was a crunching sound. Then the eyes were gone.

He staggered back, his hand over his eyes. There was a gabbling shriek in the room, it went on and on, split and spun around itself. He peeped through his fingers.

Thompson was reeling, his head drawn back and down almost to his shoulderblades. He kicked and elbowed backward. Holding him, her hands over his eyes, her knee in the small of his back, was Bonnie, and it was from her the gabbling came.

Hip came forward running, starting with such a furious leap that his toes barely touched the floor in the first three paces. His fist was clenched until pain ran up his forearm and in his arm and shoulders was the residual fury of seven obsessive years. His fist sank into the taut solar plexus and Thompson went down soundlessly. So did the Negro but she rolled clear and bounced lithely to her feet. She ran to him, grinning like the moon, squeezed his biceps affectionately, patted his cheek and gabbled.

"And I thank *you!*" he panted. He turned. Another dark girl, just as sinewy and just as naked, supported Janie who was sagging weakly. "Janie!" he roared. "Bonnie, Beanie, whoever you are—did she . . ."

The girl holding her gabbled. Janie raised her eyes. They were deeply puzzled as she watched him come. They strayed from his face to Gerry Thompson's still figure. And suddenly she smiled.

The girl with her, still gabbling, reached and caught his sleeve. She pointed to the floor. The cylinder lay smashed under their feet. A slight stain of moisture disappeared as he watched. "Did I?" repeated Janie. "I never had a chance, once this butterfly landed on me." She sobered, stood up, came into his arms. "Gerry . . . is he . . ."

"I don't think I killed him," said Hip and added, "yet."

"I can't tell you to kill him," Janie whispered.

"Yes," he said. "Yes, I know."

She said, "It's the first time the twins ever touched him. It was very brave. He could have burned out their brains in a second."

"They're wonderful. Bonnie!"

"Ho."

"Get me a knife. A sharp one with a blade at least so long. And a strip of black cloth, so-by-so."

Bonnie looked at Janie. Janie said, "What—"

He put his hand on her mouth. Her mouth was very soft. "Sh."

Janie said, panicked, "Bonnie, don't—"

Bonnie disappeared. Hip said, "Leave me alone with him for a while."

Janie opened her mouth to speak then turned and fled through the door. Beanie vanished.

Hip walked over to the prone figure and stood looking down at it. He did not think. He had his thought; all he had to do was hold it there.

Bonnie came through the door. She held a length of black velvet and a dagger with an eleven-inch blade. Her eyes were very big and her mouth was very small.

"Thanks, Bonnie." He took them. The knife was beautiful. Finnish, with an edge he could have shaved with, and a point drawn down almost to invisibility. "Beat it, Bonnie!"

She left—blip!—like a squirted appleseed. Hip put the knife and the cloth down on a table and dragged Thompson to a chair. He gazed about him, found a bell-pull and tore it down. He did not mind if a bell rang somewhere; he was rather sure he would not be interrupted. He tied Thompson's elbows and ankles to the chair, tipped the head back and made the blindfold.

He drew up another chair and sat close. He moved his knife hand gently, not quite tossing it, just feeling the scend of its superb balance in his palm. He waited.

And while he was waiting he took his thought, all of it, and placed it like a patterned drape across the entrance to his mind. He hung it fairly, attended to its folds and saw with meticulous care that it reached quite to the bottom, quite to the top and that there were no gaps at the sides.

The pattern read:

Listen to me, orphan boy, I am a hated boy too. You were persecuted; so was I.

Listen to me, cave boy. You found a place to belong and you learned to be happy in it. So did I.

Listen to me, Miss Kew's boy. You lost yourself for years until you went back and learned again. So did I.

Listen to me, *Gestalt* boy. You found power within you beyond your wildest dreams and you used it and loved it. So did I.

Listen to me, Gerry. You discovered that no matter how great your power, nobody wanted it. So did I.

You want to be wanted. You want to be needed. So do I.

Janie says you need morals. Do you know what morals are? Morals are an obedience to rules that people laid down to help you live among them.

You don't need morals. No set of morals can apply to you. You can obey no rules set down by your kind because there are no more of your kind. And you are not an ordinary man, so the morals of ordinary men would do you no better than the morals of an anthill would do me.

So nobody wants you and you are a monster.

Nobody wanted me when I was a monster.

But Gerry, there is another kind of code for you. It is a code which requires belief rather than obedience. It is called ethos.

The ethos will give you a code for survival too. But it is a greater survival than your own, or my species, or yours. What it is really is a reverence for your sources and your posterity. It is a study of the main current which created you, and in which you will create still a greater thing when the time comes.

Help humanity, Gerry, for it is your mother and your father now; you never had them before. And humanity will help you for it will produce more like you and then you will no longer be alone. Help them as they grow; help them to help humanity and gain still more of your own kind. For you are immortal, Gerry. You are immortal now.

And when there are enough of your kind, your ethics will be their morals. And when their morals no longer suit their species, you or another ethical being will create new ones that vault still farther up the main stream, reverencing you, reverencing those who bore you and the ones who bore them, back and back to the first wild creature who was different because his heart leapt when he saw a star.

I was a monster and I found this ethos. You are a monster. It's up to you.

Gerry stirred.

Hip Barrows stopped tossing the knife and held it still.

Gerry moaned and coughed weakly. Hip pulled the limp head back, cupped it in the palm of his left hand. He set the point of the knife exactly on the center of Gerry's larynx.

Gerry mumbled inaudibly. Hip said, "Sit quite still, Gerry." He pressed gently on the knife. It went in deeper than he wanted it to. It was a beautiful knife. He said, "That's a knife at your throat. This is Hip Barrows. Now sit still and think about that for a while."

Gerry's lips smiled but it was because of the tension at the sides of his neck. His breath whistled through the not-smile.

"What are you going to do?"

"What would you do?"

"Take this thing off my eyes. I can't see."

"You see all you need to."

"Barrows. Turn me loose. I won't do anything to you. I promise. I can do a lot for you, Barrows. I can do anything you want."

"It is a moral act to kill a monster," said Hip. "Tell me something, Gerry. It is true you can snatch out the whole of a man's thought just by meeting his eyes?"

"Let me go. Let me go," Gerry whispered.

With the knife at the monster's throat, with this great house which could be his, with a girl waiting, a girl whose anguish for him he could breathe like ozoned air, Hip Barrows prepared his ethical act.

When the blindfold fell away there was amazement in the strange round eyes, enough and more than enough to drive away hate. Hip dangled the knife. He arranged his thought, side to side, top to bottom. He threw the knife behind him. It clattered on the tiles. The startled eyes followed it, whipped back. The irises were about to spin. . . .

Hip bent close. "Go ahead," he said softly.

After a long time, Gerry raised his head and met Hip's eyes again. Hip said, "Hi."

Gerry looked at him weakly. "Get the hell out of here," he croaked.

Hip sat still.

"I could've killed you," said Gerry. He opened his eyes a little wider. "I still could."

"You won't though." Hip rose, walked to the knife and picked it up. He returned to Gerry and deftly sliced the knots of the cord which bound him. He sat down again.

Gerry said, "No one ever . . . I never . . ." He shook himself and drew a deep breath. "I feel ashamed," he whispered. "No one ever made me feel ashamed." He looked at Hip, and the amazement was back again. "I know a lot. I can find out anything about anything. But I never . . . how did *you* ever find out all that?"

"Fell into it," said Hip. "An ethic isn't a fact you can look up. It's a way of thinking."

"God," said Gerry into his hands. "What I've done . . . the things I could have. . . ."

"The things you *can* do," Hip reminded him gently. "You've paid quite a price for the things you've done."

Gerry looked around at the huge glass room and everything in it that was massive, expensive, rich. "I have?"

Hip said, from the scarred depths of memory, "People all around you, you by yourself." He made a wry smile. "Does a superman have super-hunger, Gerry? Super-loneliness?"

Gerry nodded, slowly. "I did better when I was a kid." He shuddered. "Cold. . . ."

Hip did not know what kind of cold he meant, and did not ask. He rose. "I'd better go see Janie. She thinks maybe I killed you."

Gerry sat silently until Hip reached the door. Then he said, "Maybe you did."

Hip went out.

Janie was in the little anteroom with the twins. When Hip entered, Janie moved her head slightly and the twins disappeared.

Hip said, "I could tell them too."

"Tell me," Janie said. "They'll know."

He sat down next to her. She said, "You didn't kill him."

"No."

She nodded slowly, "I wonder what it would be like if he died. I—don't want to find out."

"He'll be all right now," Hip said. He met her eyes. "He was ashamed."

She huddled, cloaking herself, her thoughts. It was a waiting, but a different one from that he had known, for she was watching herself in her waiting, not him.

"That's all I can do. I'll clear out." He breathed once, deeply. "Lots to do. Track down my pension checks. Get a job."

"Hip—"

Only in so small a room, in such quiet, could he have heard her. "Yes, Janie."

"Don't go away."

"I can't stay."

"Why?"

He took his time and thought it out, and then he said, "You're a part of something. I wouldn't want to be part of someone who was . . . part of something."

She raised her face to him and he saw that she was smiling. He could not believe this, so he stared at her until he had to believe it.

She said, "The *Gestalt* has a head and hands, organs and a mind. But the most *human* thing about anyone is a thing he learns and . . . and earns. It's a thing he can't have when he's very young; if he gets it at all, he gets it after a long search and a deep conviction. After that it's truly part of him as long as he lives."

"I don't know what you mean. I—you mean I'm . . . I could be part of the . . . No, Janie, no." He could not escape from the sure smile. "What part?" he demanded.

"The prissy one who can't forget the rules. The one with the insight called ethics who can change it to the habit called morals."

"The still small voice!" He snorted. "I'll be damned!"

She touched him. "I don't think so."

He looked at the closed door to the great glass room. Then he sat down beside her. They waited.

It was quiet in the glass room.

For a long time the only sound was Gerry's difficult breathing. Suddenly even this stopped, as something happened, something— *spoke*.

It came again.

Welcome.

The voice was a silent one. And here, another, silent too, but another for all that. *It's the new one. Welcome, child!*

Still another: *Well, well, well! We thought you'd never make it. He had to. There hasn't been a new one for so long. . . .*

Gerry clapped his hands to his mouth. His eyes bulged. Through his mind came a hush of welcoming music. There was warmth and laughter and wisdom. There were introductions; for each voice there was a discrete personality, a comprehensible sense of something like stature or rank, and an accurate locus, a sense of physical position. Yet, in terms of amplitude, there was no difference in the voices. They were all here, or, at least, all equally near.

There was happy and fearless communion, fearlessly shared with Gerry—cross-currents of humor, of pleasure, of reciprocal thought and mutual achievement. And through and through, *welcome, welcome.*

They were young, they were new, all of them, though not as new and as young as Gerry. Their youth was in the drive and resilience of their thinking. Although some gave memories old in human terms, each entity had lived briefly in terms of immortality and they were all immortal.

Here was one who had whistled a phrase to Papa Haydn, and here one who had introduced William Morris to the Rossettis. Almost as if it were his own memory, Gerry saw Fermi being shown the streak of fission on a sensitive plate, a child Landowska listening to a harpsichord, a drowsy Ford with his mind suddenly lit by the picture of a line of men facing a line of machines.

To form a question was to have an answer.

Who are you?

Homo Gestalt.

I'm one; part of; belonging . . .

Welcome.

Why didn't you tell me?

You weren't ready. You weren't finished. What was Gerry before he met Lone?

And now . . . is it the ethic? Is that what completed me?

Ethic is too simple a term. But yes, yes . . . multiplicity is our first characteristic; unity our second. As your parts know they are parts of you, so must you know that we are parts of humanity.

Gerry understood then that the things which shamed him were, each and all, things which humans might do to humans, but which humanity could not do. He said, "I was punished."

You were quarantined.

And—are you . . . we . . . responsible for all humanity's accomplishments?

No! We share. We are humanity!

Humanity's trying to kill itself.

(A wave of amusement, and a superb confidence, like joy.) *Today, this week, it might seem so. But in terms of the history of a race . . . O new one, atomic war is a ripple on the broad face of the Amazon!*

Their memories, their projections and computations flooded in to Gerry, until at last he knew their nature and their function; and he knew why the ethos he had learned was too small a concept. For here at last was power which could not corrupt; for such an insight could not be used for its own sake, or against itself. Here was why and how humanity existed, troubled and dynamic, sainted by the touch of its own great destiny. Here was the withheld hand as thousands died, when by their death millions might live. And here, too, was the guide, the beacon, for such times as humanity might be in danger; here was the Guardian of Whom all humans knew—not an exterior force, nor an awesome Watcher in the sky, but a laughing thing with a human heart and a reverence for its human origins, smelling of sweat and new-turned earth rather than suffused with the pale odor of sanctity.

He saw himself as an atom and his *gestalt* as a molecule. He saw these others as a cell among cells, and he saw in the whole the design of what, with joy, humanity would become.

He felt a rising, choking sense of worship, and recognized it for what it has always been for mankind—self-respect.

He stretched out his arms, and the tears streamed from his strange eyes. *Thank you*, he answered them. *Thank you, thank you . . .*

And humbly, he joined their company.

Theodore Sturgeon

Theodore Sturgeon was born in New York City in 1918. In the 1940s Sturgeon made frequent appearances in *Astounding* and *Unknown*, the leading science-fiction and fantasy magazines of their day. Though he is identified with that period which has become known as The Golden Age of Science Fiction, he has continued to publish fine works of fiction.

For several years Sturgeon served as a regular columnist for the celebrated *New York Times Book Review*. Sturgeon lives in Southern California and spends much of the year lecturing to groups around the country. He is currently at work on a major mainstream novel, tentatively entitled, *Godbody*.